DEAD ON TIME

Distantly he heard another truck coming from the Ramkhed direction. But he did not dare take his eyes off the point where the bus should appear, somehow illogically convinced that if he failed to see it at the first opportunity it would mean that it had already come.

It was only when the roar of the oncoming vehicle's engine grew deafeningly loud close behind him that some inner warning-system made him begin to wheel round.

He had one glimpse of a motor-bike, a gleam of chrome leg-guards advancing, the rushing prow of some swooping ship. He knew then, without having an instant for calculation, that it was bearing down directly on him himself. . . .

DEAD ON TIME

H. R. F. Keating

MYSTERIOUS PRESS

Mysterious Press books (UK) are published
in association with
Arrow Books Limited
62–65 Chandos Place, London WC2N 4NW

An imprint of Century Hutchinson Limited

London Melbourne Sydney Auckland
Johannesburg and agencies throughout
the world

First published in Great Britain by Hutchinson 1988
Mysterious Press edition 1989

Printed and bound in Great Britain by
Courier International, Tiptree, Essex

ISBN 0 09 9616602

1

'Dead on time, Inspector Ghote,' the Director General, Maharashtra Police, said.

He tapped the watch on his wrist.

'One of the New Tata Titan quartz jobs. An Exacto. Accurate to the second, always. Day and date also.'

'Yes, sir,' Ghote dutifully answered.

But why has the DGP specially called me here, he wondered furiously underneath. The head of the whole State police force did not usually summon a mere inspector by name. So why himself? For what?

Thank goodness he had arrived at twenty minutes past eleven, sharp, as requested. That had made it all worthwhile: checking for certain his own watch, which seemed to be more unreliable every day, was exactly right, and, when that joker, Inspector Deshpande, seeing him dial 197 had said the speaking clock itself was often three minutes slow, even ringing Sahar Airport where they had video screens flashing up the time in seconds. By way of abundant precaution.

And then, of course, after all there had been that long wait outside when he had arrived fifteen minutes – no, seventeen minutes – early. Idling all round the block. Along past the University to glance up at the big clock on the Rajabi Tower there. Across into Mahatma Gandhi Road, and a long pause there to use up more time by contemplating the clock on the wall of the Sassoon Library, *Unique Made by Mr Lund in 1858*, with its twelve little surrounding dials giving the time in New York, London, Paris, Cape Town . . . What a pity the whole thing had stopped at precisely 1.35 pm as long ago as he could remember. Then along Madam Cama Road, and back to the Oval Maidan and its tall palm-trees.

And the last-moment panic that he would after all be

late when his arm had been seized, just outside, by that madwoman insistently thrusting at him the banana peel she had been chewing and calling him 'Baba' . . .

But in the end he had arrived, as the DGP had said, dead on time.

For what? Why had he himself and no other been ordered to report at this exact hour?

The DGP was still looking, in admiration it seemed, at his new watch, the sleeve of his shirt held back by the crooked little finger of his other hand.

Ghote ventured on a very slight cough.

'Ah, yes. Er– Ghote. Yes. You will be wondering why I have asked you to come at this time.'

'Yes, sir. That is– Yes, somewhat I was wondering.'

The DGP rubbed his hands briskly together. In the quiet of the big room the sound of one dry palm against the other was startlingly loud.

'It is like this, Inspector. There was a Section 302 affair yesterday in a shop near Kemp's Corner. Young man beaten to death by, it seems, the shop-owner. Place called the Tick Tock Watchworks. Now, of course that ought to be a matter simply for the local station where it seems to have been dealt with in a perfectly satisfactory manner. The culprit made a confession, and, though he has to make it again, of course, in the presence of a Magistrate, as far as I'm concerned, the whole affair has been properly wrapped up.'

'Yes, sir,' Ghote put in, quietly respectful.

The DGP looked up at him. A tiny spasm of rage contorted his face.

'Unfortunately, Inspector,' he said, making Ghote feel as if somehow, whatever the unfortunate circumstance was, he himself was responsible for it. 'Unfortunately, the young culprit, though of the poorer classes, happens to be a cousin of the Dhunjeebhoy brothers.'

Ghote began to understand.

The Dhunjeebhoy brothers were one of Bombay's great names, Parsi industrialists with a score of different concerns under their control, next in importance perhaps

6

only to the Tata family, of the new Titan watches amid much else. So, from a small-time watchmaker who for some reason had committed a brutal murder, this cousin of the Dhunjeebhoys had leapt in an instant to become a person of influence, even if at secondhand.

In consequence Crime Branch at Headquarters was being called in, as it usually was when an offence that ought to be investigated by one of Bombay's forty-five local police stations turned out to have social or political complications. Yet that could not be the whole of it. If in the ordinary way such a case had been brought to the DGP's notice, he would have simply passed it over to the Assistant Commissioner, Crime Branch. So why now had he himself been directly summoned?

'Both brothers are coming to see me this morning,' the DGP continued, with just the merest hint of uneasiness. 'They are due' – he glanced once more at his Titan Exacto – 'in precisely six minutes.'

Ghote swallowed.

'Yes, sir?' he said.

'I can only suppose, – er – Ghote, that they intend to claim that the young man's confession was extorted from him by force.'

Ghote wondered what to reply. Confessions were beaten out of culprits when an investigating officer was certain he had the right man. It was often the only way to achieve a result. Yet it was not a method endorsed by the Criminal Procedure Code. So should he produce an exclamation of shocked disapproval?

On the other hand, the DGP, who must have risen all the way from Probationary Sub-Inspector to his present topmost rank, could not be ignorant of the way things were done.

'Yes, sir,' he said eventually, attempting to get an absolute lack of meaning into the words.

The DGP looked at his watch again.

How many seconds of those six minutes had already gone? And how much more needed to be said before the powerfully influential Dhunjeebhoy brothers appeared?

'In the ordinary way, Inspector – hm – Ghote, I would have dealt with the Dhunjeebhoys myself, given them some reassurances and so forth. But . . .'

The DGP paused long and long, in search apparently of a way to put some delicate point to an officer altogether too junior to be entrusted with such matters.

Ghote thought of the new seconds that had ticked away.

'Yes, sir?' he ventured.

'Inspector, there is one damn difficulty.'

Another pause.

'You see, – er – Ghote, the victim of the murder was a certain – '

One of the telephones on the DGP's huge wide desk, the pink one, buzzed in sudden urgency.

The DGP's mouth tightened in sharp displeasure. He consulted his Exacto once more, then reached across and picked up the pink receiver.

'Yes?'

An anxious voice quacked at the other end.

The DGP groaned out an infuriated sigh.

'Send them up then,' he said. 'Send them up.'

He turned to Ghote, putting the receiver down.

'Early,' he said. 'Damn it, four minutes and twenty seconds early.'

But already there was a clatter of footsteps on the stone stairs outside. Then a discreet knock.

'Come in,' the DGP called.

He drew the sleeve of his shirt firmly across the face of his new Tata Titan Exacto.

The two visitors ushered in by the DGP's peon were not in appearance the powerful industrialists Ghote had expected to see. Dynamism was not written all over them. Diffidence was.

Both were tall and inclined to stoop. But, though clearly there was a family resemblance, in their pale tobacco-leaf complexions, their deep-set saddish eyes and fine hooked noses, they seemed in fact to differ considerably. The older one, who introduced himself almost shyly as Homi Dhunjeebhoy, was so fleshlessly thin as to make Ghote at

8

once wonder how he continued to keep himself alive. The younger, bouncily adding that he was Bomi Dhunjeebhoy and at once appearing to regret the forwardness, though almost as lean as his brother possessed a little rounded paunch which alone gave him an air of happy good living.

The DGP had jumped up from his wide desk as soon as they were shown in and with much shaking of hands, smiling and gesturing and offers of cold drinks, tea and coffee had got them seated in two of the sprawling leather armchairs that marked out his office as that of a very senior man. Ghote, standing discreetly in the background, he introduced almost with a single word.

Then, back behind his desk, fingers steepled, he asked: 'Now, gentelmen, how can I help you?'

Homi Dhunjeebhoy leant forward in his wide armchair, like a delicate question-mark.

'Mr Director General,' he said, 'my brother and I are anxious not to take up any more of your valuable time than we have to – '

'No, no, that's just it,' Bomi Dhunjeebhoy broke in, almost hopping in his huge chair. 'Time. We know yours is valuable sir. We do not wish to take up more than one second of it that we do not need to. But – But – '

'But,' said his brother, sharply cutting in, 'we regard this as a matter, quite simply, of life and death.'

'Yes, yes. Life and death. Exactly that. I mean, you see, after all, if – if this terrible business should result in – in – '

'A verdict of guilty,' Homi Dhunjeebhoy declared hollowly from beside his brother, 'then it would indeed be a matter of death. Of death by hanging for poor young Rustom Fardoomji, who is after all our cousin.'

'Though we must admit that of late we have hardly seen the boy,' Bomi bounced in. 'Remiss of us. Remiss. Family ties. We ought . . .'

He came to a halt, sadly contemplating it seemed the lack of family contact.

His brother sonorously took up the tale.

'Rustom must be held partly responsible,' he said. 'The boy has no interest in family affairs. Otherwise – '

'Yes, yes. Otherwise we would have made sure we saw him from time to time. Entertained. Inquired. Looked after. But – But – Well, the poor fellow was obsessed. Not too strong a word, I think?'

Bomi looked across at the scraped-thin question-mark shape of his brother.

'Obsessed,' Homi gravely concurred. 'With timepieces, Mr Director General. Timepieces. He – '

'Yes, yes,' Bomi hopped forward. 'The young fellow can think of nothing else. Nothing but his watches and his clocks. Of tick and tock. Of what makes the things go and what makes them – '

'Stop.'

For a moment Bomi looked at his elder as if he had been sharply ordered to hold his tongue. Then he realised that his sentence had simply been completed for him, and tumbled into the fray again regardless of his brother's anxiety to say what had to be said as swiftly as possible.

'Yes, yes. Clocks stopping, watches going. They make up the whole of that young man's life. Not married, Mr Director General. Thirty years of age, and not married. Except to his timepieces. Yes, yes, wedded to those. Wedded.'

Homi Dhunjeebhoy leant further forward in his wide brown chair and put out a hand to restrain his brother.

'And that is why,' he said, 'my brother and I are completely unable to believe that young Rustom could have done the terrible thing he is accused of.'

The DGP seized this opportunity to produce his promised platitudes.

'Gentlemen,' he said, rather more loudly than he might have done. 'Let me assure you that the officers of my force are men of considerable experience. None of them lightly brings a charge under Section 302 of the Indian Penal Code. And in this particular instance, let me remind you, it has been done on the strength of a confession from the young man in question. A direct confession.'

'But – ' Homi Dhunjeebhoy interrupted weightily.

'But – But – But – ,' his brother broke in, in a fine rubber-bouncing splutter. 'In the newspapers, Mr Director General. One has read . . . Beatings, threats, humiliation. Torture even. I can give you instances. Let me see. Let me see . . .'

'Bomi,' his brother broke in, booming like a bell. 'We are taking up too much of the DGP's time. He is a busy man, don't forget.'

'Oh, yes, yes. Busy. Quite, quite. Not one moment more than – '

'Mr Director General,' Homi came in again. 'Let us be perfectly plain. We cannot but suspect that this confession was obtained from young Rustom Fardoomji under duress.'

'Yes, yes. Duress. Duress. It is not too strong a word.'

'Bomi – '

'Oh, yes. Time. Your time, Mr Director General . . .'

The DGP once more seized the chance Homi Dhunjee-bhoy had made for him. At more than a little length he explained how 'the Indian Evidence Act, 1927, read with the Criminal Procedure Code, Section 164' made obtaining confessions by force altogether impossible, while refraining from any mention of the fact that such confessions were from time to time obtained. Then, without pause, he launched into a fearsomely detailed account of some of the triumphs of efficiency his force had recently achieved.

'In one single day, gentlemen, no fewer than one hundred and fifteen goondas arrested, plus also eleven slumlords, plus again thirty-seven bootleggers detected and no fewer than 97,202 litres of hooch destroyed. I have the figures before me.'

He tapped impressively at one of the piles of papers on his desk. Ghote, flat against the wall in the background, suppressed the thought that the papers might contain no such figures.

The Dhunjeebhoy brothers had been reduced to list-ening in silence, Homi bending at every moment into a yet more doubting mark of interrogation, Bomi excitedly tapping at his little rounded paunch with impatient fingers.

Now Homi at last saw his chance.

'Mr Director General, I have no doubt all you say is true. However – '

'However, sir, however,' Bomi popped in. 'We have known Rustom since his childhood days. Yes, yes. And he was dreamy. That's the word. Dreamy. A sweet – '

'Mr Director General,' Homi rode over his brother, 'the fact is we cannot believe the boy committed a crime of such savagery.'

'Yes, yes, savagery. That's what we understand, sir. The body was savagely attacked. Savagely. Am I right?'

The DGP consulted for an instant another sheet of paper on the desk in front of him.

'The victim was severely battered, yes,' he said. 'I have a detailed description here. It is not too much to say the attack was savage.'

'And it is the considered opinion of my brother and myself,' Homi Dhunjeebhoy stated, 'that our cousin Rustom is incapable of savagery. Let us not take up more of your time, sir. Let us state plainly that we have come this morning to ask you to make the most rigorous inquiries into this alleged confession.'

'Oh, Mr Director General, rigorous. Rigorous, rigorous. Not a stone unturned, sir. A stitch in time . . . Not a – Not – '

'Bomi, we have made our point, I trust. Remember, the Director General has numerous duties.'

'Good gracious, yes. Oh, forgive me, sir. I fear I have gone on. Gone on at length. But – But – But, you see, Rustom means a great deal to us. The family. You understand, there are ties – '

'Bomi.'

'Oh, yes, yes, Homi. Yes, we must be going. Yes, indeed. Going.'

Homi, by way of agreement, uncurled his long body from the deep leather armchair.

'Mr Director General,' he asked, 'can I feel I have your assurance that the matter will be pursued?'

'Pursued to the utmost,' Bomi hopped up out of his chair to add. 'Any sign, sir. Any sign at all that that confession . . .'

The DGP bowed his head in acknowledgement. Sad acknowledgement.

'Bomi, time.'

'Oh, yes, yes. Waits for no man, waits not a minute. Going. We must be going. We are going.'

Bomi Dhunjeebhoy's voice trailed away as he went through the door that his brother was holding wide for him.

It closed. Ghote came back to stand in front of the DGP's desk again, to receive his orders.

'Sir,' he said, 'you would be wanting me to follow the investigation till date on behalf of Crime Branch? To make doubly certain there were no irreg – '

'No.'

The DGP chopped out the word like a blow from an axe.

'No, sir?'

'No, Inspector.'

2

Ghote felt submerged in astonishment. Surely, he thought, the DGP is not after all going to dismiss to one hundred percent a request from such influential people as the Dhunjeebhoy brothers. It was all very well to talk about 'reassurances and so forth', but for all the details he had produced about the 97,202 litres of hooch discovered and destroyed – and, now that he came to think of it, that was the exact figure, given in the newspapers even – and for all his careful quoting of the venerable Indian Evidence Act, the brothers had not been won over. They had left seemingly believing the confession that this Rustom Fardoomji had made would be inquired into, to the very bottom.

But now the DGP apparently was ordering him not to pursue the matter at all.

He almost asked once again if that was what had been said. But before he had gone that far the DGP spoke.

'No, Inspector. The damn thing is more complicated than that. And it is because of the complications that I sent for you.'

Ghote felt at one and the same time flattered and worried. Worried that he would not succeed in dealing with the complications, whatever they were. Flattered that he had been picked out as capable of doing so.

'Your name was suggested to me, – er – er – Ghote,' the DGP went on distantly, as if as he spoke he was trying to decide how he could say what he had to say. 'Suggested as a suitable officer who, if the worse came to the worst, could be . . .'

Then abruptly he made up his mind.

'It is the identity of the particular victim,' he blurted out. 'That is the trouble. He is one Ramrao Pendke, who turns out to be the grandson and sole heir of a certain

14

Bhagwantrao Pendke, Patil of a village called Dharbani, out somewhere miles away, beyond Nagpur. And Bhagwantrao Pendke is a landowner about as big as they come, who – not to beat about the bush – has got ten thousand votes in his pocket.'

Then Ghote realised what the DGP's complications were. The headman of a village with so many votes at his command, whose word, deep in the mofussils, would be law to hundreds and hundreds of illiterate petty tenants and landless labourers, was in a diffferent way every bit as influential as the Dhunjeebhoy brothers. They might have vast wealth. But this Bhagwantrao Pendke would have something as precious in today's India, votes that could turn a politician into a Minister.

But surely the mere fact that the Patil of Dharbani was the murder victim's grandfather could not be the whole of the complication. Bhagwantrao Pendke was unlikely to be offended even if it should turn out that the officer who had extracted that swift confession had been – the scathing words of Dr Hans Gross whose *Criminal Investigation* had for so long been Ghote's holy writ came back to him – too much of an 'expeditious investigator.' So long as whoever had killed the Patil's grandson was brought to justice in the end, surely he would be content.

Yet . . .

'Superintendent Verma, in charge of District Ramkhed under which Dharbani falls, happens to be an old colleague of mine from Police Training School days,' the DGP went on. 'And, as soon as the news reached him that young Ramrao Pendke had been killed, he got on to me with some private information.'

From behind his wide, papers-strewn desk he looked at Ghote sharply.

'Private information, Inspector,' he said. 'Information not a hint of which is to go beyond these four walls. Understand?'

'Yes, sir,' Ghote said.

And he could not fight away a feeling of sinking dismay.

'It appears that in the event of Ramrao Pendke's death

– something which, incidentally, nearly took place already a few weeks ago – the next-in-line to the Patil's lands and influence would be the boy's cousin-brother, one Ganpatrao by name. And that particular gentleman, not to mince words, is a damn bad hat.'

Ghote felt another massy beam lowered into place in the weighty structure being heaved on to his shoulders. If Ganpatrao Pendke was such a damn bad hat, it was very possible that he had murdered the cousin who stood between him and power, wealth and influence. But this murderer, if murderer he was, was also a grandson of the Patil of Dharbani. How content would that influential man be if it was proved that his other grandson was the killer? Or, worse, if it was half-proved? And by him himself?

'SP Verma,' the DGP was going on, 'not knowing that the watch-shop murder had been satisfactorily dealt with here, any more than I did myself at the time, thought fit to give me a private tip that this fellow Ganpatrao was a man perfectly capable of doing someone to death. And you know the old saying about paternal cousins, Inspector? Kautilya Chanakya, 250 BC?'

Ghote, who thought he probably did know the saying, more or less, had sense enough to say, 'No, sir.'

'*Paternal cousin is a naturally envious person*, Inspector. That's the wisdom of old Kautilya Chanakya, and I've no reason to doubt it still holds good.'

'Yes, sir. And you were telling also, no, that the victim in question nearly died some weeks ago? Did the said Ganpatrao make some attack on him at that time?'

'No, no, not at all. No, you see, the whole reason young Ramrao was in Bombay was that he was very seriously ill. So serious that his death was, so to speak, assured. But then an America-returned surgeon who's just set up a clinic here in Bombay, name of Yadekar, I think – something like that – succeeded to give him some sort of transplant. And from being on the point of expiring, though a patient still at the clinic, he was to all intents and purposes alive and well again.'

16

'And Ganpatrao's hopes to become heir to all those lands had vanished,' Ghote said. 'So, yes, sir, I see he then had very much more of motive. But, sir, was SP Verma telling that the said Ganpatrao was in Bombay itself yesterday at the time of the crime?'

For a moment the DGP looked a little disconcerted.

'Well,' he said, 'there you've put your finger on it, Inspector. My old friend, Verma, is in a somewhat difficult position. After all, the Patil of Dharbani is by far and away the most important individual in his whole district. The fellow may choose to stay in a village, but he is due a great deal more respect than the Chairman of the Municipal Council in Ramkhed, or anybody else. So Verma is not particularly anxious to go poking his nose into the family's affairs. Why prod the cobra's nest, as they say?'

'Yes, sir.'

'Look at it this way, Inspector. Ganpatrao Pendke may be a thoroughly dirty dog, but whatever he's done to come to police notice hitherto has invariably been allowed to lie in the dormant file. At the particular request of his grandfather.'

'I see, sir,' Ghote said.

The cloud of despondency that had hovered over him ever since he had heard the words 'private information', with their hint of things that ought to be made public being kept neatly under cover, descended fully on to him now. Damp and chilling.

It had begun to be altogether clear that, if the DGP's friend, Superintendent Verma, felt himself debarred from conducting any investigation out at Village Dharbani, that tricky task was going to be given to Inspector Ghote. But a flicker of hope sprang up.

'Sir,' he said, 'even if Mr Ganpatrao Pendke is responsible for the death of his paternal cousin, surely it would not be necessary to go to his native-place to find out if he had left for Bombay before the murder. Sir, he could all the time have hired some goonda to do his dirty works.'

'No, no, Inspector,' the DGP said, whisking the idea

17

away with a dismissive hand. 'Do you think a man like this Ganpatrao would entrust a secret that could cost him his life to a sopari he had hired? Or at the least lay himself open to lifelong blackmail? No, no. Ridiculous.'

'Yes, sir,' Ghote said, realising the DGP was almost certainly right.

If Ganpatrao Pendke had killed his cousin he was bound to have come to Bombay for the purpose. Which meant that he in turn would have to go out to Village Dharbani and conduct the investigation which SP Verma was too much of a bootlicker to conduct himself, to find whether Ganpatrao had or had not been in Bombay at the time in question.

'So what I want you to do, Inspector,' the DGP went on, hammering Ghote's last hopes into the ground, 'is to get yourself out there and, without disclosing your identity as a police officer thereby bringing trouble down on poor Verma's head, quietly ascertain just exactly where Ganpatrao Pendke was yesterday morning.'

'Yes, sir.'

The DGP leant back in his tall desk-chair, a burden off his mind.

'In any case, – er – Ghote,' he said with sudden affability, 'I dare say the whole Ramkhed end of the business is no more than a mare's nest. The investigation here is under one Assistant Inspector Lobo, a chap I've had my eye on for some time. Thoroughly keen and reliable. A tip-top officer. He won't have gone far wrong, take my word for it.'

'Yes, sir.'

Ghote could not help asking himself briefly how it was that a fellow of assistant inspector rank only could have got himself so well into the DGP's good books. He would have his promotions accelerated no doubt. Yet he himself was so little known to higher authority that for almost all this interview the DGP had had difficulty remembering his name.

And then something else was borne in on him. That he had in fact been picked out for the task that had been thrust upon him because, if his investigation should somehow earn the displeasure of the votes-rich Patil, any ensuing trouble could conveniently be visited on his own head and no one else's.

For a moment the DGP appeared still to be reflecting pleasurably on Assistant Inspector Lobo and the rapidity with which he had obtained a confession in the case. Then he rubbed his hands briskly together once more, pulled back the sleeve of his shirt and consulted his new Exacto.

'Right,' he said. 'Well now, I've promised to take lunch at home today. A grandchild's birthday. Must honour the occasion. So I've had a train looked out for you, – er – Ghote, and . . .'

He scrabbled for a slip of paper.

'Ah, yes, the 14.15 hours for Nagpur. You'll have to make your own way from there to Village Dharbani. But I dare say by the time you get back to Bombay you'll find AI Lobo has got a detailed confession properly recorded in front of a Magistrate and that will be that.'

'Yes, sir,' Ghote said.

He clicked heels in salute and turned to go, not without momentarily allowing a disloyal thought to enter his head. If this wonderful AI Lobo was going to have the whole business wrapped up in such short order, was it truly necessary for him himself to go all the way out to Dharbani and risk getting into a devil of a soup?

But orders were orders . . .

Then, as he went down the stairs and out into the road, another thought struck him. It was – he looked at his ancient watch – not yet a quarter to twelve. His train did not leave VT Station till a quarter past two. So, even after going home and packing a suitcase, he ought to have time enough to call in at the station covering Kemp's Corner and the Tick Tock Watchworks nearby. And there at least he could make himself discreetly better acquainted with the facts of the case. Because, if he could do that, when he arrived at that remote Village Dharbani he would be in a very much stronger position. It would be all the easier then to find out how likely it was that Ganpatrao Pendke, the damn bad hat, had been responsible for killing his cousin rather than the watch-shop owner, Rustom Fardoomji, so rapidly lined up as the culprit by Assistant Inspector Lobo, DGP's pet.

Provided he went carefully, it need never come to the ears of the DGP that he had ventured to go just a little against those orders to keep the Dharbani possibility strictly confidential. And – it occurred to him suddenly – he had a certain advantage here. One Sub-Inspector Miss Shruti Shah.

He had worked alongside SI Shah out in the suburbs not many months before. It was a case in which a young schoolteacher, who in a love match had married the daughter of a high-up municipal councillor, had then killed her. A tragedy that had for weeks given him periods of grey sadness. The murderer, tormented by his inability to provide his new wife with the comforts she had been used to, and yet more by the obsessive jealousy she had soon shown, leading her even to time to the minute how long it took to bicycle back from his school to their one-room flat, had in the end beaten her to death with her own wooden belna as she had been rolling out chapattis. He had afterwards made a pathetic attempt to lie his way out of the crime. SI Shah had had no difficulty in seeing through his story, and he himself had had even less to do than usual in keeping his watching brief on the investigation. But he had been much impressed with the humane yet unflinching way Shruti Shah had handled her pathetic killer. And in the short while they had worked side by side they had become friendly.

More – a great piece of luck – he had heard that she had recently been transferred to the Kemp's Corner area.

And, yet more good luck, when, suitcase in hand and wifely complaints over his sudden departure still ringing in his ears, he arrived at the station he was told that SI Shah was due back from her lunch break almost at once.

He decided then to stroll up and down outside to wait for her. He was hardly anxious to meet the DGP's star, AI Lobo. But before long he had begun to think he had made a mistake. The minutes ticked by, five, ten, twelve, and there was no sign of Shruti Shah. His suitcase grew heavier and heavier in his hand, and there was no shade anywhere.

He remembered now that Shruti, though a model officer in every other way, intelligent, quick, thorough and sympathetic as well, was a congenitally bad time-keeper. She had not once during the week they had worked together, met him at exactly the appointed hour. She had always arrived behind time in a desperate hurry, hair falling down, uniform sari tugged awkwardly over her shoulder, full of incoherent excuses. And this despite a habit she had – she had told him about it quite early in their acquaintanceship – of permanently keeping her watch five minutes fast. Adding, not much to his surprise, that in fact she never succeeded in tricking herself. She was, he had realised almost as soon as he had met her, much too quickly intelligent to let herself be deceived in this way.

He had found this unpunctuality, her sole fault, endearing then. But now, with time going by before that train to Nagpur, he began to feel differently.

He turned once more and walked slowly in the other direction, sweat gathering on shoulders and back. Should he give up the idea of finding out that little extra about the crime at the Tick Tock Watchworks and get off in good time to VT Station?

'Inspector Ghote, it's you.'

SI Shah had come up behind him in a rush. She was looking every bit as dishevelled as he had seen her before, face glistening with perspiration, a heavy shopping-bag swinging at her side, a strand of hair running from forehead to lower lip.

'Shruti,' Ghote said, 'I have been wait – I had hoped I would see you. There is one favour . . .'

'My God, but come inside. Ek minute just. There is a phone call I must make. I am running behind time also.'

She glanced at the slim watch on her wrist, and gave a

little grimace at, once again, not having tricked herself by altering its hands.

Ghote grinned. He could not help it.

'I will come in,' he said. 'But I cannot stay long, I have a train.'

He followed Shruti's scurrying figure into the station.

Her phone call took her a good deal longer than the 'ek minute' she had promised. But, listening with half an ear, Ghote had to recognise that she was not wasting the time. Evidently it was a tricky matter – something to do with a girl being possibly detained against her will – and he could only admire the way she was dealing with it.

But at last she put down the receiver and turned to him, and he was able to explain what the discreet favour he needed was.

'Well,' she said, 'Mike Lobo is playing this one altogether close to his chest. But, if you are wanting, I can at least show you the scene.'

Ghote looked at his watch.

Yes, there should be time still if it did not take too long.

The Tick Tock Watchworks, when Shruti Shah led him round to the lane just off busy, prosperous Kemp's Corner where it stood between a cheap eating-place called the Sri Krishna Lunch Home and a small barber-shop, the Decent Electric hairdresser, came as something of a disappointment. He had had only the vaguest notion of what he might see there that would somehow eventually perhaps show up expeditious AI Lobo. But when he was confronted by the blank, pulled-down metal shutter of the little shop he realised that there could hardly have been anything to learn without having first arranged to get inside.

'Well, there it is,' Shruti Shah said, as they pushed through a circle of idlers, small boys, beggars, youths with cigarettes dangling from their mouths, dallying office messengers, still staring hopefully at the rust-streaked shutter behind which a murder had happened. 'You know it was a watch company salesman who first saw the body?

He came into the shop and found the place deserted. The victim, badly beaten up, was lying on the floor just inside. So he phoned the station, and Mike Lobo came round, twice as fast as light as usual, just in time to meet a traffic constable bringing back the owner. Mike guessed he had been absconding, nabbed him and straightaway got a confession.'

'Just only like that?'

'Just only with a few slaps and some hair pulled and probably a little more,' Shruti Shah answered wryly. 'Mike's an expert.'

'And why did this owner fellow do it?' Ghote asked, remembering only just in time that he had better not let even Shruti learn he knew the man's name was Rustom Fardoomji.

'Well, as Mike says, police has only to prove means and opportunity and motive can go to hell. I am quoting. Hey, but look.'

Ghote turned in the direction she had indicated. A neatly dressed, busy-looking man with a brush of a moustache, carrying a flat black briefcase, had come to the back of the little crowd round the shuttered shop and was staring at it almost transfixed.

'A piece of luck for you, Inspector,' Shruti Shah said. 'That is the man who was finding the body. By the name of Saxena. I had a word with him yesterday when Mike was making out the FIR on the case.'

The First Information Report on the affair was a document Ghote would dearly have liked to have had sight of. But this chance meeting with the watch company salesman who had discovered Ramrao Pendke's battered body might be almost as rewarding.

He took one quick glance at his own watch – was it still going to time? – and saw that he had a few minutes in hand at least.

'I would very much like to talk,' he said to Shruti.

She gestured the salesman across.

'Sub-Inspector Miss, good morning,' he greeted her.

'You would be asking yourself what for I am here again, isn't it?'

'Well, yes, Mr Saxena,' Shruti Shah answered. 'That I was very much wondering.'

The watches salesman produced a smirking grin under his brush of a moustache.

'Oh, it is most easily explained,' he said. 'Most easily. You see, it was coming into my head this morning itself that this shop may be up for selling, now that poor Rustom is no longer on the spot. And, though I am most happy in my job – '

He came to a stop, hauled up the left sleeve of his shirt and revealed, on a hairy forearm, not just one watch but four, strapped one above the other.

'Hindustan Machine Tools products,' he said. 'Look, each and every one telling exact same time. *HMT – timekeeping within everyone's reach.* Our slogan itself.'

Abruptly he yanked the sleeve down again. But not before Ghote had noticed that the uppermost watch was in fact two minutes behind its fellows.

Evidently Mr Saxena realised what he had seen.

He grinned his uneasy grin again.

'Yes, well,' he said. 'I was altogether forgetting to wind up same this morning. In my state of excitement, you understand. Because – Because of what I had thought about taking over this Tick Tock shop.'

Another smirk of a grin under the thick moustache.

'You see, it is these Tata Titan fellows. They are moving into the field, you know. Future is not too assured.'

'You definitely expect this Mr Rustom to be found guilty and his shop to be available?' Ghote asked sharply.

'What else to think is there? The body was in his shop. Rustom himself was absconding. No other explanation.'

'Well, at least that is what Assistant Inspector Lobo is believing,' Ghote commented. 'But you seem to know Mr Rustom well. Tell me, please, you were not at all surprised at what he had done?'

'Oh, yes. Yes. Altogether surprised. I mean, a chap is

not coming into a shop and finding one dead body on the floor without feelings of surprise, no?'

'But is it that you were surprised when you learnt Mr Rustom had been charge-sheeted?' Ghote persisted.

Mr Saxena shook his head, this way and that, up and down.

'With the human being you cannot ever be telling,' he said at last. 'That is my experience. Absolutely. Why, last month only Rustom would not take one single HMT watch. Not one. Titans only, he was saying. Titans. What nonsense and rot.'

He lifted his sleeve again, as if to show that in the intervening minutes none of his three lower HMT watches had varied from conformity by as much as one second.

And Ghote, looking idly at the array on that hairy forearm, saw that each one of the three said twenty-two minutes to two. He ought to be off at once if he was to get to VT Station in decent time to buy a ticket and catch the 14.15 train to Nagpur.

'Look. Shruti,' he said, 'I must be off. But thank you very much for the help you have given.' He dropped his voice. 'And – And not a word to Mike Lobo, please.'

He began to go. But he had hardly lugged his suitcase beyond the fringe of the small circle of onlookers when he felt his free arm grabbed by what seemed like a claw of steel. A harshly croaking voice in his ear demanded, 'Time kya? Time kya?'

He turned.

It was a madman who had grabbed him, a bushily grey-bearded fellow, dressed only in a pair of filth-grimed cotton trousers with a shirt flapping open to reveal a chest covered in festering scratch marks and a long ugly wound or scar running down under the rib cage. A waft of filthy breath, sour with the rottenness of food gone bad before it had ever been eaten, assailed his nostrils.

'Time for bus to be starting, yes?' the fellow went on, voice raw as a crow's. 'Time for bus. Oh, sahib, sahib, I was bus-starter before . . . Yes, one first-class job. And then came Saturn.'

Ghote let his case drop, took the hand that had fixed so ferociously on to his arm and tried to loosen it.

'Saturn?' he asked, hoping to distract the fellow's attention.

Two mad creatures in one day, he thought. It was hardly fair. First there had been that woman with her banana peel just before he was due to go in to the DGP. And now this fellow, who once, if what he was saying was true, had been employed getting buses out of the depot neither before nor after the correct time and now was well past the limits of sanity.

'Oh, sahib, I am under the curse of Saturn. Astrologer foretold all. Seven years under Saturn in my horoscope. Oh, why did I have it cast?'

'But – But that is perhaps nonsense only,' Ghote said, still trying to prise away the grimy claw.

'No, no, sahib. True, true. From the first day he told it. My job retrenched. Then no money. Turned out from the room we had. Wife was dying. Son gambling, gambling, and then, when I had got all he needed to pay off those fellows, running away. So many rupees, gone, gone, gone. No money, no wife, no son, no watch. Oh, sahib, sahib . . .'

Ghote had managed to force back only two of the grime-flaked fingers. He thought of his train. If he could do no better than this he would still be here at 14.15 when it left.

'Let go, let go,' he shouted into the fellow's face.

'Time kya? Time kya, sahib? Bus must start.'

'Will you let go?'

'Now, gently, gently.'

It was Shruti Shah. Seeing his predicament, she had come up behind the madman and now she put a coaxing arm around the filthy, flapping shirt on his back.

Her crooning reassurance worked almost magically. Ghote felt the claw grip slacken. He slid his arm away. Shruti was still hushing the wild fellow, but she contrived to glance away to Ghote with a grin of complicity and a nod of the head that told him to make off while he could.

He stooped, grabbed his suitcase, looked hastily up to the lane end, spotted the yellow roof of a stationary taxi and ran.

He got to VT Station with a decent amount of time in hand and breathed a sigh of relief before paying off the taxiwalla. He marched hurriedly into the huge pillared concourse, trying to remember where exactly the ticket office was.

In a moment he saw it. And above its windows the implacable painted notice *Closed for Accounting 14.00 to 14.30 hours*. The windows were shuttered. He looked at his watch. It was 14.01.

3

So Inspector Ghote travelled 'WT' to Nagpur, without a
ticket for the first time in his law-abiding life. And at the
end of his long journey he contrived to stroll out of the
night-quiet station unchallenged. He booked himself in at
the Skylark Hotel, the first he came to in the dimly-lit
city. In bed there he read for a few minutes the guide-
book someone had left behind. He decided to buy, if he
could at the Bharat Stores, whose advertisement in the
guide's pages promised *Aeroplane Quality at Submarine
Prices*, a genuine Nagpuri sari for his wife to make up for
this sudden call away. He considered briefly the book's
assurance that he was here 'far away from the clog clog
of machines, the whizzing trains, the blaring horns and
sirens' and that the people in this unhurried part of India
were 'very urbane and hospitable, yet at times as nasty as
anybody.' And with that tiny warning jab in his ears he
fell asleep.

First thing in the morning he set out to discover the
times for the long-distance bus that would take him to the
nearest point on the highway to Village Dharbani. To his
dismay he found it almost ready to depart. No submarine-
price sari for Protima just yet.

For three hours or more the chugging vehicle took him
through the sun-scorched countryside. Past the orange
orchards round Nagpur itself they went, into the cotton-
growing area, through the little town of Ramkhed, where
in the police station SP Verma would be at his desk safe
from any possibility of upsetting the powerful Patil of
Dharbani. Finally they came to the setting-down place for
the village.

As the bus pulled away in a cloud of puffing dust, Ghote
looked about him, senses alert.

He was, he realised abruptly, back home in a way.

Home, not in familiar Bombay, but in the countryside in which he had spent his boyhood. A mile or so in the distance, down a meandering earth track, he could make out Dharbani itself, huddled in the shadow of a low hill. It was evidently a village a good deal larger than his own native-place. But it was bound to be still, he thought, of much the same sort. And as different from Bombay as milk from water, not just in that Nagpur guide-book's freedom from the clog clog of machines and whizzing of trains, but in the very time that it moved by.

Here hours would no longer be ticked out in Sahar Airport's digital seconds. Time would not be measured even in days and weeks, but in the slow round of the six seasons, Spring into the Hot Weather, Hot Weather into the Rains, Rains into Autumn, Autumn into Winter, Winter into the Cold Weather, Cold Weather into Spring once more.

And, he thought, coming back to the present with a swallow of apprehension, in the village ahead, where everybody had all the time in the world to stop, to stare, to wonder, it would not be at all as easy to make inquiries as in Bombay. There the police were an everyday sight. An officer was answered if he questioned. There people understood they were in danger if they kept silent of a swift slapping or being hustled into the lock-up. But here there would be, if he remembered village ways rightly, only sullen unwillingness. Yet before the day was over he had to find out, if he could without any official powers, whether or not Ganpatrao Pendke, grandson of the village's powerful Patil, had been away from home at the time his cousin-brother had been beaten to death in Bombay. If he were to fail, it was more than likely AI Lobo would march his man in front of a Magistrate and get that possibly dubious confession formally recorded.

He cleared his mouth of the dust from the departing bus, straightened his shoulders and set off along the track to Dharbani and its secrets.

The path by no means led straight to its objective, though it could have nowhere but the village to go to. It jigged and jogged this way and that, as if no one walking its length could ever be in any sort of hurry. Here it skirted a miserable tree. There it slanted off towards a rock, time-sunk deep in the dusty earth, its side marked by a smear of bright red paste that showed it was an object of worship. But, Ghote observed, the path, for all its aimlessness, was not unused. Besides buffalo hoofmarks and the ruts of the lumbering carts they pulled, bicycle tracks criss-crossed each other plentifully.

So the inhabitants ahead are accustomed to go some way out into the wider world, he thought. Dharbani, unlike his own native village in his boyhood, had been touched by the hurrying world, if only lightly. Once or twice, indeed, he even made out the tracks of a motor-cycle, and a powerful one, too, to judge by the long scatters of earth it had sent spurting away at the path's twists and bends.

So, he thought, I will not be able to count all the time on my memories of village life. A mistake I must not make.

He marched steadily on.

At what he judged must be some two-thirds of the way to the village he saw the path seeming to lead to a field where a dozen or so women were at work, backs bent in the glare of the sun, harsh-coloured saris tucked between their legs. Would they, if he stopped to talk, give him an idea of how things stood in the village ahead?

But, well before he reached the field, the meandering path took a turn away. He abandoned the idea of approaching the women in favour of finding someone later likely to be more awake to the village's secret, inner life.

He came to the outskirts soon enough, a string of untidy mud huts with roofs of curling palm leaves. The quarter, he decided, where such necessary people as tanners, workers in leather, washermen and the barber would be segregated from the higher castes. So Dharbani had not altogether joined the modern, bustling world too busy for ancient distinctions.

Outside the last of these separate huts a shoemaker was

30

at work, squatting bare-chested on the dusty earth. Ghote crossed over to him, realising well that his approach had been long noticed, for all that the fellow was pretending to be wholly absorbed in the stout thread running from his needle, round the big toe of his outstretched foot and back to the thick-soled chappal he was slowly stitching together.

'Ram, Ram, mochiji,' Ghote said loudly, causing the cobbler at once to look up with a tremendously badly acted show of surprise.

'Is this Village Dharbani?'

The man gave him a glance full of malign suspicion.

'Since you have come, you must know that.'

Ghote sighed inwardly. No use with these slow-witted villagers opening a conversation with any sort of courtesy question . . .

Direct attack then.

'Ganpatrao Pendke, has he returned home yet?'

But direct attack was not the way either. At the fired-out question the shoemaker simply lowered his head and put another coarse stitch into the thick sole of the chappal.

Ghote waited to see whether he was, in the timeless way of the countryside, merely making up his mind about how to answer. But the fellow's silence persisted. Another stitch went into the chappal.

Ghote turned away.

Well, he thought, one thing at least is clear: Ganpatrao Pendke is not a man whose business it is wise to talk about.

He would have to go cunningly if he was to learn, without news of his approaches getting to the ears of the Patil, anything at all about the fellow. Let alone where he had been forty-eight hours before. If the people he contrived to question had any clear notion of what was meant by forty-eight hours . . .

He walked more slowly onwards.

The huts on either side of the dusty road after a gap of a hundred yards or so became better built. Roofs here were of corrugated iron held down by heavy stones. Holy tulsi plants grew in tubs or hanging pots outside each one. Through open doorways he glimpsed women blowing at cooking fires to keep life in them or poking sticks delicately under them. Outside, men sat idly and children played or sprawled on the ground. Dogs prowled and sniffed. Chickens scratched for sustenance. A donkey, tethered to a stump of tree, shook its long ears at him as he went by.

But he made no new attempt to learn anything more. He was going to need time in plenty to extract information. Of that he was now certain. However short time might be.

Soon he came to the vague square that marked the village's centre. Would the Patil's house be somewhere near? Did his grandson, Ganpatrao, still live there in the joint family?

He saw no building that seemed large enough for the home of a man with ten thousand votes in his pocket. There was only the village temple, old and crumbling, its forecourt dominated by a single squat stone pillar with projecting from it half a dozen little stone shelves or brackets. With a jolt, he recognised the object as precisely similar to the pillar that had stood outside the temple of his own, long-ago village. That, too, had had those little shelves. And he had once in a fit of youthful curiosity, or even anti-religious rebellion, asked the temple's pujari what the projections were for. Only to be told sharply that they had always been there, and that was all anybody needed to know.

A row of prosperous-looking shops stood to one side of the square, half-hidden behind an ancient banyan tree, its rope-like roots dangling to the ground to provide a pleasant shade for a surrounding stone bench, now unoccupied. Through the tree's knotty tumbling branches, a tall metal pole holding an electric lamp thrust itself incongruously upwards, rust-patched. One more sign of the progress that had edged in.

Then, as he advanced further into the rubbish-strewn, track-marked square, he caught sight, just into one of the lanes leading away from it, of a chaikhana. A cup of tea there would provide him with a fine excuse to sit opposite the half dozen villagers on its benches. If he waited long enough, surely out of suppressed curiosity someone would eventually open a conversation. Then it might take little more than half an hour – he glanced at his unreliable watch, but at once realised that whatever it said, right or wrong, had no significance here – before he could lead the talk round to the Patil and then on to his grandson.

He made his way across, circling a black goat tied to a heavy stone, stepping boldly over the open drain on the far side and wrinkling his nose a little at its blatant odour, past a group of chattering women with big brass pots drippingly tucked on hips or balanced on heads, evidently returning from the well. As their laughter and gossip suddenly ceased at the sight of a stranger he did his best to seem to take no notice.

The chaikhana, small and tin-roofed, was presided over by a grossly fat individual wearing only a splash-stained dhoti tucked into one of the folds of his wobbling belly. On the clay stove at the back on his open-sided establishment a large black kettle sullenly puffed. Above it there hung from a plastic strap a transistor radio, feebly wailing filmi music from distant Bombay.

Ghote ordered tea and watched the proprietor as he poured it milkily from the kettle into a steel tumbler and from that at maximum height so as to cool it into a large white chipped cup. This, when he judged the right moment had come, he set on a saucer with a pattern of blue flowers, much too small for the cup. Ghote took it and made his way over to one of the two benches placed opposite each other outside.

Somewhat to his dismay the two young men who had been sitting on the bench sharing a cigarette promptly got up and moved away, nudging each other and whispering. However, the row of three elderly villagers on the other bench, each slurping tea from a saucer carefully held in front of him, their cups on the ground at their feet, stayed where they were, staring into nothing between sips, letting time flow past.

How long would it be before one of them broke into speech?

Ghote slowly drank his cooling tea and waited. It was plain to see that the men opposite, for all their solemn staring, were gradually becoming consumed with curiosity about this stranger who had descended on the village like an avatar of a god coming down to earth. But none of them ventured a word or even a sign of acknowledging his presence.

Why should they, he thought. They had all day. They were in no hurry. Perhaps they had never been in a hurry all their lives long.

By contrast, the thought of Assistant Inspector Lobo, the expeditious, came into his head. How different someone like that was from these old men. Yet was Lobo's way of going about things perhaps after all the right one? And, worse, had he by his expeditiousness arrived at the right culprit in the Tick Tock Watchworks case? Was he in truth improving an already shining image in the eyes of the DGP behind his big desk back in Bombay?

Should he himself, then, try to speed things up here? Lean forward and open a conversation? The thought of his rebuff on the outskirts of the village at the hands of the shoemaker deterred him. No, there was no room here for anything expeditious.

He saw he had emptied his cup, got up and asked for another – the milk in it had tasted like buffalo's – and tried to drink even more slowly. But all too soon the level of the pale brown liquid had got dangerously low. How many cups could he manage before the elders opposite broke down and spoke?

He got up again and asked the bulging-bellied chai-khana owner for something to eat. He was offered a couple of chapattis and some pickle, with rather suspicious haste. As soon as he took a first bite he realised why the fat fellow had been so quick to pass them across his counter. They seemed to be composed as much of grit as of flour.

He eyed the rest of them. Would he have to grind

his way through every mouthful before those old men addressed a word to him?

But his breakthrough, when it came, arrived from quite another quarter. As he sat, beginning himself almost dreamily to let the minutes drift past, he felt suddenly a sharp tap on his shoulder. Starting round with sweat springing up on his forehead, he saw behind him a very old man, much more ancient than the men on the bench opposite. His stained white beard straggled to his waist. His face was lined and seamed under its dirtyish red headcloth.

And the old creature was speaking. Speaking to him. Although what he had said seemed almost as incomprehensible as if it was part of the dream he had been half-way into.

'Oh, you may think I have been here all my life. But not so, no, no, no.'

'You have been here all your life?' Ghote hastily took up the ancient fellow, snatching at this sole strand of communication that had been granted him, wildly lacking in logicality though it had seemed. 'So you are a man who has travelled? Someone who has seen the world, is it?'

'I was born in this village,' the old man answered, infuriatingly indirect.

He lowered himself on to the bench, and, giving his beard a thorough scratching, seemed to have lapsed already into a silence as impenetrable as that of the elders on the other bench.

Ghote licked his lips, and tried furiously to hit on a way of carrying on the conversation. But he need not have worried. The ancient fellow eventually finished his beard scratching, and, in a voice as cackling and uncertain as before, spoke again.

'Things were different then. Yes, yes. Then, you know – ' he laid a hand on Ghote's arm – 'then if you caught a cold they gave you honey with ginger and some tulsi leaves in it. It did not make you better, but the cold went in the end. But now . . . Now if they have cold, people want it to go before it has properly come. They take the bus all the way to Ramkhed and buy those things like stiff pieces of worm. They pay and pay for them. And the cold goes. They want to be cured all at once of their ill. Ah, we live in the age of evil. The age of evil. The age of Kali.'

Ghote ground his teeth in frustration. When at last someone had spoken, what was he getting but a long rigmarole about the evils of modern days? And from someone so old that plainly he was half out of his wits? How would he ever discover from this creature whether or not Ganpatrao Pendke had been at home two days ago?

'So I ran away,' the straggly bearded old man said with sudden inconsequence.

Ghote pounced.

'Yes, yes. You said: you have not been here all your life. You have seen the world, isn't it? You have seen – ' he thought he glimpsed a way of getting to where he wanted – 'you have seen bad men and good, no? Good men and bad. Tell me – '

But his tortuously arrived at lead was abruptly snatched away.

'I went to Poona,' the ancient fellow said, shaking his arm urgently. 'You know where is Poona?'

'Yes, yes. But – '

'Many, many soldiers in Poona. And somehow I had heard they wanted more. The big, big war was happening. Many soldiers were needed. So I walked to Poona. In this village I was trapped like a frog in a well, and I was at the height of my manhood then. I was full of juice. So I, too, became a soldier.'

Would the old fool never let him get a word in?

'I was in Africa. You know where is Africa? I was there. We fought. We fought the British. We got them out. In Africa, yes. You know where is Africa?'

Oh God, the damn fellow cannot even remember which side he was on, or where he did his fighting, Africa or here in the Independence struggle. If he did any fighting at all.

He is not far from being, out of sheer age, as mad as

that bus-starter who grabbed me outside the Tick Tock Watchworks, *Time kya? Time kya?* And if he is as confused in his mind as this, will whatever I do manage to get out of him about Ganpatrao Pendke be any good to me?

But then something the wandering old fellow had said mysteriously twanged an altogether different chord in his head. Running away. Rustom Fardoomji, too, was said to have run away. And been brought back to the scene of his crime. Almost at once. By a traffic constable, to be arrested by expeditious AI Lobo. But was there not something somehow wrong with that? How had the constable known Rustom Fardoomji was to be brought back as a culprit? The sequence of events was back to front. So was Lobo definitely wrong too? And was the solution of the watch-shop murder, after all, to be found here in Dharbani?

'But now,' the old soldier was cackling on, 'we have the panchayat. In those days people used to go to the brahmin's house, and he would say what was right or wrong. But Government is saying we must be having democracy. So there is a panchayat. And at the head of those five men we must vote for is the Sarpanch. Bapurao, son of our Patil, is our Sarpanch. Bapurao's son is known by the name of Ganpatrao, you know.'

Home, Ghote thought in a burst of delight. Home, home, home. Ganpatrao Pendke arrived at.

Yet, surely, Ganpatrao's father cannot be head of the village panchayat council. The DGP had definitely stated that Ganpatrao was now, with the death of his cousin, heir to the Patil. So how could Ganpatrao's father still be alive?

But, never mind. Ganpatrao's name had been spoken. How now to take advantage of that?

'Ganpatrao,' he said loudly into the ancient's ear. 'Is he a good man? A bad man?'

'No.'

What the devil did that mean? He had been too hasty, damn it.

'No,' the ancient soldier said, clutching again at Ghote's

shirtsleeve. 'No, Bapurao is dead. Sometimes I forget things. But, yes, Ganpatrao is dead. No, no, no. Bapurao is the one who is dead. Now. Last year. So Jambuvant, who is the husband of the Patil's daughter, has been made by him Sarpanch of our village. And what happens? You have a dispute with your neighbour. You take it to the panchayat for their decision. You pay the Sarpanch, as head of the panchayat twenty-five rupees to tell the other four how to vote. And your neighbour pays him thirty. So the Sarpanch refuses any decision, and the dispute remains. Now, when I was a boy the brahmin settled everything. Oh, these are evil times, evil, evil.'

Oh God, on to evil times again. And Ganpatrao lost.

'Yes, yes. Evil times. The age of Kali. Evil. Evil. You are knowing Ganpatrao?'

And the old fellow actually stopped for Ghote's answer. For a moment.

'Ganpatrao, the greatest murderer alive. I myself know it. I heard him say it. He killed his cousin-brother, you know. Killed him. And when the brahmin who serves the Patil's house – he is just only a boy, but a brahmin is a brahmin – when that boy comes to the house each day, does Ganpatrao show him any respect? No, no, no. So last year – no, the year before – just after the monsoons, he killed his cousin-brother Ramrao. You are knowing Ramrao?'

Ghote sat amazed. Ramrao, Ramrao Pendke, the victim of the Tick Tock Watchworks murder back in distant Bombay. Was this old man, actually a witness to Ganpatrao confessing to the killing? But – But how could the old fool have been a witness to that confession if it had been made, as he seemed to believe, two years ago? Or perhaps one year ago?

Damn it, Ramrao Pendke had been battered to death in Bombay only some forty-eight hours ago. So how could, how possibly could this wandering-witted idiot have heard Ganpatrao confessing to the murder a year ago? Or, no, two years ago even?

It made no sense. No sense at all.

Was it, though, somehow conceivable that some rumour was flitting here and there about the village? A hint that the day before yesterday Ganpatrao, Ganpatrao the nefarious had killed his cousin-brother in Bombay?

But could the times fit for that? Surely it must take some little while for even the tiniest hints of such a secret to become a matter of common gossip for this idiot of an old soldier to pick up? But, if he had not, then how was it he was saying this about Ganpatrao? Was it no more than a recollection of something the old fool had heard long ago coming to the surface now? Some talk of a quarrel between the cousins and somebody saying what they imagined Ganpatrao might have liked to have done?

And, damn it, the answer lay there in the old man's head somewhere. In its inevitable place in the layers and layers of time laid down there.

Ghote was swept by a consuming spasm of rage. He would have liked to jump up, seize the old man by the shoulders and shake and shake him until somehow the right one of those layers of time came to the top and he could take from it his right answer.

But there was no doing that. The years layered there inside had collapsed and subsided into one another like the floors of some rickety Bombay building succumbing at last to the toll of many, many disintegrating monsoons. If the old fellow had once seen or heard something that might even now be of use, it was lost. Lost for ever.

Rage towering up to obliteration point, Ghote did now jump to his feet. Jump to his feet and, almost snarling aloud, stamp away.

4

It took Ghote a good long while to calm down. To seem to have been on the point of finding out something about Ganpatrao Pendke at last, and then to have been presented with a tale of murder some two years before the victim had been found dead, it was infuriating beyond endurance. And time had gone by. He had sat outside that wretched chaikhana for heaven knows how long waiting for the tea-slurping elders to open a conversation so that his inquiries should not be obvious, and in the end it had all been a waste of time.

With anger boiling in him, at countryside life and ways, at himself, he tramped here and there about the big village, along close-crowded, rubbish-strewn lanes, past scores of the little houses, their open doorways giving glimpses of everyday goings-on within, past children playing in the dust, past more than once the same cluster of men gambling with a pack of greasy cards, past the village blacksmith's, the tree outside his hut adorned with a dozen hanging bicycle tyres and orangey inner tubes. He stopped short once only, when turning a corner at the end of one more narrow, urine-smelling, dung-fires aromatic lane, he found himself not twenty yards distant from the sole two-storey building he had come across, a big, blank-walled, startlingly white-painted place that could only be the house of the Patil.

He had wheeled round then, as if confronted by a buffalo gone crazy. Plagued by the taunting thought that, while he himself had spent all that time getting nowhere, back in Bombay expeditious AI Lobo might well have persuaded Rustom Fardoomji to repeat his confession in front of a Magistrate. Whether that confession was obtained by fair means or foul, once made, rescind in court later though Fardoomji might, he would have a hard time escaping being found guilty. While all that he himself had to set against such a case was the garbled talk of a man so advanced in years that he did not even remember whose side he had fought on long ago in Africa, or perhaps here in India. That, and the belief of the two Dhunjeebhoy brothers that the relative they hardly knew would not have committed a crime of such brutality. A belief based, perhaps, on no more than the feeling of those two very respectable figures that no family member of theirs should be mixed up in murder.

At last, exhausted more by sustained fury than by his tramping march, he slumped on to the low wall surrounding a small whitewashed shrine near one edge of the village, a little red flag drooping from a bamboo mast above it. For as much as ten minutes – though he had ceased almost entirely to make any semi-conscious count of time – he sat on, too tired even to think any more.

But then, glancing up, he found he was looking straight into the open doorway of one of the village's more prosperous houses – its roof was covered in red Mangalore tiles – and he was seeing a scene that took him back to his boyhood days while simultaneously sending a prickle of revived hope through his numbed brain.

All he had seen was a man, seated on the hut's floor, having his underarms shaved by a barber. But the sight recalled for him, in an immediate flood of memories, the itinerant barber who had served his own village together with four or five others nearby. And the great thing about that man was that his duties, besides shaving beards and from time to time heads and underarms, as well as performing minor pieces of surgery and prescribing occasional herbal cures, included acting as a messenger between one village and the next, one household and another. He was the carrier of news, good and bad, and the maker of marriages. And, perhaps really more important than any of this, it was his unofficial duty to be the retailer of plain gossip.

More, the barber of his youth had had a wife who performed similar offices for the better-off womenfolk, paring nails, rubbing away hair on legs with pumice-stone, cutting out corns, decorating the soles of brides' feet, and gossiping and match-making. Between the pair of them, man and wife had known almost everything that went on in the four or five villages they used to visit, everything openly spoken of, very nearly everything kept secret.

So, surely, the barber here, whisking his open razor now on the stone slab at his side as he squatted next to his client, testing the sharpness on the inside of his arm, rapidly applying lather from his little brass basin and wiping the excess off on the ball of his thumb, surely he would know all about Ganpatrao Pendke. Surely he would be able to produce, if handled right, something more solid that the breath of a rumour from an ancient solider so confused he could not tell one war from another.

He sat waiting on the shrine's low wall till the barber, chattering hard all the time, had finished his task. At last the fellow – he seemed to be in his active early fifties, short, rather monkey-faced, bow-legged, wearing only a green and red headcloth and the invariable dhoti draped round his waist – went striding off along the lane, walking rather faster than anybody he had yet seen in the unhurried village. He contrived in a few moments to catch up with him. He fell into step and risked at once opening a conversation.

'Namaste, Barberji,' he greeted him. 'I used, you know, to love watching the barber at work in my own village as a boy. If it had not been for caste, I would have liked nothing better than to have been a barber myself. Going here and there, seeing life, hearing of people's troubles and their good fortunes.'

There was a moment when he thought the fellow, talkative though he had seemed at his work, was not going to respond. But it was a moment only.

'And I myself, I have never wished to be anything but a barber. I was born to be a barber. My father before me was born to be a barber. His father before him was born so, and his before him again as long as the world has been.'

He could not have sounded more friendly, and Ghote realised that, if he himself wanted to learn something from the barber, the barber was more than ready to learn all he could about this stranger in the village to have some good fresh gossip to pass on. So he gave him as many details as he could about his family and early life, his wife's name, his son's age, how long he had been married, his father's name and profession of schoolmaster, his sisters' names, their husbands' occupations. And, if he carefully avoided saying he himself was a police officer, what did it matter?

It mattered, he soon found out, quite a lot. Because the moment he had finished his somewhat embroidered account, the barber asked him directly the one question he had foolishly not prepared himself for.

'So what is bringing you to Dharbani?'

He swallowed.

And inspiration came. He grabbed it with both hands.

'I had learnt that Dharbani is a prosperous place,' he said, recalling the electric lamp rising up through the banyan in the square and the row of well-stocked shops behind it and coupling that with a quick memory of Mr Saxena of the watches-covered forearm in Bombay and the reason he had given for coming to look at Rustom Fardoomji's shop. 'And I am by trade a watch-maker. So I am thinking this would be a good place to set up a shop.'

The barber burst into laughter.

'Oh, my friend,' he said, 'you have come to as unlucky a place for you as you could. You are not going to find any timepieces to mend in Dharbani. Never. The Patil has a clock in his house, yes. But it stopped, to my knowledge, four seasons past. And he has never thought of winding it since. No one else round about has anything of the sort. Why should we? We can see when the sun comes up, and when it is dark we can see that we can no longer see. We do not need any clock-watches to tell us such things as that.'

Ghote felt totally deflated. He ought, he realised, to have foreseen everything the barber had said. Had not his own boyhood days been just as the fellow had described? He had made the comparison more than once since he had been in Dharbani. In spite of the place's touches of the modern, it was really almost unaffected by the counting of minutes and hours.

But evidently his mistake had put the barber into an even better frame of mind. He went chattering cheerfully on.

'Yes, yes. No clocks and watches here. True, times have changed a little. There is the bus now. It can take you into Ramkhed whenever you are wishing. There is even a girl from the outcaste quarter here who goes on it every day to work as a steno for a lawyer. She went to school, you know. We are that much of forward-looking here. But you will not find any watch on Sitabai's little wrist. Bangles only, my friend. Bangles such as they have always been, if nowadays they are coming from Bombay or somewhere instead of being made here itself.'

'A forward-looking place?' Ghote asked, recovering enough to try to steer the talk again in the direction he wanted it to go. 'Tell me, is the Patil, despite that clock he has forgotten to start up, is he then a forward-looking man?'

'No, no,' the barber answered, plainly delighted to have the chance of laying out a character study he must have worked on over the years. 'No, Bhagwantrao Pendke, Patil of Dharbani, believes that things were well long ago when he was a boy, and, as much as is in his power, he means them to stay that way here for ever.'

'And a great deal is in his power?' Ghote asked.

'Oh, yes, yes. Government in Delhi may rule India. But, as they say, Delhi is far away. The ruler in all District Ramkhed is the Patil here. He is the one who says what is the law. Not any Chief Minister in Bombay, not the Collector in Ramkhed, not those swines of police there.'

Ghote swallowed the 'swines of police' without a catch. He was getting nearer, surely.

'So if I myself lived in Dharbani,' he said cautiously,

44

'and was a good friend of the Patil, I could commit as many crimes as I was liking? Is that the way of it?'

'No, no. Once more wrong.'

They had come out of the village now and were walking through the fields. Evidently the barber was on his way to some neighbouring smaller place.

'No,' he went on, 'you could do what is against Government law only if Patilji thought it was not wrong. He is a just man. But it is his own justice.'

So would the Patil, Ghote thought, protect his grandson Ganpatrao if he was convinced he had committed murder? He had, according to SP Verna, committed a good many lesser offences, things that at least ought to have got his name on to the police Bad Character Roll, and the Patil had arranged to have them all ignored. But murder? Would the Patil consider murder as something against Government law but not against his own? Perhaps it would depend on what his feelings were for each of his grandsons. If, for some reason, he had nothing good to say of the sickly Ramrao and delighted in the nefarious exploits of Ganpatrao . . .

He decided to explore the barber's opinions of the Patil a little further, a little nearer dangerous ground.

'I was saying, if I was just only a good friend of the Patil,' he ventured. 'But if it was a matter, for example, of a relative? Does the Patil have sons who might commit serious crimes?'

'Ah, no. Patilji has lost his sons. Lord Yama has taken each and every one. But grandsons he – But one grandson he has remaining. His first grandson, Ramrao, was murdered, you know. Yes, just two days ago. In Bombay. Where such things happen.'

'Murdered? Does anybody know why? Do they know who did it?'

'Yes, yes. It was some shop-owner there. In Bombay such people will beat you to death for rupees ten only.'

Ghote dutifully shook his head over the wickedness of the big city.

'Terrible, terrible. But you were saying, the Patil has one more grandson at least.'

'Yes, yes. One only now. After that just only a daughter. And what a grandson.'

'He is a good man, this one remaining?'

'No, no, no, no. Ganpatrao is the greatest rogue in all District Ramkhed. He is drinking. And the girls he has seduced . . . The people he has ridden down on that motor-bike of his also . . . Chee, chee.'

Ghote, walking steadily along the narrow, dust-powdery path between the fields beside his splendidly useful source of information, wondered if he dared push the talk yet nearer his objective.

'The greatest rogue in District Ramkhed?' he said. 'And does he, this Ganpatrao – it is Ganpatrao? – does he go so far as to do these wicked things beyond Ramkhed? Does he go to Nagpur? To Bombay even?'

Had he risked too much? Would the barber feel he was being asked unnecessary questions? Wonder then whether this too-hopeful watch-maker really was what he had said he was? Would he go and talk to the Patil about him?

But it seemed not.

'Oh, Ganpatrao has been in Bombay,' the barber answered, clearly happy to be able to relay so much juicy gossip to someone who had heard none of it before. 'Yes, that is where he was learning such bad habits. The Patil sent him to college there. He sent both his grandsons. But while Ramrao did well and learnt much about getting rich, Ganpatrao learnt just only about drinking and whoring. Oh, if he could have got more of money out of his grand-father he would have stayed and stayed in Bombay. Often he is saying it.'

'So does he go there still when he can? Was he . . . Was he perhaps there just only three-four days ago?'

It was not a very clever question. It risked, if anything did, alerting the barber. But he had been able on the spur of the moment to think of no more cunning way of obtaining that one vital piece of information.

However, the barber simply wagged his head ambiguously.

'Perhaps, yes. Perhaps, no. Who can say? With that motor-bike where can he not go? To Nagpur it is easy. And then all places are there for him on the train.'

Ghote sadly admitted to himself that he had failed to have had the tremendous piece of luck he might have done. For a little he walked in silence along the dust-soft path scarcely wide enough for the two of them.

'The Sarpanch was away three-four days ago,' the barber suddenly said, turning with happy crudeness to an as yet untouched subject for gossip-mongering.

'The Sarpanch?'

Ghote's mind was at once a-whirl with questions, hopes. Surely that memory-dazed old soldier had said that the Sarpanch of the village was the Patil's son-in-law. Indeed, that must be why the barber had abruptly mentioned him. And had he himself not just learnt that, after Ganpatrao, the Patil had no other male heir? Just his one daughter? So this Sarpanch would have almost as much to gain from Ramrao's death as Ganpatrao. And the Sarpanch had definitely left the village shortly before Ramrao had been beaten to death in the Tick Tock Watchworks. So could it be . . . ?

'Yes, our Sarpanch, Jambuvant Dhoble by name. He is the husband of Patilji's daughter, you know. Patilji said he was to be voted Sarpanch when Bapurao, the father of Ganpatrao, was no more.'

Yes, so he was right. Here, surely, unless it proved the Sarpanch had returned within two days was another suspect. And, if what that muzzy idiot of an old soldier had told him was true, that the Sarpanch took bribes from both sides, then he was probably as much of a bad hat as Ganpatrao himself.

But how to obtain some hard evidence against him? Or against Ganpatrao? How to get hold of something more definite to set against AI Lobo's case than the mere fact that someone with a motive might have been away from his home at the time of the victim's death? Something that would make his own name with the DGP?

Till now all he had learnt had been rumour and guess-work, better though it was than the state of total ignorance he had been in when he had first set foot in the village. But very likely the DGP would dismiss mere hearsay out of hand. And the barber, plainly, had little more to tell, if anything.

Then it came to him.

If what the ancient soldier at the chaikhana had said, though muddled, was more reliable than he had believed, as the barber's gossip had tended to confirm, then perhaps one other thing the old man had spoken of was more than the mere confusion of a mind that had lost all sense of time.

The boy brahmin. The old soldier had said that a boy brahmin, presumably the son of the regular village priest who had perhaps died early, was accustomed to visit the Patil's house every day to perform the necessary rituals. Surely that boy would know, if anybody, whether Ganpat-rao had been absent from the family home.

So how to find the boy? Not easy without asking direct questions that, in a village like Dharbani, would at once provoke questions in return, questions it might be difficult to answer.

He thought.

'Tell me,' he said at last, 'does the Patil keep to all old customs? Are prayers said in his house each day?'

'Oh, yes, yes. Patilji is a good man, I was saying it. He would not think any day had begun unless the brahmin had visited his house.'

'And the brahmin . . . I expect he had been going to that house for year after year?'

Once more the barber was delighted to put this ignorant stranger right.

'No, no, no. The brahmin we had for some years was expiring. So now it is his son who goes to the Patil's house.'

48

'Ah, yes. And if your brahmin was a man of many years, I suppose this son of his is well used to the work?'

'No, no, no, no. No, the brahmin now is a boy only. Luckily he was old enough to take up the task when his father was dying. He was just past twelve. He had received his sacred thread.'

'So he is twelve-thirteen only now? You know, I would like to see that boy. To do a brahmin's work at that age, it is something Dharbani can be proud of.'

'Yes, yes. You are right for once. That boy is very, very good.'

'So where is it I could see?'

Was his inquiry too sudden? Apparently not.

'Oh, that is easy. The boy goes each day after he has visited the Patil's house to the old temple on the hill. No one else is going there these days, but the boy goes. He is saying the god has called him. He is a boy in a thousand. In two thousand.'

'Yes, that I can believe. So, I think, if you will forgive – '

But, just as Ghote was hurriedly turning to go, the barber seized him by the elbow.

'Look,' he said. 'Look.'

Ghote turned in the direction the barber indicated. Coming round a bend in the path where at the corner of a field a straggly bush had obscured the way ahead there was a tall man, young, wearing not a dhoti but western dress, a brightly coloured check shirt and blue jeans. Even at a distance he would be seen to walk with a tremendous swagger, and his face could be seen to be decorated with a pair of thick curling moustaches.

Ghote turned to the barber.

'Who . . . ?' he asked.

But he already knew the answer before the barber spoke.

'It is Ganpatrao, Ganpatrao himself.'

5

For a few moments Ghote stood where he was, rooted to the ground in a tangle of emotions. To be suddenly confronted with the man he now believed, despite the existence of a confessed killer, was most likely to be the actual murderer of the watch-shop attack back in Bombay, that was bad enough. But Ganpatrao Pendke was also the man he had been ordered not to investigate directly, the man he had spent all the long morning in Dharbani trying to find out about without drawing attention to his inquiries. And here the fellow was, coming strolling towards the place where he himself stood on the narrow field-path, looking as if he already owned every square inch of the wide, sun-bleached countryside around.

At his side the barber hastily stepped back in among the low-growing thorn bushes that lined the path.

For an instant Ghote contemplated refusing to do likewise. What if he stood his ground, let Ganpatrao Pendke come face to face with him and then, defying his strict instructions, announced that he was a police officer, come from Bombay for the purpose of investigating the murder of Ramrao Pendke? Would the shock rattle from the man strolling towards him an immediate admission of guilt? Or at least some sign that would confirm he was indeed the watch-shop murderer?

But wiser thoughts at once prevailed. The trick might not work. And the DGP's anger would be terrible. It could result in his promotions being blocked for ever. Or he could end up being transferred to the Armed Police in some remote, dacoit-ridden, corruption-thick area to eat away his days till the end of his service.

He stepped back beside the barber. A thorn dug painfully into his left ankle above the shoe.

'Ram, Ram, Ganpatraoji,' the barber said with loud obsequiousness.

The murder suspect was upon them.

And, without a word to acknowledge the greeting, with scarcely a glance, he simply walked straight past.

Ghote stood there till the fellow was almost out of sight. The barber, plainly thinking there was nothing that could be said, stepped back on to the path and scuffled a foot in its yellow powderiness.

Eventually Ghote, feeling he could scarcely return to the subject of the Sarpanch's absence, repeated his excuses about wanting to go at once to admire the boy brahmin, and, taking care not to walk too quickly and risk overtaking the swaggering Ganpatrao, he set off back to Dharbani.

It took him a full hour before he neared the top of the low hill on the other side of the village where the old temple the barber had spoken of stood. It had been a long, hot climb with the sun now high in the sky. He was wet with sweat from shoulders to calves, and cursing himself for not having taken time to visit the chaikhana again and drink some tea or even risk another couple of gritty chapattis.

But then he saw the boy.

A slight figure in purest white dhoti and upper garment, he was sitting cross-legged, an image of stillness in front of the years-erased image of the god. If only from that very stillness he seemed to Ghote to be years older than his own son, always snatching at life's opportunities like a darting gecko snapping up flies.

In the scanty shade of a scrubby tree Ghote waited and watched. At last the boy brahmin showed signs of ending his silent prayer.

Ghote stepped forward, taking care to plank down his shoes on the rough-hewn paving-stones of the temple's forecourt to draw attention to his presence. At the sound the boy rose to his feet and turned to see who had made the long climb up the hill.

Ghote, not for years feeling particular respect for priest

or religion, nerved himself up to stoop and touch the young brahmin's feet.

But the boy, with unassuming simplicity, stopped him.

'You have come to worship the god?' he asked.

Ghote hesitated. Should he lie to ingratiate himself with this youthful pujari who might have information he badly needed? But some subconscious instinct warned him not to use the least trickle of deceit.

'No,' he said. 'No, I have not come to worship. I have come because I want you to tell me something.'

Still, however, he hesitated to put his request directly. He had thought, as he had toiled up the hill in the sun, that there would be no difficulty in using his adult authority simply to demand from a boy what he needed to know. But now, confronted with the young brahmin's plain serenity, he wondered whether he could ask his questions at all.

Yet he must.

He swallowed, dry-mouthed.

'I have come to – ,' he began. 'No. No, it is that I want to trust you with a secret.'

'Yes?' the boy asked, with a lack of either eagerness or reluctance that belied all the more his actual age.

Ghote gathered his thoughts.

'I have to tell you,' he said, 'that I have been sent here to Dharbani all the way from Bombay to – To learn something about – '

His good intentions faltered.

'To learn about the people who live here,' he finished on a lame lie.

'It is social study?'

Damn, Ghote thought. Damn, damn, damn. Why had he let himself be fooled by the boy's air of withdrawnness into thinking he was not as other boys? Of course the son of a village brahmin would have gone to school besides learning from his father his religious duties. And, of course, even in remote Dharbani nowadays such ideas as social studies might be spoken of in the classroom, even if no more than that.

But he did let himself be betrayed by doubting that instinct that had told him the boy was not a person to fob off with half-truths. Someone like him deserved better than weak evasions.

He took a breath.

'No, not a social study,' he said. 'And I think after all I cannot tell you why exactly I have come here. But I want you to answer some questions.'

'If I know the answers.'

Well, perhaps after all he had got to where he wanted. He cleared his throat.

'You go each day to the house of the Patil?'

The boy considered the question for a long moment. Then apparently he decided it was something he could answer.

'Yes, I go there each day.'

'And there do you see the Patil's grandson, Ganpatrao? He stays in the house?'

'Yes. He is staying there. With his wife. But they are not having any children.'

Ghote felt a little jump of delight. Another nugget of information. If Ganpatrao Pendke had no children, and from the tone of the boy's voice was not likely to have them, then his uncle by marriage, Jambuvant Dhoble, Sarpanch of the village, must be the next heir after Ganpatrao to the Patil's lands and influence. Could it be that, for this reason, it was he rather than Ganpatrao who had got rid of Ramrao at the Tick Tock Watchworks?

But Ganpatrao was to the fore now.

Ghote licked his lips.

'Please tell me,' he said to the upright, white-clad figure standing still and composed in front of him, 'tell me, was Ganpatrao away from the Patil's house two-three days ago? Was he away long enough to have gone to Bombay?'

This time the boy considered his reply at greater length.

Ghote realised, clearly as if it was written out for him on the time-eroded stones at his feet, that the youngster had realised from the way he had put the question that a great deal lay behind it. He was weighing whether answering would be to break a trust.

At last the boy spoke.

'Four days past in the morning, when I was going to that house, I saw a water-pot with mango leaves in it by the doorway, and I knew that I must go back and take care to come again later.'

'I see,' said Ghote, who did not. 'But perhaps you did not understand what I was asking. I want to know if Ganpatrao was away from his home three days ago.'

The boy regarded him with a steady, limpid-eyed gaze. And said nothing.

Ghote, standing looking down at him, could do no more than attempt to direct at him a beam of thought that would induce some answer. He knew that it would do no good to put the question in words a third time.

Minutes passed. Ghote did not dare to look down at the watch on his wrist to see how many of them, two, three or even four. But in the end he realised that there was nothing left for him to do but leave. The boy had decided, for whatever reason, that he would tell him no more. And nothing, no beam of thought, no demand in words, was going to shake that placid resolve.

Ghote muttered a goodbye, and the boy gave him a reply, calm as ever.

He turned and began the long walk down to the village, upbraiding himself at every step as soon as he was out of the boy's sight. But what else could he have done, he asked. Should he have threatened the boy? Cuffed an answer out of him? But he knew he would have learnt no more. Should he have offered money? To that boy? To the god of the temple even? But, no. Again he knew he would have got nothing more. Nothing more than that rigmarole about a water-pot and mango leaves –

And then the inner vision of such a pot with two or three sharp-pointed, glossy leaves floating in it called back to him in a single instant his boyhood. It had been his mother who had always insisted on putting a water-pot with mango leaves in it by the doorway when anyone . . .

Yes, when someone was setting out on a journey. And, something more. Yes. Yes. His mother, too, had believed it was unlucky to see a brahmin when anyone was departing from the house.

So the boy had been tactful enough, four days ago, when he had seen the water-pot and the mango leaves in it by the doorway of the Patil's house, to take himself out of the way so that a departing traveller would not encounter a brahmin.

And he himself could have been told this only because it was an answer to his question. His question about Ganpatrao. The boy had been indicating to him, without breaking the trust he felt he owed, that he knew Ganpatrao Pendke had left on a journey four days ago.

But what to do next? The DGP was hardly going to be so impressed by the tale of a young brahmin, a water-pot and some mango leaves as to believe his favoured Assistant Inspector Lobo was wrong about the Tick Tock Watch-works murder and that he himself had got a case against a killer who had shown no signs of guilt, much less had poured out a confession. However strongly, having seen the boy and spoken with him, he himself was convinced that he had been given an incriminating fact.

But, if it was Bombay that Ganpatrao had set out for that morning, how would he have made the journey? Scarcely by motor-bike, all four hundred miles. Indeed, the barber had said as much, had said that Ganpatrao could go by motor-bike to Nagpur and afterwards on to anywhere he liked by train, even to his favourite Bombay.

Could he check at Nagpur Station? With hundreds of passengers travelling each day it would be a slim chance at best. If he could persuade the DGP that Ganpatrao was likely to have been in Bombay when the murder had taken place, the full resources of the city police could be used to check hotels and to question the many idlers always to be found in the streets in such places as Ganpatrao was likely to have been. But the DGP would need harder evidence than what he could bring him now before ordering an operation on as massive a scale as that.

But, wait. There was the Sarpanch. He, too, had most likely been absent from Dharbani at the time of the murder. The barber had stated that. Now, if he could convince the DGP that there was a good case against the Sarpanch as well, then perhaps some investigation in Bombay into both suspects would be permitted.

The Sarpanch had no motor-bike. So how would he have made the journey? Simply, surely, by setting off on the bus to Nagpur.

And . . . And there was something else he had learnt from the barber that should help him there. Something he had heard from that chattering gossip without at the time realising it could be useful. There was a girl who each morning went by bus from the Dharbani stopping-place on the highway into Ramkhed. The outcaste who had learnt enough to become a steno and take dictation from a lawyer in Ramkhed. What was her name? Yes. Sitabai. Sitabai. She ought to be able to tell him if the Sarpanch had been on that bus one recent morning.

And not many hours from now, he thought, Sitabai will be getting down from the bus on her way home.

He calculated. Yes, he could afford to wait here in Dharbani until the time the bus came on its second trip of the day from Nagpur and Ramkhed. He could then question the girl as soon as she had arrived and with what he had learnt wait till the bus had reached the far end of its journey and pick it up again on its way to Nagpur. He might even get a night train and be in Bombay in the morning with enough evidence to impress the DGP. Or, if he had to spend the night in Nagpur, he would have time after all to buy Protima that aeroplane quality, submarine price sari before catching a morning train.

He felt a wave of hopefulness.

But before very long that began to fade away. In the hours before the bus was due from Ramkhed with Sitabai the steno on it there was nothing for him to do. He dared not risk making more inquiries. He had learnt enough, more than he could have hoped for. To go about trying to add a crumb or two extra would be to put himself in danger of his presence in the village coming to the ears of the Patil.

He disposed of a short half-hour of all he had to get through by visiting the chaikhana again, and insisting on getting something to eat better than gritty chapattis. But after that there was nothing to occupy the time.

And it passed so slowly. He found he was looking at his watch almost before its hands had moved from the time he had looked at it before. And then he kept lifting it to his ear to make sure it had not stopped. Silently he cursed the villagers he saw going about their lives in complete obliviousness to the prickle of punctuality. And looked at his watch again. And again.

He arrived eventually at the bus setting-down point far too early. The bus in any case, as he knew from his morning journey, hardly kept up with the times laid down in the timetable at the bus-station in Nagpur. But the thought that he might miss Sitabai if somehow for once the bus happened to run early had sent him walking out to meet the girl an hour or more before it was possible for her to arrive.

He sat on the low grassy earth-bank beside the narrow dusty black ribbon of the highway in the shade of one of the bushes that contrived to grow there and watched the traffic thundering along. There was surprisingly much of it, more than he had realised when he had travelled the same stretch of road in the bus. Trucks were coming by at frequent intervals, brightly painted, rattling vehicles hurrying goods of all sorts from one place to another.

Yes, he thought, I am hardly more than a mile away from lost-to-time Dharbani itself, but here the world of schedules and appointments is all the time noisily going by. That truck coming up now with *Public Carrier* in those nicely painted, differently coloured letters on its front, it is going at full speed to meet one deadline somewhere. Some person is even now perhaps looking up at a clock to see how much longer it would be before it arrives to be unloaded. And, just down the path behind me, in the Patil's house the clock has stopped four seasons past and nobody has remembered to wind it.

But the bus. How much longer before that would come?

He looked at his watch for the twentieth, thirtieth, fiftieth time. Was it in any case still right? And, if it was, how late was the bus going to be?

Or could it have come already? No. No, surely, that was impossible. However badly to time it was running, it could not have reached the setting-down place an hour before it was due.

Two more trucks, running one behind the other, came into view, rattled and thundered up, thundered and rattled away in a double cloud of dust.

Silence descended. Slowly the dust settled. Ghote looked at his watch once more. From the village, away down the winding hoof-marked path there came the faint sound of a donkey braying to the wide, washed-blue sky above.

Then, very distantly, the sound of a motor engine. The bus? Was this chug-chug different from the noise the trucks made?

He strained to hear.

No, it was clear that once again only a rattling, hoarse truck was coming full-pelt from the direction of Nagpur. And a minute or two later it came into view. Soon it was possible to make out behind the windshield the driver, a mauve-turbaned Sikh, crouching happily over the wheel, his accompanying 'cleaner' apparently asleep beside him.

Surely the bus was late now. But how late might it be on its afternoon run? Would the driver have waited to pick up regular travellers who for some reason had let the time go by and been in danger of missing their ride? Perhaps the lawyer in Ramkhed who employed Sitabai had fallen into conversation with a client or a friend and she had not dared to leave his office without taking permission. Did that sometimes happen? And would the girl have somewhere she could sleep the night in Ramkhed if it did?

Another truck, battering along in a cloud of dust and

a waft of noise, this time with a human cargo, twenty or more labourers, bare-chested and grimed with dirt, being taken from heaven knew where to heaven knew where in an endless round of drudgery. One of them, perched on the truck's tail-board, took it into his head to wave.

But after it, emerging softly from the disappearing welter of noise, surely there was a different steady chugging sound.

And, yes, yes, yes, a moment later the bus came into sight. The same vehicle he had travelled out in, its roof piled high with bundles, baskets and cases, more baskets dangling from its sides.

Slowly it ground its way towards him, and then with a short squeal of brakes came to a halt. Its door opened. A girl in a green cotton sari, lunch-box in hand, stood on the step for an instant, clambered down. No one else got off. The bus jerked into motion again, drew away belching bluey-black exhaust smoke.

The outcaste steno was not the pretty girl Ghote had somehow imagined as, time and again, he had rehearsed this meeting in his head while watching the highway's trucks thundering by. Her face was noticeably pock-marked, her nose sharp and angular.

He marched straight up to her.

'You are one Sitabai by name?'

She looked at him quickly, a mixture of fear and pertness in her eyes.

'Who are you?' she demanded, though at once seeming to regret the boldness.

Ghote knew now that he was going to have no trouble getting what he wanted out of her. He had questioned too many girls not unlike her in Bombay, outwardly hard-shelled but inwardly floating on seas of uncertainty, petty thieves, servants from the country, prostitutes.

'I am wanting to know just only one thing from you,' he snapped out. 'You tell me without any nonsense and lies, and we would hear no more about it. You will keep your mouth shut: I will forget all about you.'

He had not even had to tell her that he was police. He

knew that she knew, that she was hearing the voice of authority she had heard before and knew she must cow down to.

'Yes?' she breathed, hardly audible.

'Now, three or four mornings past one Jambuvant Dhoble left Village Dharbani. Did he travel on the self-same bus as yourself? Yes or no?'

'The Sarpanch,' Sitabai whispered, the look of fear coming more clearly on to her face.

'Never mind if he is Sarpanch or schoolmaster or whatever, was he or was he not on the bus?'

'Yes. He was. Yes. He came almost late. He sent a servant, running, running before him. The bus had to wait. Five minutes, more. I do not know. Then – '

Ghote cut sharply in on the girl's frightened flow of words, an outpouring of anything she hoped might please.

'Did he go past Ramkhed, the Sarpanch? Was he going to Nagpur itself?'

'He sat just only behind me. He was beside that man who is at Tata Institute in Bombay. One Mr Raghu Barde, he who is always and always coming back to his village of Khindgaon to help the villagers there who are very, very poor. He is sending the baskets and cloth they are making to Bombay. He is saying it is *vital* – ' she dropped the English word into her terrified stream of Marathi – '*vital* for them to stay happy as they are and not have to leave the village where they – '

'Stop. Never mind all that. Are you telling that Jambuvant Dhoble was talking with this individual? What was he saying to him? What?'

'I am telling, I am telling. The Sarpanch was saying he also was going to Bombay for three-four days. He was saying they could go together.'

'Enough. Now, listen, say nothing of this to any person whatsoever. Understand? To no one. And then you would hear no more.'

He had no need to make the threat any clearer. The mere smell of police would keep the girl's mouth shut.

Not a word of his inquiries would get back to the Sarpanch or to the Patil.

'Go. Go home. Now.'

Sitabai took to her heels. After twenty or thirty yards one of her chappals kicked itself off her foot. She stumbled to a halt, stooped and scrabbled it up, snatched off the other and with the pair of them clutched in one hand and her lunch-box in the other ran off again. To safety, to the familiar hut where she had lived all her life in the outcaste quarter, to its sparse comfort, to escape from the stinging flick she had received from the great nasty world beyond.

Ghote sat himself down in the shade of his roadside bush. He had learnt all he needed. Even a little extra, that 'three-four days' the Sarpanch had said he intended to stay in Bombay.

There would be an hour at least now before the bus returned to take him back to the nasty world, its demands and its schedules, its murders and its extracted confessions to murder. Above him the sky was clear. The heat of the day was just beginning to wane. He sat holding his knees, breathing the cooling air. In front of him the road, running a thin black line to north and south, seemed to have lost the last of its traffic. Not the least sound of a grinding, rattling truck. A bird in the bushes nearby ventured a few notes of song.

And when he got back to Bombay, he thought, he would have something worth taking to the DGP. He had done his work better than he could ever have hoped.

He had been sitting at ease, letting the minutes slip by, for little more than half an hour when he heard voices on the path from the village behind him. He felt a twinge of annoyance. He would have liked to have stayed alone hugging his triumph to himself. But he shrugged. Others after all had a right to take the bus into Ramkhed.

Then, as he carefully avoided turning to look at the newcomers in the hope that they would leave him to his thoughts, a voice spoke loudly from right behind him.

'You are to come. Patilji would speak with you.'

6

For an instant Ghote thought of resisting. Who were these men – they were a brutal enough pair, one squat and bulging with knotted muscle, the other less well-built but with a deep scar under one eye that told of no-holds-barred fighting – who were they that they should order him to accompany them to the Patil? He would refuse. He had the bus to catch. And if they attempted to use force, let them try, tough as they looked, and see what would happen.

But then he knew that refusal, whether it led to a physical encounter or not, would be pointless. Here within a mile or so of Dharbani he was in the heart of the Patil's territory. In the grasp of a man who, as the talkative barber had said, was more powerful than the Government in Delhi, than any State Minister in Bombay.

Eventually he was bound to be hunted down and dragged in front of the man. All right at some later distant date he might be able to claim justice. But the Patil's influence could well be too strong even for that.

'Very good,' he said, 'if Patil sahib is wishing to see me, I also am happy to see him.'

Neither of the Patil's messengers answered a word. Not without a sinking inner feeling of apprehension, Ghote set out with them back along the winding path to the village.

For a little he asked himself who it might have been who had told Patil he was in Dharbani. The barber? The boy brahmin? But it might have been anyone who had seen or heard him, the elders on the bench at the chai-khana, anyone.

In the village he was marched – he felt this was what was happening though not a hand was laid on him – through the narrow lanes, across the square and at last to the tall two-storeyed house he had seen just once as he had gone about the place earlier. As they entered it he had a confused impression of richness. Rural richness. He glimpsed just before they went through the wide outer doorway, broad enough to admit a groaning bullock-cart, a pair of modelled peacocks on the wall above, painted in bright detail down to the last eye on the last feather. The outer wall itself, he saw as he was led into the courtyard beyond, was so thick that there was room in it for a narrow stairway leading upwards.

Inside, he saw that the wide courtyard was opulently encircled by low open-fronted rooms in almost all of which stood huge baskets plastered with mud and heavy, if his boyhood memories were anything to go by, with grain. Above, to one side, there was a long platform where more grain was stored in fatly bulging sacks. Corresponding to it on the other side was a veranda with on it, lined up next to each other, a bed covered with a rich coloured cloth and a shiny red rexine sofa that might have come straight from Akbarali's Department Store in Bombay.

And, sitting precisely in the middle of the sofa, was the person Ghote knew instantly must be the Patil.

He was huge. Weighty as the bulging sacks of grain in his store. Age had slackened the skin of his face and left it hanging like a blotched bag under his heavy turban. But the eyes in that face were plainly still as shrewd as in the prime of manhood.

No, not just shrewd, Ghote thought as, walking away from his two heavy-muscled escorts, he mounted the wooden steps up to the veranda. The Patil's eyes were also those of a man who gave orders, who had given them for many long years and had seldom found them disobeyed.

'Namaskarji, Patil sahib,' he greeted him, determined to retain what initiative he could.

The Patil looked up from the game of chess he was playing – his opponent appeared from the three broad white lines across his forehead to be the village astrologer – and then, having taken the merest quick glance, looked down again at the chess-cloth laid out on a small table beside him. After a moment his hand went out, strong, fat and age-mottled, and with cautious deliberation he moved his rani diagonally from one corner of the cloth to the other to take an opposing vizier, clicking the two pieces together in loud triumph. The astrologer, a shrunken, shrivelled old man, cross-legged on the floor, uttered a tiny squeak of dismay.

The Patil turned and gave Ghote now a long, steady look.

'So,' he said at last with as much deliberation as he had shown in moving his chess queen, 'you have spent the day going here and there in my village, talking with this person and that. You have put out questions about myself. You have put out questions about my family members.'

He gave a quick, almost mischievous half-smile.

'You look surprised, Stranger sahib,' he went on. 'Do you not know what life is like in a village? You cough in the morning when you are squatting out in the fields and your wife has prepared ginger juice and honey when you come back in.'

'Well, yes, Patil sahib,' Ghote answered cautiously. 'I am knowing that. I spent my boyhood in a village, and went out to the fields every morning like everyone else. But surely it is not surprising that someone should want to learn all he could about such a man as the Patil of Dharbani.'

The attempt at flattery was a mistake. The Patil's heavy-jowled face under the thickly wound turban darkened in an instant.

'Do you think I have lived eighty years sucking my big toe that you try tricks like that on me? Now, what for did you come here? I am asking.'

No help for it, Ghote thought. I can hardly claim once more to be a watchmaker wanting to set up shop here. The Patil would see through a lie like that in a moment, would see through the best lie I could invent.

No, however much trouble with the DGP it might get him into eventually there was nothing else for it but the facts.

64

'Patil sahib, let me tell you the whole truth. I am a police officer. I come from Bombay. And – '

'It is my Ramrao,' the Patil broke in, his voice changing in an instant from heavy threat to desolation. 'You have come because of his murder. My sweet boy they were raising almost from the dead.'

And Ghote felt at once he was no longer facing an opponent, an opponent who was bound to inflict on him an ignominious defeat. A rush of pity swept up in him for this grossly huge old man, powerful though he was. It was plain to see that Ramrao's death coming, as he had put it, when the boy had been almost miraculously rescued from a fatal illness had struck him to his very core.

But the wounded old man was still aware, alert, ready to put himself, as always, one step ahead.

His shrewd eyes glinted, and not with tears.

'Yet I was hearing from that fool, SP Verma, they had found out who had killed my Ramrao. Some watchmaker fellow wanting to rob only. That was what SP Verma was telling. So, why now are you here in Dharbani?'

Again Ghote thought that only the truth would do.

'Patil sahib,' he said, 'it is not cent per cent certain that the murderer was after all that watchmaker.'

'And why is that? How can it be that one day you policewallas are saying it was a watchmaker who deprived me of my life's remaining joy and next day they are saying it is not? How is that? How?'

Ghote bit his lip.

Impossible to say to this man of influence that other men of influence, perhaps of greater influence, had declined to believe in the watchmaker's guilt, and that it was for that reason alone he had been sent to make inquiries in Dharbani. But there was hardly any other reason to give.

Except one.

There was one reason in logic why it was at least doubtful that it had been the influential Dhunjeebhoys' cousin who had killed Ramrao Pendke. A reason that had come into his mind only here in Dharbani when that gabbling old soldier had talked about running away from the village.

'Sahib,' he said, looking straight into the Patil's large, time-blotched face, 'there is just only this one doubt. You see, the watchmaker who has been accused of the murder was not in his shop when the – when your grandson was found. It was just only when an officer from the nearby police station had arrived on the spot that the watchmaker was brought back there by some traffic constable. Now, how was it that this constable knew the watchmaker was absconding? The times, you see, are not very well fitting. There was not enough for – '

'Times-times,' the Patil broke in with quick rage. 'Do not be talking to me about your times for this and times for that. That is what you city people are not understanding. What does it matter whether it is one minute more or five minutes less? I will tell you what is mattering, Mr Police. It is not how you can eat up time, gobble, gobble, gobble, as fast as you can because you are fearful there is not enough of it. It is letting time go through yourself. It is being there and knowing and feeling what is happening at each and every moment. Knowing everything and feeling it, that is what you should be doing with time.'

Ghote felt a surge of hot resentment. What the old man had said might be true enough, though it would be hard to act in accordance with his philosophy when you were a police officer in hurry-scurry Bombay. But it had nothing to do with what he himself had realised about the case against Rustom Fardoomji. He had seen that false jump in logic speedy AI Lobo seemed to have made, in the logic that none other than the DGP appeared to have accepted. But this old, authoritative man in front of his chess-cloth had simply refused to consider what he had said.

Yet in a moment he found that, if the old man in his disdain for city people's notions of time had blinded himself to the meaning of that lapse in logic, he was still full of the shrewdness that had kept him for so many years lord and master of his wide lands and all who lived in them.

'So,' he said, before Ghote could respond, 'if you are now not believing, Mr Police, that this watchmaker is the man who must be hanged, who are you believing it should be?'

More truth? But how could he say to this man of power that he believed it was his own grandson, the nefarious one he had nevertheless protected from the consequences of all his illegal activities, who had committed the murder? Or even that it was the work of the Sarpanch, the man he had married to his daughter and had put into his present office?

But what else was there to say?

He looked down in perplexity, and saw, hardly seeing, that on the chess-cloth the Patil had achieved an invincible position. His opponent, the shrivelled old astrologer, evidently had seen it too, since he was making no attempt to play in his turn.

We are two of a kind, old man, Ghote thought. The Patil is too good for us.

'Nothing to say, Mr Police?'

'Patil sahib . . .'

No, nothing to say.

'Then I will tell you what you are wanting to talk, and not daring. You are wanting to tell that the fool of an SP in Ramkhed has whispered in some ear that my Ganpatrao was liking to kill his cousin-brother.'

'Patil sahib, I – '

The huge old man gave a sudden malicious grin, showing a mouth long devoid of any teeth.

'Oh, you bewakoof,' he said, 'did you not think I had very well seen that for myself? Do you think that because I stay in Dharbani and do not choose to go and be the big man in Ramkhed itself, as that ne'er-do-well Ganpatrao is wanting to do, do you think I am as foolish as the donkeys who bray in the village streets?'

'No, Patil sahib. I have spoken with you for just only

67

three-four minutes, but already I am knowing you are not at all a foolish man.'

'Good. You are not so much of an owl as that SP fool in Ramkhed.'

'Then yes, Patil sahib,' Ghote said, with a spurt of recklessness, 'I do believe it is possible – possible and no more – that it was Ganpatrao who killed his cousin-brother. He was not here in the village itself at the time the murder took place. That is so, is it not? I have yet to find out that he was in Bombay then. But I will do it.'

'Good. Good, little Mr Police. Then I will tell you what you have not yet found out. Yes, Ganpatrao was in Bombay. He told a servant he was going there. And two days afterwards my Ramrao was dead.'

Now tears had filled the old man's deep, fat-sunk eyes. Ghote waited for a little.

'There is one thing more that I can tell you, Patil sahib,' he said eventually. 'It is that your son-in-law, who is Sarpanch of this village, went also to Bombay at that time.'

The eyes in that big, blotched face glinted in approval through the tears that still hung in them.

'Good again. Good. So I will give you some more. That greedy satan of a grandson of mine, who must have been a rat in his last life, and my son-in-law, who is no satan but slippery as a cobra, they plot and plan together. They think I do not know it. They think that because they go creeping off, each one on his own, into Ramkhed and talk and plan and drink there that I do not know each and every time. And that I do not very soon find out what matters they have been talking.'

'It was murder they were talking, Patil sahib?'

'No, no. No, no. If murder was in their hearts, together or each one of his own, then they did have sense enough not to let out such thoughts. No, their plots and plans are about what they would do with my wealth and lands when I am no more. Those I am knowing and knowing.'

He chuckled, and a trail of saliva, red-tinged from a paan he must have been chewing, began to trickle from the side of his old-man's loose-lipped mouth. He rolled round on his shiny rexine sofa and spat into a big brass spitoon behind.

'You know what that idiot Ganpatrao is wanting to do?' he demanded.

'No, Patil sahib.'

'He is wanting to go to Ramkhed when I am no more and build there the biggest house of all with – with – '

Chuckles overflowed again, and he stopped to wipe tears, now of laughter, from his rheumy old eyes.

'With above – ' he managed to get out at last. 'Above, a tower for a clock. A clock. He wants nothing more than to see a clock of his owning standing up above entire Ramkhed. He is wanting to have built a tower like one you are having in Bombay, some Tajabi-Dajabi Tower.'

'The Rajabi Tower, Patil sahib? The one that is over the University in Bombay?'

'Yes, yes. Rajabi. A Rajabi-pajabi tower on top of his house with in it a clock. No. Three-four clocks. What for could anyone be wanting such?'

'To tell the time by, Patil sahib,' Ghote suggested with caution. 'So that everyone in Ramkhed will tell the time by his clocks?'

'And what for would they be wanting to know what minute-minute it is? What for do people like that want their this-clocks and their that-clocks, their house-clocks and their alarm-clocks, ping-a-ling-a-ling? What for when there are sparrows in the eaves to wake you each day with their twittering? What for do they need two clock-hands sticking this way and that when you have only to look up in the sky to know how much of the day has passed? Answer me that.'

But what the old man had ranted and roared on about had alerted Ghote to just what time it must now actually be, and to how little must remain before the bus came to take him back to Nagpur and on to Bombay.

He took a look at his watch.

He could have wished to have done so surreptitiously in view of the Patil's scorn. But he knew that those eyes, old though they were, would detect any manoeuvre, however adroit, and despise him for it.

But he was despised in any case.

'Oh, ho, Mr Police, now you even are looking at that little whirligig on your wrist, like a merry-go-round at a mela only. Why do you do it? Does it matter what it is telling you? And it is most likely lying also.'

Stung because his watch was quite probably lying – it had been erratic for the past few weeks – Ghote could only stammer out by way of answer. 'The bus, the time.'

'The bus? The bus? Oh, no, you are not taking any bus, Mr Police. There is work here for you to do. You are to find out if that satan Ganpatrao, or Jambuvant Dhoble who I myself was making Sarpanch, is the one who killed my poor Ramrao.'

Ghote felt as if he had been slapped in the face. He had begun quietly thinking to himself how well he seemed to have got out of the situation the DGP had plunged him into by ordering him to come to Dharbani in secret. He had seen himself going back to Bombay and reporting all he had now learnt and adding that the Patil had gone so far as to give him aid in his task. And now he was being commanded – commanded – to stay here in Dharbani.

'But – But – ' he stammered, 'if – if I stay here tonight where would I sleep?'

It was feeble, and he knew it. But no other thought had come into his head.

'Sleep? Sleep? Sleep where you are dropping, Mr Police. Go at those two fine bastards until you are dropping, and then sleep. Come here then, and I will have beds for you more than you can count.'

Ghote found he had now adjusted himself to the situation. The only thing to do, after all, was for the time being to obey the Patil's command. Perhaps, indeed, he would be able to bring the investigation to a successful conclusion in time to go back to Bombay and tell the DGP that Rustom Fardoomji was not the only suspect in the case before he made that formal, frightened confession.

'Very well, Patil sahib,' he said. 'I will do what I can. So let me first see your grandson. He is in the house?'

The Patil's eyes narrowed to two thin glinting slits.

'Oh, yes,' he answered, 'Ganpatrao is in the house now. But soon he will be going. To Ramkhed. To sleep with whores. And he thinks I do not know how he creeps out each night.'

He gave a rich chuckle and spat again into his brass spitoon.

'He makes a servant he thinks he can trust push that big, big motor-bike I was giving him down the road until I would not hear its noise. And I do not hear it. But I hear what that servant has to tell when he is coming back. I hear all, or I would have the skin from his back only.'

Ghote felt puzzled. Why had the old man not told him to go at once to see Ganpatrao, if he knew he was on the point of roaring away to Ramkhed on his powerful machine?

'So what you would do,' the Patil said, leaning forward on his sofa, 'is to go down the path to the highway and, when you are seeing that motor-bike, you must send the servant back to me and catch Ganpatrao there where he is not expecting.'

'Very well, Patil sahib.'

It was good thinking, most probably.

'It is almost the Hour of Cowdust now,' the Patil went on. 'And that is when Ganpatrao is sending the man to push-push that motor-bike out. He is believing that because of the dust rising when the cows are coming back to the village I cannot see. But I have got something better than old eyes in my head, Mr Police. I have got ears to hear what I can make people tell. So, go now and be there. Go.'

'Yes, Patil sahib, at once.'

'Yes, Mr Police, go and find which of those two was killing my Ramrao, and see that he is hanged. Hanged.'

71

7

Ghote left the Patil's house almost at a trot. Although the huge old man had said nothing particularly to indicate there was any danger of him failing to reach his ambush place before Ganpatrao, he felt impelled to go as fast as he could. But his hurry lasted only a very short time.

The evening was too beautiful. He had hardly gone past the shoemaker's hut in the outcaste quarter when he encountered the first of the cows being driven idly back from where they had been grazing all day. Their hooves were stirring the dust of the path as they went. It rose in the langorously swirling clouds he so well remembered at the Hour of Cowdust from his childhood.

The floating dust could hardly make a screen dense enough completely to hide Ganpatrao's motor-bike being heaved along to its rendezvous. But it was turning the light, which during the day had been one single harsh brightness, into something soft, glowing and golden. And, since the sun was at last sinking towards the horizon, there was a wonderful coolness in the air that at once lifted the spirits.

Yes, he thought, why hurry after all? That servant with the motor-bike will not be going any faster than he need. Why should I? There will be time enough.

So he wandered onwards, easily and amiably as the cows came in twos and threes towards him with a small boy or two armed with frail pieces of stick occasionally forgetfully urging them on.

How different these animals are, he reflected, from the skinny-ribbed scavengers of the streets in Bombay, almost as sharply acquisitive as Bombayites themselves going about their grabbing, not-a-moment-to-lose business. Here each flop-eared animal seemed sleek and contented, calmly approaching the evening tryst with the milking-pail, swaying gently from side to side, sending up with each easy pace one more puff of dust to add to the floating cloud around and above.

Tranquillity grew in him with every step. The DGP's urgency fell into place in his mind. He would take his time here in Dharbani. The Patil had made it impossible for him not to do what he could towards finding out if Ganpatrao had killed his cousin in the Tick Tock Watch-works, or if the murder had been the work of the Sarpanch. Very well, he would do what he could. And eventually, whatever the outcome, he would go back to the DGP and report. Perhaps he would have facts to tell that would put AI Lobo in his place for ever.

Overhead, the sky was deepening in colour swiftly and steadily. The kites that had wheeled endlessly over the village all day, black winged outlines against the washed-out blue above, were circling lower now, making their last descending forays on little running rat or neglected morsel.

Then, almost exactly where he had expected, he saw Ganpatrao's motor-bike. The servant, who had laboured to push it silently all this way, was leaning against its saddle. A leaf-wrapped beedi in his mouth sent a trickle of dark grey smoke up into the evening air.

He went over to the fellow, at the same easy pace he had adopted from almost the first moment he had met the returning, unurgent cows, and gave him the Patil's message.

He stood then and watched the man disappear into the now fast-waning light. Up above, a star had faintly appeared in the deep-bluey sky.

After a little he decided to take up a position behind the big motor-bike with its wide handlebars decorated with black leather streamers and its great curving chrome leg-protectors like the shields of an advancing army. He leant against the wide saddle. If he opened his shirt front, bunched it behind him and stood quite still, in the gloom he would look not unlike the bare-chested fellow Ganpat-rao had sent out.

The shock of discovering he was someone else would do nicely to put Ganpatrao straightaway at a disadvantage. It would be as well to start from as strong a position as he could when tackling the haughty individual he had seen strolling through the fields in the morning ignoring him as he stood among the thorns beside the path with the barber. Ganpatrao certainly had self-confidence, if no other good qualities. Anything that would rattle him was worth doing.

In silence he stood waiting.

All around the crickets had begun their night of shrill churring, on and on, monotonous and unending. In the distance he could hear occasional faint sounds from the village, a voice raised in shouting, the bray of a donkey, a dog barking.

Then at last he made out, coming softly and steadily towards him, padding footsteps in the now almost completely settled dust of the path. Padding and somehow insolent footsteps.

He braced himself.

As soon as the swaggering figure of Ganpatrao was near enough for him to be able to make out against the pallor of his face the twin deep rolling curls of his moustache he came swiftly round from behind the big gleaming motor-bike.

'Shri Ganpatrao Pendke, I am wanting one word with you.'

Ganpatrao's swagger dropped from him like a loosened dhoti falling in a heap round the wearer's ankles.

'What – Who – Who are you?'

The check-shirted figure came nearer.

'Yes,' he said, still with quick-jumping anxiety, 'I have seen you before. Today, out in the fields. How do you know my name?'

'I know your name, Mr Ganpatrao Pendke, because it was my duty as a police officer to find out such.'

'Police? You cannot be police. I know every policeman in this district from SP Verma down.'

'I am not at all an officer of this district,' Ghote replied,

74

happy to have the opportunity of reinforcing the threat he represented. 'I am one Inspector Ghote, Bombay CID, detached for special, confidential duty here in Dharbani.'

But the extra edge of threat appeared now not to have the effect he had calculated on. In the fast-gathering dusk he thought he saw Ganpatrao begin to resume his habitual arrogance.

'Well, Inspector, I cannot see how your special duty is of any concern to me. So I will bid you goodnight.'

Shoulders back, head lifted, he set off to go round Ghote to his waiting, chrome-gleaming machine.

Ghote moved firmly to block his way.

'Mr Pendke,' he said, 'I am thinking my duties here are very much concerning yourself. It is on account of you only that I have been sent here.'

Ganpatrao Pendke looked down at him. In the deepening gloom it was not easy to read that face adorned with its heavy curling moustaches. But Ghote thought its expression was hovering, delicately poised, between sharp aggression and snickering fear. He decided he must strike at once, and strike hard.

'Where were you on the morning of Tuesday last, being March the ninth?' he barked out.

'I – I – In Bombay. I was in Bombay.'

Then, after a long pause, with a trace of returning jauntiness, he added 'If you must know.'

'Oh, yes,' Ghote said. 'Well I am aware that it was in Bombay itself that you were. But what I am asking is: where in Bombay were you in the morning of that selfsame day?'

'What the hell business is that of yours?'

But Ghote had stamped on too many attempts at bluster from young men with money in their pockets to be over-awed by this spurt of hardly achieved confidence.

'What business?' he snapped back. 'It is police business, Mr Pendke. Answer, please.'

For a moment it looked as if the tall young man was not going to respond. But the moment hardly lasted.

'I – I was looking over the inside of the Rajabi Tower,

if you must have every last detail. I suppose you know what the Rajabi Tower is?'

'I am very well knowing what and where is such,' Ghote answered, seeing for an instant again the tall clock tower he had peered up at as he had prowled about waiting for it to be time to report to the DGP and receive the awkward order that had sent him out here. 'But I am not thinking that you were visiting Bombay just only for that. Was it? Was it?'

His grabbed-at bluff seemed to have gone home. In the fast-going light Ganpatrao's face took on a look of darting uneasiness.

'You were going to Bombay on account of your cousin-brother, Mr Ramrao Pendke,' Ghote charged, hammering home the advantage he felt he had gained.

Ganpatrao licked his lips under the thick black curl of his moustaches.

'But – But that was only natural,' he answered, forcing the words out. 'He – He had been most serious. We had thought he would die. But then they had succeeded, so they were saying, to bring him back to life. So naturally I went to see him, to find out if he truly was well again. How – How was I to know that next day he would be murdered? That was nothing to do with me. Nothing.'

At this moment Ghote wished with twanging intensity that he had something more to go on, something with which to press home the ascendancy he had achieved. To break his suspect at last.

If only he had been able when he had visited the station where AI Lobo was holding the wretched Rustom Fardoomji to get hold of that First Information Report on the murder . . . What he wanted now above all was some hard facts to face Ganpatrao with. Some times. *Where were you at just exactly 11 am? Oh, yes, so you say. So where were you at 10.47?*

Armed with hard information to be able to put questions like that he could break Ganpatrao in ten minutes. Or perhaps find definitely that he could not have been his cousin's killer and that therefore his uncle by marriage,

Jambuvant Dhoble, the Sarpanch, was the man to go for. But he had not got one single one of those facts.

Deprived as he was, he could only utter a threat which he hoped might be effective.

'Nothing to do with you, the murder of your cousin? Are you expecting me to believe that, Mr Pendke?'

'Yes, by God, I am. Why should poor Ramrao's murder be anything to do with me, Inspector? He was my cousin-brother. We grew up together here in Dharbani. We shared things. Why on earth should I want to batter the poor fellow to death?'

'Batter him to death?' Ghote retorted, though inside he sensed he was moment by moment losing ground. 'And how is it you are knowing victim was battered to death, please?'

Ganpatrao gave him a supercilious smile, black moustaches curling more deeply.

'For the simple reason, Inspector, that your superior officer, SP Verma, so informed us. And now, if you please, I must be on my way.'

And Ghote knew then that there was nothing more he could do to detain his suspect. He had lost.

Whether Ganpatrao was or was not the man who had killed his cousin in the Tick Tock Watchworks, unarmed with any ammunition of facts and times, he could only withdraw.

He stepped aside from the big motor-bike.

Ganpatrao marched across to it, swung a leg over its wide saddle, sat for a moment, tall and proud, before kicking the engine into violent, roaring life. He flicked at a switch and the machine's powerful headlamp sent a beam of dazzling white light out in front of him, turning in an instant everything around into blotting-out darkness.

Then, with a redoubled roar of sound, he plunged off down the path towards Ramkhed and its doubtful pleasures.

Ghote set off slowly back towards the village. The serenity with which he had waited to tackle his suspect had been gale-blown away. If he had been able to have his wish at that moment, he would have summoned from thin air the bus he had not been in time to catch and in it been steadily rumbled back to Nagpur and then have been able to go on to Bombay, to his home, to oblivion. But the time for the bus had long gone past, and there awaited him in the village only the task he had been set with such authority by the Patil. To find who had killed the Patil's favourite grandson, and to make sure that person was hanged.

And that person might or might not be the Sarpanch of the village, Jambuvant Dhoble. Jambuvant Dhoble, who if what that wandering-witted ancient soldier had spoken of had any basis in fact, was one of those people in the area the Nagpur guide-book in the Skylark Hotel had described as being 'as nasty as anybody.'

A sudden disquieting thought shot in to add to his depression.

In a village like Dharbani, or his own boyhood one, news of any sort travelled with the speed of fire spreading from hut to hut. And there could hardly be a more interesting piece of news in Dharbani at this moment than the presence in the village of an inquisitive stranger who had had a long talk with the grandfather of the murdered heir to the wide lands around. So, if the Sarpanch had not already learnt of his being here, he was likely to do so very soon. And, once he had become aware of that, he was likely enough to have a shrewd idea of what this stranger had come to Dharbani to find out. He would have time in plenty, if he indeed had beaten his nephew Ramrao to death in Bombay, to prepare alibi after alibi.

And, damn it, he himself did not even know where the Sarpanch's house was.

By now he had got well back inside the village, already with the coming of darkness shut up and inhospitable. Through the doorways of huts here and there, true, he could see the glow of cooking fires or the occasional dim light from the flickering floating wick in a clay lamp or the orangey gleam of the rarer electric bulb. But he doubted whether, if he had the temerity to knock and ask directions, he would get any very welcoming reply. The Sarpanch might not be a figure as all-powerful as the Patil, his father-in-law, but he must yet be someone feared throughout the village.

He heaved a sigh of blanketing frustration.

And at once saw, by the pallid light of the lamp thrusting up through the dangling air-roots of the banyan in the village square, the one person who should be able to extricate him from this one more infuriating dilemma. The aged astrologer who had been the silent victim of the Patil's prowess on the chess-cloth was coming towards him, tapping his way along with the aid of a stick.

'Panditji,' he called out.

The old man came hobbling up.

'Ram, Ram, my good sir. So we meet again.'

He looked up at Ghote through the steel-rimmed spectacles askew on his nose with a little wry smile.

'Do you know,' he said, 'I have been playing chess with the Patil for more years than I am able to count, and never once have I beaten him.'

Ghote felt a rush of warmth for this cheerful old man he had almost completely ignored on the floor opposite the overwhelming Patil.

He smiled.

'But could you have beaten him, Panditji?' he asked. 'I suspect that perhaps you could.'

The old astrologer grinned back at him, his spectacles glinting pale yellow in the light of the lamp inside the banyan.

'Yes,' he answered, 'I could perhaps have trapped his rajah. But would that be to beat him in the end?'

Ghote savoured the reply. He felt that in hostile Dharbani he had found an ally. Perhaps an ally who could do little to help him. But an ally whose simple existence gave him courage.

'Panditji,' he said, 'there is one thing you can do for me. You can tell me where is the house of the Sarpanch.'

'My son,' the old man answered, 'I can do more than that for you. I can take you there myself. It would not be

79

easy for you to find it in the darkness of the night and on the other side of the village.'

He turned to lead the way back in the direction from which he had been coming.

'But Panditji,' Ghote said, 'you were coming this way. Just only give me directions.'

'No, no. What else can an old man like myself do? I have all the time I want. I sleep little. I do not care when or how much I eat. Come. Come. We would be there in the time it takes to chew a paan.'

Ghote set off beside his new-found ally, hope-filled once more. But almost at once he began to regret having accepted the offer the old man had made. Bent-backed and bandy-legged he walked appallingly slowly, and it was possible that even at this moment someone in the village was flitting along the darkened lanes towards the Sarpanch's house to warn him about the mysterious stranger who had had that talk with the Patil.

He attempted to compensate for the tortoise-like speed of their progress through the shut-up, silent village – how Bombay would be buzzing at this time of the evening, he thought – by asking about the Sarpanch. Any information he could gather about the suspect he was about to interview might be helpful. But the astrolger did not seem to realise that what he had to say about the Patil's son-in-law could be of interest. He answered only in the briefest way before falling back into commenting on their progress through the village.

'It is just here when I was a boy only that I was bitten by the dog belonging to one Motiram.'

Hobble, hobble, hobble.

'In a hut down that lane – you would not be able to see it now in the dark – there lived a woman by the name of Yamunabai, who was making the best sweetmeats I have ever eaten. But she has been dead these many years. Yes, dead.'

Ghote, forcing himself to take the shortest of steps so as not to outpace his guide, wondered with fierce impatience how long the old man must be able to keep a paan in his mouth if their journey was to last, as he had said in the time-vague way of village life, 'as long as it takes to chew a paan.'

One piece of information about the suspect he was being led so slowly towards he did, however, manage to acquire. It confirmed the ramblings of the old soldier at the chai-khana. The Sarpanch, it seemed, had certainly used his position as head of the village council, at least once, to line his own pockets. There had been a big irrigation scheme, and a sum of Government money had been allo-cated to Dharbani. But the work had never been carried out. The Sarpanch, though, had shortly afterwards made considerable improvements to his house.

If I ever get to see that house, Ghote fumed. If inside it at this moment there is not someone warning the Sarpanch about myself and what perhaps has been overheard of my talk with the Patil. *Find which of those two was killing my Ramrao, and see that he is hanged.* Now in all probability he would come up at his destination against hedge after hedge of spiky lies.

Politely he expressed indignation about what the astrol-oger had told him, although he knew that such milking of public funds as the Sarpanch had contrived was common enough.

'But the Patil,' he asked, 'did he not prevent his son-in-law? The Patil is a good man, is he not?'

'Oh, yes, Patilji is good at heart. But he has his manhood also. If people had lost what should have come to them, more fools they, he is saying.'

'Yes. I understand.'

In silence they crept further along. Ghote wondered whether to ask again to be given directions. But he had not the heart to reject the old man's kindness. Especially now that he himself had felt that here was his only true source of support in these alien surroundings.

Perhaps talk would make the old man, whose stick seemed to stay stuck to the tramped earth under them for whole seconds before each new forward pace, proceed a little faster. He racked his brains for something more to say.

At last he recalled his recent encounter with, not an astrologer, but a man oppressed by astrology, the mad bus-starter he had been rescued from by Shruti Shah. The fellow had wildly claimed that Saturn had entered his astrological house and in absolute consequence he was suffering seven years of disaster. Did this kindly old man equally deal out such punishments, poring over his scratched palm-leaf predictions?

'Panditji,' he said, 'tell me, if a person born at such-and-such an hour at such-and-such a place is coming under the influence of Saturn, is he bound to have seven years of bad luck? Is there no escape from that?'

The old man stopped his doddering walk and turned to face him.

He almost exploded with anger at this apparent failure of his little ruse. Were they now going to stay where they were all night?

'My son, my son,' his aged guide said, 'is it that you yourself have come under such influence? Has your jatak been cast and revealed this?'

'No, no. No, no. It is – It is just only somebody I was meeting.'

'Well, if this friend of yours has truly fallen under the doom of Saturn, if that planet was truly found in the tenth place in his house, then it is there. It has come to be there, and it will take its seven years to traverse his life. It cannot be hurried by as much as one minute, and it will not stay one minute less than its proper period.'

Ghote, seeing in his mind's eye the mad bus-starter, bushy-bearded, shirt flapping to reveal a wealed and wounded body, demanding with fierce insistence *Time kya? Time kya?*, asked almost with anger, 'Is there no hope for him? No hope at all?'

'Oh, there are ways to counter such bad influence, yes, yes. If this friend of yours is undertaking many pujas, if he is burning much ghee, if he is chanting many, many mantras.'

Abruptly he chuckled.

'Patilji is believing a jatak may be changed by bribing the man who cast it,' he said. 'When his grandson Ganpatrao was to marry and the jatak I cast foretold the girl would be a cobra to him he was giving rupees fifty to have it altered. I told him it would be better to get the girl married to a sugarcane stick and let Ganpatrao have someone else. But he was insisting. So I let him understand I had changed the jatak, just like I am letting him win at chess always. And the marriage took place. But, though Patilji had trapped my rajah on the chess-cloth, it was the planets who were beating him in the end. The girl had one daughter only, a child that died, and now the doctor sahibs are saying she is not able to have another.'

At last the old man turned and began hobbling onwards again. Ghote walked beside him thinking.

So Ganpatrao can never have a son to inherit in his turn the Patil's lands and influence. And that makes his son-in-law, the Sarpanch, next-in-line now that Ramrao has been killed. So he did have reason enough for murder. As I shall bear in mind. If I ever reach the fellow's house.

But at that moment, turning a corner, there in front of him in the light of a slowly rising moon was the second largest house he had seen in Dharbani. It possessed, in fact, just a single storey and its walls were of unpainted clay. But it was large enough and had other signs of affluence about it. Its roof too appeared to be covered with tiles from distant Mangalore. Its wide door was of heavily carved wood, and under that there shone the bluish glint of light from a neon tube.

The aged astrologer bade him farewell, acknowledged his thanks, offered a blessing and set off, step by careful step, the way he had come.

Ghote stood and looked at the wide door in front of him. Nothing for it now but to knock and demand entrance.

8

Jambuvant Dhoble, Sarpanch of Dharbani, when Ghote
was led to him by a servant, might well have been
mistaken for a servant himself. He was dressed in a
grimed, long-tailed shirt over a baggy, red-striped, very
dirty pyjama. Short and chubby, his round, pudgily
double-chinned face had, two, three or four days' growth
of greyish beard.

Was the cheerful, chatty barber ever turned away when
he came to the house on his round, Ghote wondered. And
was that out of meanness? Or was it perhaps out of a
cunning desire not to draw attention to a prosperous life?
And was that why the fellow's clothes were so far from
clean? A man who had electricity in his house and lived
under a wide roof of fine tiles from faraway Mangalore
ought easily to be able to afford to pay one of the village
dhobis and have a clean-washed shirt every morning of
his life.

He was at first a little surprised, too, at the affability
the Sarpanch showed. He plastered frequent smiles on his
face as he ushered him to a seat in the cool of the inner
courtyard. Even if he was in no way guilty of his nephew's
death, Ghote thought, it was strange that he should be so
immediately friendly towards a CID inspector coming to
ask about his recent visit to Bombay.

But perhaps someone had, as he had feared, reached
him with news of his presence in the village while that
interminable walk with the astrologer had been dragging
itself on. Yet, even if that were not so, surely he was being
more hospitable than he need be.

Now he was ordering a servant to bring a fresh meal.

With only the little he had been able to eat at the
chaikhana during the day inside him, Ghote felt
constrained to accept, though he hardly liked the idea

of questioning a suspect while he ate the man's food. Nevertheless, as soon as the food had come – the large metal thali he had been brought was generously piled with a variety of good things – he began putting his questions.

While he did so he endeavoured as much as he could not to disclose his lack of precise knowledge about the exact time the murder had taken place in Bombay on the morning of Tuesday, March the ninth. And he found, to his inner satisfaction, that he was able to put a good many questions without mentioning precise times.

The Sarpanch, reaching across with greedy fingers every now and again for some choice morsel on the thali, seemed to be answering with extreme fullness. Yet little concrete emerged.

It was only, indeed, when, after the almost completely cleared thali had been taken away, the little fat man let slip the Patil's name that Ghote realised why he was co-operating so fully. It was not because he had had advance warning from some friend of this CID walla's visit. It was because he must have had a message from the Patil ordering him to answer to the full any questions that were put to him.

And he was doing what he had been told to do. Except that the answers he gave, though lengthy, amounted in the end to no more than that he had spent the morning of the murder, or part of it – it was never clear how large a part – with his nephew Ganpatrao in looking over the ancient, dominating Rajabi Tower at Bombay's University building.

'Yes, but at what time exactly were you leaving there?' Ghote asked, for the fifth or sixth time.

'I have told, Inspector. I cannot truly say.'

He leant forward and pushed his wrist clear of the grimy cuff of his long shirt.

'Look,' he said. 'Look, I am not having any timepiece. I am not able to afford.'

Then he had the impudence to reach across, flick back Ghote's own sleeve, expose his desperately unreliable watch and add: 'I am not an Inspector of Police with money from above offered always.'

Ghote could not stop himself reacting.

'Well, if you cannot answer, or will not, then I must go.'

He stood up.

And immediately the thought came into his head that he had neatly been made the victim of a cunning move to avoid further questioning.

But the Sarpanch was cleverer than this. With many quick smiles coming and going on his pudgy, beard-fuzzed face, he insisted that Ghote should stay, thereby covering himself from the Patil's wrath while at the same time leaving no opportunity for any more questions.

'It is too dark for you to be finding your way now to anywhere you can sleep. To the house of my dear father-in-law perhaps? No, no. You must stay here. I offer your goodself the best bed I am having.'

With defeated reluctance Ghote accepted. And found his dislike of the Sarpanch redoubled when, after the servants had dragged two charpoys out into the cool of the courtyard, the Sarpanch calmly appropriated the obviously better one for himself.

It took Ghote then a long while to get to sleep. To begin with, the strings of his charpoy, alternately too taut and too sagging, cut into him whichever way he turned. Then, within minutes, the Sarpanch, some ten yards distant, began to snore so loudly that it looked as if he was still awake and making the noise deliberately.

And all the while his mind kept going whirlingly over everything said during his long session of questioning. Had there been some tiny illogicality he had missed? Was there some change in the repeated versions of how the Sarpanch had spent that morning in Bombay which would give away a false alibi? Had the fellow betrayed somehow his greed to inherit the Patil's wealth and position? In some single careless word?

But he could hit on nothing. Indeed, what he remembered most clearly, and gratingly, from all the answers he had received was a moment when it was borne in on him that in his unsatisfactory earlier encounter with Ganpatrao his one seeming triumph had been no more than the result of a misunderstanding.

The Sarpanch had said at some stage that the day before Ramrao's death the two of them had visited him at the clinic where he had had his life-saving operation.

'We were very much wanting, you understand, Inspector, to make sure our dear Ramrao was truly restored to health, as we had all been praying.'

And at the clinic, he had continued by way of emphasising how little he could have wanted Ramrao dead, he and Ganpatrao had discussed a scheme which Ramrao had had in mind before his illness to exploit some large deposits of manganese near a place called Khindgaon at the furtherest extreme of the Patil's lands.

'Ramrao was hoping to start operations as soon as the Patil – '

He had broken off abruptly then and twitched out one of his quick smiles.

'That is, as soon as the time should be ripe.'

And the Patil's certain objections to such change removed, Ghote had added to himself.

It was then that he had realised that, when he had said to Ganpatrao by way of bluff that he believed inquiring after Ramrao's health was not the real reason he had gone to Bombay, Ganpatrao must have thought that somehow he had learnt of this mining project. He must have been momentarily frightened then that he might tell the Patil. So that one moment of triumph of his had been gained not from his own astuteness but by mistake.

Perhaps, though, Ganpatrao still believed he himself knew of this secret plan. So should he try tackling that arrogant young man again, and make use of that?

Or not? Was it not rather his duty to leave Dharbani if he could? After all, the Patil had no right to order him to conduct investigations here, impossible though it had been to refuse earlier. He had been sent here by the DGP simply to find out whether it was possible that the antisocial Ganpatrao could have been in Bombay when his cousin-brother had been murdered. He had done that. He had done more than that. He could take now good arguments to the DGP for proceeding to investigate more deeply in Bombay both Ganpatrao and the Sarpanch. AI Lobo's Rustom Fardoomji was certainly now no longer the only strong suspect.

So he was free to go.

But was he? Would the Patil have taken precautions to keep him in the village till he had named his beloved grandson's murderer? Well, at the least perhaps he ought to find out.

He turned over once again on the torturing charpoy. One more over-stretched string bit into his hip.

And once more he began to go over that interminable, evasive interrogation of the Sarpanch. Surely there must be something he had heard that might let him satisfy the Patil that the fellow would soon be brought to justice? But perhaps there was not. Perhaps even, back in Bombay, AI Lobo was right.

He longed for sleep, for being able not to think. But sleep obstinately kept away, throbbing with fatigue though his brain was.

The noises of the night loomed over him as if each tiny sound had been picked up on a microphone and was being dinned into his head from loudspeakers. The incessant squealing of the crickets, which in his village boyhood had been a sound that seemed simply part of the night, made, he had believed when he was small, by the circling stars above. A jackal in the distance howling and howling while he waited, tense, for the next mournful cry.

No, he thought, Bombay. It is my first duty to report to the DGP. I am an officer of police. I have my orders.

The light of the moon, now high in the sky, was shining into the courtyard, strong as a searchlight. In a few minutes, moving inexorably, it would strike his face. Then sleep would become absolutely impossible. And he needed to get sleep. He must wake early if he was to get to the bus stopping-place before anyone saw him and informed the Patil.

And he would not manage it. The creeping moonlight, steady in its advance as time itself, would reach his face and . . .

Then he found it was not moonlight but daylight. The sparrows in the eaves under the Mangalore-tiled roof of the house must have woken him.

But what time was it? His last thoughts had been that he must get away early to the bus. Now how late was it?

The Sarpanch on the charpoy at the other end of the veranda was still asleep, though no longer snoring. It seemed to be quite light.

Blinking gumminess from his eyes, he peered at his watch.

It said 3.20.

It could not be 3.20. There was too much light, far too much. It must be later, a great deal later. The bus, it might even have gone already. Or at any minute now it would be at the stopping-place, if his memory of the timetable back in Nagpur was right. If the driver paid any attention to the timetable's figures.

Furiously he shook at the watch.

And then he remembered how, despite the strangeness of his surroundings, he had managed to keep to routine the night before and wind it. So it must have stopped.

He shook it. He put it to his ear. Silence. He looked at the hands again. Still 3.20. He snatched at the winder and twiddled it for all he was worth. And the hands had not moved.

Broken. Broken. The damn thing was finally broken.

He did not know the time. He could not, here in time-less Dharbani, find it out.

He leapt from the torturing charpoy then, and, without waiting to see if there was anybody about or to do anything by way of smartening up the clothes he had slept in, he ran to the wide wooden door of the house, tugged its bolts open and hurried out.

He ran in what he hoped was the right direction for the

89

outcaste quarter and the path to the highway. There was scarcely anybody about, but he knew there would be no point in asking such people as he saw in the distance what time it was. Daytime, would be their answer. It was all they would know.

He tried, as he trotted along, dry-mouthed, to see how high in the sky the sun had reached. But beyond deciding that at least the day was not very far advanced, he found, though, like all the boys in his village days who had been able to tell by the sun how much they were in danger of being late for school, he once had had the knack, he had lost it altogether now. He had relied for too long on a watch. On the watch that now seemed to have stopped for ever. At 3.20.

He trotted on, at least increasingly confident he was heading in the right direction. And before long he found he had, indeed, hit on the outcaste quarter – he glimpsed the surly shoemaker emerging yawning from his hut – and the winding dusty path that would lead him to the bus.

And then he was at the stopping-place, panting from his long loping run. And the highway in front of him was silent and empty under the slanting cheerful rays of the early sun. There was not even anyone already waiting for the bus, not even Sitabai the steno, his witness that the Sarpanch could have been in Bombay to batter to death the heir to the Patil's lands.

I am in time, he thought. At least I am in time. The highway is still traffic-free. Those battering trucks thundering along have not yet begun their day. Good. Good.

He sank down on to the grassy earth-bank, taking care to keep well in the shadow of a low-growing thorny babool tree where any messengers sent by the Patil would not be able to see him before he had warning.

Then, letting out a great sigh, he looked at himself ruefully. His night at the Sarpanch's sleeping in his clothes had done nothing for his appearance. His shirt was limp with sweat and his trousers were creased so comprehensively that they might have been bundled up under a stone and left for days. Certainly, before he went to see the DGP back in Bombay he would have to get a change.

He looked along the road again.

And at once he was possessed by the notion that it was by chance only that there were no noisy, roaring, rattling trucks on it. Perhaps the bus had already come and gone, bearing Sitabai to her lawyer's office in Ramkhed, leaving him stranded here once again to come under the Patil's orders.

He jumped up and craned forward at the road's edge, peering in the direction from which the bus to Ramkhed and Nagpur should come. All was calm and still. Only the birds twittering foolishly in the bushes broke the silence. Then from behind him he did hear the sound of an engine. He turned briefly and saw a truck coming thudding and rumbling from Nagpur. As it passed him and went away along the black, dusty highway into the distance he saw its load was something bulky wrapped under a bulging black tarpaulin. It vanished. For a little the dust it had raised lingered. Then that, too, vanished and there was only the far horizon to look at.

Would the bus appear there? Ever? Had it really come and gone? He must have been here now almost half an hour – to judge by his vague feeling for the passing of time – and there had been no signs of life other than that one truck. So was the bus coming chugging towards him? Or was it not?

Distantly he heard another truck coming from the Ramkhed direction. But he did not dare take his eyes off the point where the bus should appear, somehow illogically convinced that if he failed to see it at the first opportunity it would mean that it had already come.

It was only when the roar of the oncoming vehicle's engine grew deafeningly loud close behind him that some inner warning-system made him begin to wheel round.

He had one glimpse of a motor-bike, a gleam of chrome leg-guards advancing, the rushing prow of some swooping ship. He knew then, without having an instant for calculation, that it was bearing down directly on him himself.

He started to fling himself sideways.

And there was a blaze of pain as the machine struck him full on his side and sent him, tossed like a hollow plaster statue, far into the verge.

9

Ghote never knew how long it was that he lay unconscious in the deep grass beside the highway. He calculated afterwards that it could not have been for many minutes because, when he had come to, the pock-marked face of Sitabai the steno was looking down at him. She was kneeling by his side, wiping blood from his neck with the end of her sari. Shakily he had sat up then and in a moment or two had felt clear-headed enough at least to ask what had happened. She had replied that coming to wait for the bus – 'It is always late on this day when it has so many baskets made in Khindgaon to take up' – she had just seen one of his shoes protruding from the grass.

'It was good that I saw, or you would never have been found.'

He had then a brief, horribly disquieting vision of his body, life ebbed away, lying there first for the vultures to pick it clean, then, over years, sinking deeper and deeper into the ground, at last to be lost altogether.

After all, he thought, as his state of dazed bewilderment lessened a little, nobody is knowing exactly where I am. Yes, DGP sahib knows I was to go to Dharbani, and, yes a search would be undertaken. But those searchers might not at all have found my body, and –

And then Ganpatrao Pendke would have got away with murder, perhaps for the second time.

Because he was suddenly certain, although he had not actually seen who it was who had been riding the motorbike that had swept down on him, that his attacker had been Ganpatrao. Returning from a night of lust in Ramkhed, he must have impulsively seized his chance to get rid of someone he believed somehow knew of that plan he had shared with his dead cousin to start up manganese mining as soon as the Patil was no more.

But, hardly had Sitabai put those spirallingly unpleasant thoughts into his head about what might have happened to him had she not found him, than she announced that the bus was approaching. Without at all working out whether it was the best course of action or not, he asked her to help him into it.

It was only when he had actually got back to Bombay, hours later, that he came fully to his senses. The whole journey remained a blur in his head, lit only by short periods of clarity when he had had to force himself to pay attention to his surroundings. He remembered seeing tottering loads of new-made baskets being taken off the bus at Nagpur railway station when he had had to make himself go in to find out about trains to Bombay. But had he managed at Ramkhed to thank at all Sitabai for what she had done for him? After the harsh treatment he had meeted out to her in order to find out what he had needed to know about the Sarpanch?

Then there had been another, longer period of full attention when, a little later, he had learnt that he had missed the train. He must then, he realised afterwards, have made up his mind to go by air. Somehow he had had sense enough to get into a taxi and go to Nagpur Airport. And he could remember getting a ticket there, and his relief when he had found he had actually got money enough to pay for it. And at some point – was it at the railway station or the airport? – he had drunk, one after another, three cans of sweet, dark-red, fizzy Thums Up. Or had he? Had that been a delusion brought on by raging thirst?

It must have been some time about then, however, waiting for the plane, that he had become conscious of what a state he was in. There was the blood from his neck, which Sitabai had made some effort to wipe with her sari but which had left a wide stain, stiff and rusty-brown, on his already limp and sad shirt. His trousers, he found, had a long rip in them on the left side, almost from hip to calf, and they, too, were stiff here and there with dried blood. And he was bruised. Bruised and bruised again.

He had felt incapable of discovering exactly how much. But he was aware that his ribs on the left as well as the whole hip and the thigh below it jabbed fierily whenever he moved. His cautious, dazed explorations had, nevertheless, reassured him. He seemed to have no broken bones and his wounds, though more plentiful than he was prepared to count, were no worse than severe grazes.

So, once safely landed in Bombay, he had felt it his duty to get to a telephone and ask the DGP's secretary for an immediate appointment with him.

It was with more than a little relief, however, that he failed to get it. After much delay the secretary informed him that DGP Sahib could not see him until 6 pm, and that that would have to be at his residence between other appointments.

He both fretted at the check and welcomed it. He fretted because, as he had recovered, he had found his mind full of a throbbing determination to pin the Tick Tock Watchworks murder on to Ganpatrao Pendke. Or, just possibly, failing that, on to the Sarpanch. It was clear to him that one or the other of them must be responsible, perhaps both jointly. Each of them was plainly capable of murder, as the Dhunjeebhoy brothers had protested their young cousin was not. Each of them had a good motive for wanting Ramrao back dead, as he so nearly had been until his operation at the clinic. Rustom Fardoomji's motive, on the other hand, despite his confession to AI Lobo, was altogether unclear. Both Ganpatrao and the Sarpanch had, too, been in Bombay when the crime had been committed, even though they had produced some show of having a joint alibi.

The enforced delay before he could put all this to the DGP was welcome because, as he had recovered in mind from the attack, he had become increasingly aware of how bruised and battered he was in body. The thought of going home and being cared for by Protima was wonderfully cheering. It would be a breathing space. He needed that.

And he could be sure at home of having it, even though he was returning without the Nagpuri sari he had promised himself to bring as a peace offering.

And, he thought with sudden confused dismay, even though he would come without the suitcase he had left at the Skylark Hotel, supposedly far away from 'the clog clog of machines, the whizzing trains, the blaring of horns and sirens.'

So it was rested, freshly clothed and much comforted by wifely applications of turmeric-and-sugar for his bruises and May and Baker's Propamidine cream for his cuts that he presented himself at six o'clock that evening at the DGP's flat on the fourteenth floor of a towering block called Sunny Hours. Or, as it turned out, since his efforts at home to get his watch going again had failed, at twenty-five minutes before six.

The servant, who had answered his ring at the bell and gone to tell the DGP he had arrived, returned promptly with a message. It was a terse echo of his master's voice. The correct time was 5.35 exactly, and Inspector sahib's appointment was for six precisely.

As the darkly gleaming door of the flat was being closed almost in his face, he manged to blurt out a request that the man would come and re-admit him at six. Sheepishly he added that his watch was broken.

He stood then in the marble-chip blankness of Sunny Hours' fourteenth-floor lobby and cursed. He was bringing urgent information about a serious crime. He was almost able to name the man or men who had committed it. And he was being made to wait.

Surely just in obedience to the DGP's mania for absolute punctuality.

He leant against the wall beside the flat's gleaming blank door and let himself grow into a sullen huddle. And, as he did so, he became gradually aware of a high, piping voice that seemed to come from nowhere directly to mock him.

'Sixty seconds, one minute. Sixty minutes, one hour. Twenty-four hours, one day. Seven days, one week. Four weeks, one month. Twelve months, one year. Ten years, one decade. Ten decades, one century. Sixty seconds, one minute . . .'

Eventually he realised what it must be. There must be a little girl in the flat opposite, No. 14B, and she was repeating and repeating an English homework lesson.

'Sixty seconds, one minute. Sixty minutes, one hour. Twenty-four hours . . .'

But then, when he did not know how much time had passed, five minutes or fifty-five, the door of Flat 14A abruptly swung back. The DGP's servant was there.

'Six o'clock, sahib. On dot.'

He followed the man in.

The DGP was sitting in his drawing-room in the middle of a large flower-patterned sofa. Here and there in the big carpeted room were other chairs, deep and springy, covered in the same bright material. There were small tables, too, in much-polished wood. There were vases of flowers, tall and resplendent. There were statues on the tables, of various gods and goddesses in ivory, bronze and wood. There was a bookcase filled with leather-bound volumes. There was a large television set, its white cloth dust-cover lying on the floor beside it.

'Inspector,' the DGP said, 'let me tell you, it is as bad to be early for an appointment as it is to be late. I like to see my officers presenting themselves at the time stated. Neither before, nor after.'

Thrusting out his left arm, he consulted the shining new Titan Exacto on his wrist.

'The time now,' he said, 'is precisely fifteen seconds past 6 pm.'

'Yes, sir,' Ghote said.

Inwardly he raged. Things could hardly have got off on a worse foot. And, besides, what the DGP had stated was not really true. Surely it was not so bad to be early for an appointment as it was to be late.

'Well now,' the DGP went on, 'I take it, Inspector, that, since you have insisted on coming to see me yourself, you have got something more to report than that this fellow – what's his name? – Ramrao Pendke was safely at home at the time of the murder.'

'Ganpatrao, sir,' Ghote felt bound to put the correction. 'Mr Ramrao Pendke was the victim of the occurrence. It is his cousin, Mr Ganpatrao Pendke, you sent me to Village Dharbani to make inquiries concerning.'

'Yes, yes. Ganpatrao. What about him?'

Ghote took a deep breath.

'Sir, I was finding out in Dharbani that, Number One, Ganpatrao Pendke was in Bombay at the time Ramrao was murdered. Number Two, that he is not able to account to one hundred percent for his movements on the morning of March the ninth last. Number Three, that now his cousin, Ramrao, is dead, Mr Ganpatrao Pendke is direct heir to the great wealth of his grandfather, the Patil of Dharbani, and that it is also very much his life's ambition to use such wealth for the building of a very fine house in the town of Ramkhed with a clock tower even, similar to the selfsame one of the Rajabi Tower here, sir.'

'Hm.'

Ghote had hoped that he might have had a more favourable response. But, he reflected, at least the case he had made against Ganpatrao had not been thrown out altogether.

'And sir, there is yet one more matter.'

'Very well, Inspector.'

'Sir, in Village Dharbani there is also residing one Jambuvant Dhoble, son-in-law of the Patil, and for the reason that Ganpatrao has no living child and his wife is unable to conceive further, the said Jambuvant Dhoble, Sarpanch of the village, is next-in-line to the Patil's wealth after Ganpatrao, and, sir, he was in Bombay also at the time of the murder.'

'And does this Dhoble fellow have any sort of alibi, Inspector? You made such inquiries as you could along those lines out there, I hope.'

'Yes, sir, I was making. Sir, both Jambuvant Dhoble and Ganpatrao claim only that at some time on the morning in question they were visiting together the Rajabi Tower. But no more than that, sir.'

'Hm.'

The DGP flicked a look at his watch.

'No, Inspector,' he said, 'I don't think we will waste any more time over that precious pair. Bad hats, I dare say, but what case is there against either of them to compare with a perfectly good confession to murder?'

'Sir,' Ghote burst out, unable to stop himself, 'has the watchmaker then repeated his confession before a Magistrate?'

The DGP's forehead creased for an instant in disapproval.

'I understand he has not, Inspector, if it's any concern of yours. I gather AI Lobo feels a period of suspense is necessary to bring the culprit fully to the right frame of mind. A perfectly sound decision.'

'But, sir,' Ghote hurled into battle something he had not intended to mention. 'But, sir, the man Ganpatrao was attacking myself, sir. Just only this morning. He was riding one powerful motor-cycle at myself, sir.'

The DGP sat up straighter on his flowered sofa.

'Why didn't you report this at once, Inspector? An attack on a police officer. Did you attempt to arrest the fellow?'

'Sir, I was not able. I was rendered unconscious, sir. And also I did not to one hundred percent see him.'

The DGP frowned sharply.

'Let me get this quite clear, Inspector. You were run down by a motor-cycle. I see now you're carrying yourself pretty stiffly. Very well. But you did not see who was riding the machine at the time? Yes?'

'Yes, sir. I was attacked from the rear, sir. I was noticing just only at the last second. But I am believing it was Mr Ganpatrao Pendke, sir. Definitely.'

'I see, Inspector. And on the strength of some fleeting impression you expect my old comrade-in-arms, SP Verma out at Ramkhed, to have the grandson of the most prominent citizen in his District put behind the bars like a common criminal?'

'No, sir. No. Sir, I was just only citing as additional evidence, sir.'

'Hm. Well, I can't say I much care for any of your evidence, Inspector, additional or not. I cannot set in hand inquiries into the lives of respectable citizens on such utterly flimsy grounds as you have brought me. It's out of the question. Dismiss, Inspector, dismiss.'

Ghote felt overwhelmed beneath a surge of despair. All right, the evidence he had gathered together was not strictly conclusive, and the confession AI Lobo had extracted was, on the face of it, altogether weightier. But those two out at Dharbani were certainly not innocent as new-born babes. It surely ought to be worth looking into their activities in Bombay at a time when a man they both had good reason to want dead had been murdered. And yet just because the DGP had so much faith in Lobo . . . And because the Patil was a man of such influence . . .

But what was there he could do?

Leadenly, and not without a twinge of sharp pain, he clicked heels in salute, and turned to go.

And, as he wheeled round, out of the corner of his eye he just caught the DGP looking once again at his new Tata Titan watch. Whether it was the word 'Tata' that set off some buried train of thought in his mind, or whether it was some other cause altogether, he found at that instant a dozen different things he had heard or half-heard during his time away from Bombay had run together into a whole coherent possibility. An altogether new possibility.

He turned back and faced the DGP.

'Sir,' he said, 'there is one more thing I should be informing you of. There is one more suspect in the case, sir. One who is not at all influential. Sir, there is a fellow working at the Tatca Institute. Of Fundamental Research, sir, here in Bombay. One by name of Barde, sir. It is Raghu Barde. His native-place is located at a village called Khindgaon, some miles distant from Dharbani but altogether within the purview of the Patil there, sir. And, though this fellow is working at TIFR, he is very much still interested in this Village Khindgaon, sir, which is altogether a poor place. So he is spending much of time to assist his fellow villagers to sell in Bombay baskets they are making and cloth also that they are weaving. He is believing it is vital for them to pull themselves up by their bootstrings only. It is Gandhian principles, sir. But, sir, I have also been learning that Mr Ramrao Pendke, the murder victim, had a plan to start up manganese mining at Khindgaon, sir. Such would destroy the rural peace of that place. So it is possible that the said Raghu Barde would go to the lengths of murder to stop same, sir.'

The DGP had at least allowed him to get his whole string of facts and suppositions out uninterrupted. He stood now awaiting the verdict.

'Yes, Inspector. Yes, that's more like it. You say this fellow started life as a simple villager, eh?'

'Yes, sir. Yes.'

'Then why the hell didn't you tell me about him straightaway? However, since you have got round to it at last, follow it up, Inspector. Follow it up. Find out all you can here about the fellow, and I'll send word to Lobo to keep his man on ice a little longer. Might be no bad thing in any case, given all the circumstances.'

'Yes, sir. Thank you, sir. And, sir, should I also just only make some inquiries, in a hundred percent discreet manner, sir, into those other two?'

'If you must, Inspector. If you must. But I am warning you, cause any trouble and I shall know who to blame. Yes?'

'Yes, sir. Thank you, sir.'

Despite his stiff side and tender bruises, Ghote ran all the way down the green-and-white marble-chip stairs of Sunny Hours, too impatient to wait for the lift and the khaki-uniformed liftwalla who had brought him up, much too early, to the fourteenth floor. Outside, he hailed a taxi and had himself driven through Bombay's tumultuous evening traffic, halted and freed and halted again, to the police station near Kemp's Corner.

It had come to him the moment he had been given permission to continue his investigation that what he had to do before all else was to obtain the fullest possible details of the actual murder. The exact time it had taken place, the names of any witnesses, any and every circumstance connected with it. Then perhaps he would be able to see if there were links between it and Ganpatrao Pendke and the Sarpanch. Then, too, he would be able to question Raghu Barde at the Tata Institute a great deal more effectively than he had questioned Ganpatrao at the Hour of Cowdust out on the path from Dharbani or the Sarpanch in his house while the fellow stole titbits from the thali he had put before him.

At the station he was told, to his mounting delight, that AI Lobo was inside.

And there he was, sitting on the corner of a table thick-piled with papers and files dusty with age, a short, athletic-looking fellow, bar signs of a thickening waist, with a round face enlivened by a pencil-thin sharp moustache. He was wearing a bright pink shirt with in its pocket three silver-clipped pens.

Introducing himself, Ghote stated at once that he had the DGP's permission to take an interest in the Tick Tock Watchworks murder.

He had been ready for Lobo to take instant offence, as many station officers did when someone from Crime Branch was allocated to a case they were handling. But the reception he got was far from cool or guarded.

'Yeah, man,' Lobo said at once, 'thought Crime Branch would be round sooner or later. Big tamasha, this. But let me give you the full works. Come and chew a cup of tea.'

Ghote expected to be taken to the station's canteen. But instead Lobo led him out to a small restaurant. Its proprietor, sitting behind his cash desk, received them with obsequious smiles. A waiter hurriedly cleared a table.

'Tea, Inspector?' Lobo asked cheerfully. 'Or, better, do you want Nescafé? Or a cold drink? Have a cold drink and something to eat. They bring me only the best here. On the house, of course.'

'I will take tea only,' Ghote said, his suspicions of Lobo wrinkling up again.

As soon as the waiter had brought their order – Ghote realised that his tea was a Special, in a large cup, full to the top, with a spoon in the saucer, while Lobo had two egg sandwiches and a cold Mangola – the Assistant Inspector leant forward and spoke in a confidential undertone.

'We can do this nicely between us, I hope, Inspector. Don't go thinking I'm one of those boys who always tries to blind any Crime Branch walla. Jesus, they ought to know better. Give and take, that's what I say. I help you, you help me.'

'Very well, AI,' Ghote said cautiously. 'So, tell me please, what exactly do you believe took place at the Tick Tock Watchworks?'

'Oh, simple enough, man. This Ramrao Pendke came in there, loaded with money. You could tell that from the body even. Gold Rolex on his wrist. And, guess what, that was stopped at the time of the murder. God, would you believe? Just like a crime film. But there it was in real life. This Rustom Fardoomji had beaten and battered him so much that he actually hit the watch. Stopped it dead. At 11.08. Good evidence, that. And you know something else? The bloody watch was a fake. A fake, man. Genuine Swiss, made out at Ulhasnagar. I happened to catch sight of the little layer of lead inside, put in to make it the same weight as gold. Keep my eyes open, you know. By Christ, yes.'

'But what evidence have you got that it was Fardoomji himself who did the battering?' Ghote asked.

'Evidence? One confession. Came popping out of him like a stone from a double-ripe mango. Hardly had to touch him. Still, nice to have it all wrapped up so quickly.'

'But if he was so quick to confess,' Ghote said, 'is that at all fitting with him being a person who would batter the victim in the aforesaid manner? Breaking the watch even?'

'Fitting farting, man. You go worrying about getting every least little thing to agree, you're there all day and all night. And in the end you're no better off than you were in the beginning. No, get a nice confession, and that's quite enough for me. Got to get him to repeat before a Magistrate, of course. But he'll do that when the time comes, God bless him.'

'Are you sure, AI?'

'Swear to God.'

Ghote stretched across the little marble-topped table and pulled his Special tea towards him. He took a careful sip.

'All the same,' he said, 'I would like to see the fellow.'

'Hey, man,' Lobo abruptly exclaimed, reaching forward to Ghote's wrist, bared as he had pulled his tea towards himself. 'You not got a watch? How's that?'

Ghote felt a dart of resentment at the interruption.

'Broken,' he said curtly.

'Then I'm just the guy you're needing, Inspector. See this.'

Lobo shot out his own wrist to reveal on it the most complex watch Ghote had ever seen. Large-dialled and black-faced, it had two smaller dials within it, a large sweeping white second-hand, a day-and-date window and what was surely a compass as well.

'Japanese,' Lobo said. 'Bet there aren't half a dozen like it in entire Bombay. Smuggled only last week. Super job. And, now, look at this.'

He dug into his back trouser pocket and in a moment plonked on to the table another watch. Not quite so large, with a glintingly shiny chrome surround, a copper face and a multi-faceted glass.

'Wore it for more than a year,' he said. 'See, second-hand in gold, anti-magnetic, water-resistant, everything. Let you have it for fifty bucks. Bargain of the year. Got my initials and motto on the back. But you can easily get the initials changed, and the motto you can keep. *First past the post*. Do you some good.'

'No, thank you,' Ghote said. 'I will be getting my own repaired.'

'As good as this? I bet not. This is a watch that makes people look at you, man. I hate to part with it.'

'No, all the same. I am preferring my own.'

He thought then how unreliable his watch had, in fact, been for months past. And, little though he liked Lobo, he thought as well how, if he was to learn every fact and detail about the Tick Tock murder, he was going to need all the co-operation he could get from this pink-shirted 'expeditious investigator'. The very words the great Dr Hans Gross had used, rich with scorn, read by himself a hundred times, came back to him. *When our artistic Investigator is sufficiently skilled in suppressing the difficulties and obstacles that may prove troublesome in quick work, he will well deserve the title of 'expeditious'*. But he fought them down.

'Look, AI,' he said, 'let me after all borrow your watch for two-three days. Then if I am liking, I will buy and forget my old one. How is that only?'

'Fine, fine,' Lobo said, thrusting the watch across. 'Keep it a week, keep it a month. But give me my fifty chips at the end, eh?'

'We would see,' Ghote answered, secretly resolving to take his own watch to the repair shop near his home as soon as possible.

He strapped the copper-faced, shiny object he had been lent round his wrist.

'And now,' he said, 'let us go back to your lock-up, and I will see what I make of this culprit of yours.'

AI Lobo looked across at him.

'Sorry, Inspector,' he said. 'Not possible. God bless you.'

10

Ghote had sat back in blank astonishment at the flat declaration that he was to be prevented from seeing the man who had confessed to killing Ramrao Pendke. Evil suspicions scurried like scorpions through his mind, confirming in a moment all the doubts he had felt about Lobo's handling of the murder.

He was on the point of ripping into the fellow and insisting, with all the authority of his superior rank, on going at once to question Rustom Fardoomji when second thoughts made him hesitate. He could get to see the influential Dhunjeebhoys' cousin later. When it came down to it, no one could stop him. Certainly not this jumped-up DGP's pet. He would make sure of that. And in the meanwhile he still needed the fellow's co-operation.

Just as much, he thought, as Lobo must see himself as needing co-operation on his part, to be obtained either by the sort of flattery he had been using up to now or by cunning evasiveness, so as to put off any interview with Fardoomji until after a formal repetition in front of a Magistrate of his confession. He might need only as short a time as twenty-four hours. But need it he would.

Yet, if Lobo wanted that minimum of twenty-four hours, that, too, was quite long enough to give him himself plenty of opportunities to demand to see Fardoomji. And then, if indeed it looked as if that confession had been beaten out of the fellow, it should not prove too hard to make it clear to him that fear need no longer prevent him asserting his innocence.

But in the meanwhile he could do with seeing the First Information Report on the case. That would have in it all the exact times and circumstances. He ought to have more to go on then that bare 11.08 at which the dead man's watch had stopped.

If he failed to get co-operation from Lobo, he could always carry out an investigation in spite of him. But, without his aid, everything would take twice as long and in any inquiry time was never on the investigator's side, however dangerous it was to be artistic and expeditious.

So in the end he contrived a mock-careless shrug and said that of course there was no hurry to see Fardoomji. 'He would not be running away, isn't it?' And, swallowing the last of his Special tea, he rose to go.

What he might do, he thought, was to start at the beginning of the victim's day and get hold of some accurate times for that. Armed with those, he could later make sure of seeing the First Information Report and add from it to a timetable of events. It came swimming into his mind's eye at once, a neat, tabulated list of events, each with a time against it. It would make the whole business totally clear.

And he could make his start without any assistance, or possibily any hindrance, from AI Lobo. The DGP had told him the name of the America-returned surgeon who had apparently restored Ramrao Pendke to life. Yadekar, it had been. Dr Yadekar. No difficulty in finding out where his clinic was and going to see him.

Stepping out of the restaurant, once more to the greasy smiles of the proprietor, he consulted his newly-borrowed watch. And found its gold hands against its copper face and its heavily faceted glass rendered it nearly impossible to read. Eventually with not a little turning and twisting of his wrist – he saw Lobo pretending not to notice – he made out that it was nearly half-past seven. Almost certainly too late to find anyone responsible at the clinic, even when he had located it.

Bed, he thought, suddenly very conscious of his aches and bruises and drained of energy after a day that had begun so long ago, and in such a disabling fashion. But a long, long night's sleep. And then see how AI Lobo matched up to an investigation not at all expeditious.

And next morning, his bruises again the better for an application of turmeric-and-sugar, he found in the telephone directory that there was a Shrimati Usha Yadekar Clinic at an address in swanky Altamount Road. Ringing as early as he dared, he was given an appointment, not by Dr Yadekar himself but by his wife, Dr Mrs Yadekar.

That was not, however, until ten o'clock. 'I have my duties, Inspector,' the sharp voice, with a tinge of American in its accent, had said. 'The care of patients must take priority.'

So, before setting out, he realised he would have time to visit the Big Ben Watch Stores, where he had always in the past taken his watch or the family clock for repair. He wondered why he had. He disliked the proprietor intensely and had once sworn never to enter his shop again, only hardly had that word 'never' entered his mind than the thought of all the minutes, hours, weeks and years it implied had made him hastily rescind that inner oath.

The reason he disliked the man he always thought of as 'Mr Big Ben' so much was his habit of handing out moral advice along with his mended clocks and watches. Sometimes this would take the form of a maxim delivered at parting. More usually it came as a carefully written card prominently propped among the dusty clocks in the little shop's window bearing more words of sage warning.

As he approached the shop now, he saw that a new card had been placed in its narrow window. *Punctuality is the Politeness of Princes (Rajkumars)*, it read. He nearly turned away at the door. But he badly wanted to give back to AI Lobo the copper-faced monstrosity on his wrist. So he quickly slipped the damn thing off and hid it away, the better to be able to claim he was without the means of telling the time.

Mr Big Ben took the old watch he had seen on not a few occasions before, fastened his glass to one eye, opened the back and peered at it.

'Balance staff worn, winder detached also,' he announced eventually.

'It can be mended?'

'Oh, yes. I am able to mend anything.'

108

'And how long would it take?'

'Try in one week. Or more.'

'One week?'

Fury flared up in him, a paper fire.

'Listen,' he shouted, 'I am a police officer, as you well must be knowing. A police officer is most often required to state the exact time to one hundred percent. Now, are you going to get that watch mended at once, or are you not?'

'My son, there are things in this world that cannot be hurried. If I set to work on this watch, throwing the parts here and there, racing and pacing, what would happen? You would never see your watch going again. No, no. Haste makes waste, that is one good old truth. Haste makes waste.'

'But I am saying I need that watch. I need it now. By tomorrow at the least. I must have it.'

The old man shook his head in negation. And with pleasure, Ghote thought bitterly.

'Then you must take it to some quick-flick fellow. I can work no faster than I am able to work. But, if you want that repair to be a repair which is not going to go wrong again as soon as you are putting it on your wrist, then you must leave it with me.'

Ghote stood poised, caught by indecision. He would have been delighted to have seized the watch, stamped out of the shop and gone to 'some quick-flick fellow.' But he knew of nowhere. And Mr Big Ben had, at least, always been reliable in the past. Each time his own watch had had to be mended it had been for some new fault. At some unknown shop he might be made to pay and pay, and still not get the job done properly.

'Oh, very well,' he snapped. 'Keep the damn watch. Take your time. I will not care.'

'Yes, yes,' old Mr Big Ben said, putting the watch on to a shelf behind him.

Ghote saw with flaring dismay that the shelf held a dozen other watches and half a dozen clocks, all stopped, all silent.

'Next week,' Mr Big Ben wheezed. 'Try Tuesday. But I am not promising.'

Ghote turned to go.

'And remember: "if you can fill the unforgiving minute with sixty seconds' worth of distance run, yours is the Earth and everything that's in it, and – which is more – you'll be a Man, my son!" Shri Kipling is saying it.'

And with those clangingly moralistic words echoing in his head, Ghote hurried off to the Shrimati Usha Yadekar Clinic.

The house in Altamount Road where Dr Yadekar had established himself was a large white-painted building, notably spick and span among Bombay's customarily years-marked edifices, with a garden in front of it, if a large dried-up stretch of grass and a much overgrown archway could be called a garden. Ghote extracted the time from AI Lobo's unreadable watch, now on his wrist again, to make sure he was not too early, the DGP's advice of the day before coming back to him like the taste of a too spicy meal. Then he went up to the wide front door under the imposing portico and rang at the bell there.

A neatly uniformed servant answered and asked him to wait. In the reception hall he sat himself cautiously on one of the half-dozen well-sprung velvet covered chairs dotted about and looked around him. The room, which was large and impressively well decorated, was dominated by a sculptured panel set in one wall, evidently dating from when the house had been in private hands. It depicted a timeless and bouncingly unreal mythological scene of full-breasted maidens entertaining with dance and music a languid young man. On either side of it there hung, in stern contradiction to its voluptuousness, framed certificates of medical degrees. Dr Yadekar's, ranging from a Bombay MB to awards in surgery from America, were on the left. Dr Mrs Yadekar's – another Bombay MB and US qualifications in psychiatric medicine – were on the right.

Ghote had just time to wonder whether he would have the courage to ask a lady apparently so formidable, in learning and in position in the social structure, for the small details of her patients' routine that he needed to know when the servant returned. He was asked to follow.

They went up a flight of stairs to a consulting-room furnished all round with clinical-looking steel cupboards. It smelt, faintly, of antiseptic. From behind a glass-and-steel desk Dr Mrs Yadekar rose to greet him, a trim, starchily severe figure in a short white tunic and white trousers, dazzlingly clean.

For a moment Ghote managed to think how like her outfit was to the salwar-kameez many smart Bombay girls wore. And how unlike in its utter lack of gracefulness. Then Dr Mrs Yadekar descended on to him.

'Inspector, I shall give you any help I can. Of course. The late Mr Ramrao Pendke was our patient. But I must warn you, I can spare you five minutes only.'

Ghote licked his lips.

'Thank you, madam,' he replied hastily. 'I am thinking you would already have spoken with Assistant Inspector Lobo in charge of the case from the local police. I am from Crime Branch.'

'No, Inspector,' the doctor said. 'I have in fact seen no one from the police at all. To my surprise. But, frankly, I put that down as just one more example of Bombay not being as efficient as the States where my husband and I were pursuing our careers until my father-in-law decided to take sannyas and left us his practice here.'

Ghote was as much struck as Dr Mrs Yadekar by AI Lobo's not even paying one visit to the clinic. And some of his astonishment must have leaked into his next, merely polite inquiry. 'Your father-in-law was taking sannyas?' because Dr Mrs Yadekar sighed sharply.

'Yes, Inspector,' she said, 'you do well to show surprise. I myself find it hard to understand how a man trained in scientific principles, a doctor, could abandon a perfectly good practice to become no more than a wandering beggar. But after my mother-in-law's decease that is precisely what happened. We don't even know where he

111

is now. In Benares, I guess. You know what they say: *Thora khana aur Banares rahna.*'

Ghote was more surprised to find that a lady with so much of America about her allowed herself to speak as much Hindi as *A little to eat and to be in Benares.* But he felt his alloted five minutes must be fast going. Quickly he turned to something that had puzzled him as he had thought about the circumstances of the murder on his way to the meeting.

'Please,' he said, 'can you be telling me how it was that the late Mr Ramrao Pendke was able to be outside this clinic at the time of the attack upon him? What exactly was he suffering?'

Dr Mrs Yadekar looked at him with something like shock.

'Surely at least you read our noticeboard outside?' she said. 'We specialise here, Inspector. Already we have a considerable reputation for our work. Renal. It is Renal.'

'Please?' Ghote said, entirely baffled by this last, American-intoned word.

'Renal, Inspector. Renal. Diseases of the kidneys. My husband is a brilliant surgeon who was specialising in Renal in the States. So when his father gave up his practice here and asked us to return we altered its nature and set up this clinic. I mean, we could hardly tolerate the usual kind of practice here, those billboards advertising *Consult in All Kinds Diseases, Phthisis, Catarrh, Sterility, Constipation.* Really.'

The vigour of her denunciation almost silenced Ghote, especially as he had realised he did not even know exactly where in the body the kidneys were.

But one thing about them he did know.

'So you are here doing transplant?' he asked, hoping to regain ground.

'Of course. One of the few advantages of practising in India is that at least a regular supply of organs is available from donors willing to sell.'

But now the thought that there were people who actually sold their kidneys sent him back into a state of dismayed bewilderment.

'They give up their kidneys, their renals, for money only?' he stammered.

'Hardly their kidneys, plural, Inspector. The body cannot function without kidneys. You ought to know that much at least. But with one kidney a human being can remain in a relatively healthy state.'

Something in the doctor's high-minded, clinical attitude made Ghote react. He found he wanted nothing more than to hit on something that would knock her from her perch.

'So you are taking out kidneys from the poors and putting in the rich?' he asked, scarcely hiding the venom.

'Where such a course is indicated, yes,' Dr Mrs Yadekar replied, loftily as ever. 'In other cases artificial substitution of renal function may be preferable. We have imported the latest dialysis apparatus.'

Conscious though he was that his stipulated five minutes must be fast running out, Ghote was still unable to refrain from one more attempt to unseat this cool, America-returned practitioner.

'The donor, as you are calling him, and the person who has paid for his kidney, do they meet?' he asked. 'Does a cash handover take place even?'

'Of course not. Of course not. Do you know nothing of medical ethics? The donor never knows – That is, the recipient is always unaware of the source of the replacement organ. That goes without saying.'

The look she gave Ghote made it plain he had been guilty of an unpardonable offence.

How now will I be able to obtain her co-operation, he asked himself with sudden bleakness.

But then the tiny hesitation in what she had said came back at the last second into his mind. Did it indicate a weakness? He probed.

'The recipient is always unaware?' he asked. 'Is it never happening that a man who has been paid to give up his one kidney finds out who is getting same?'

Dr Mrs Yadekar shot more upright on her tubular steel chair. She darted at Ghote a look of frosty inquiry.

'Have you been questioning my servants?' she said. 'The man who admitted you?'

'No, madam, no.'

'He didn't tell you about the clerk I dismissed? Come, Inspector, I have a right to know.'

But Ghote had recovered enough now to speak with some cunning.

'This clerk,' he said, 'why exactly were you dismissing?'

Dr Mrs Yadekar tightened her lips into a fierce line.

'The man had no legitimate reason to object,' she said. 'He quite needlessly allowed that donor to know who was to benefit from his surgery.'

'And this man, this clerk, he was very much upset by his dismissal?'

Dr Mrs Yadekar smiled, coolly.

'You would hardly expect him to be overjoyed, would you, Inspector?'

'No. No, I am supposing not.'

Ghote thought of putting one more question about this possibly embittered clerk. But from the doctor's continuing expression of lofty amusement he doubted if he would get anywhere. And he was urgently aware, too, of how much more of his allotted five minutes had already gone by. He reverted instead to the prime object of his visit.

'Madam,' he said, 'kindly be telling. Mr Ramrao Pendke, at what exact time of the day of his murder did he leave this clinic? Was it with or without permission?'

'It was with permission, Inspector,' Dr Mrs Yadekar replied, in tones a great deal less haughty. 'Exercise is indicated for patients after surgery. Mr Pendke would have left here at 10 am precisely. That day he was to walk down to Kemp's Corner, then along to the August Kranti Maidan, to go round that park once, at a steady pace, and then return. He should have reached here before twelve noon.'

'And when he did not, you were taking some steps?'

'Yes, yes. We called the police station. Eventually they called back to say he had been attacked and killed. Eventually.'

As much to restore the image of police efficiency as anything, Ghote asked a different question.

'And what visitors was Mr Pendke having in the time immediately before his decease?'

Dr Mrs Yadekar, without a word, swivelled round in her chair, pulled open a filing cabinet, extracted a black-bound book and flipped rapidly through its pages.

'Yes,' she said, 'he was visited on Monday last, that is the day before he was attacked, by, one, his cousin Mr Ganpatrao Pendke, accompanied by an uncle, Mr Jambuvant Dhoble.'

'And by Number Two, who, please, madam?' Ghote asked, tucking away the confirmation that Ganpatrao and the Sarpanch had seen Ramrao so soon before his death.

'By two,' Dr Mrs Yadekar answered, 'a Mr Raghu Barde. I remember the occasion particuarly since, as we do not normally permit two visits in one day, I gave my personal agreement. Something, I may say, I regretted almost at once. I understand some sort of quarrel took place, a rather violent quarrel. An occurrence that might well have retarded recovery.'

Ghote felt a flame of elation. So, not only had Ganpatrao and the Sarpanch been here to see Ramrao, but Raghu Barde had actually seen him too. Barde, the man who believed it was vital – Sitabai the steno's word of English came back to him – that his fellow villagers at Khindgaon should achieve modest prosperity by their own efforts and not as the result of the monster manganese mining operation that Ramrao had planned. Barde had met Ramrao here and there had been a violent quarrel.

Then there was the fact that, if he himself had easily learnt Ramrao's precisely timed pattern of exercise, so could Barde have done. Have learnt of it and known then how to follow his victim until an opportunity to strike occurred.

With a little more luck it should not be long before AI

Mike Lobo had something else to think about besides palming off unwanted watches.

'Please, madam,' he said, hardly able to conceal his excitement. 'What like was looking this Mr Barde?'

'It's odd you should ask that, Inspector,' Dr Mrs Yadekar replied. 'Because he had a rather strange appearance. He's pretty young, in his early thirties no more, but he's almost completely bald. Coupled with him being very tall, well up to the two-metre mark, he's not anybody you'd forget you'd seen.'

Another piece of luck coming from an inquiry he had made in wanting every last piece of information. A man as curious in appearance should not be difficult to trace from witnesses at or near the murder scene. From anywhere along the walk that had led Ramrao Pendke to his death.

'Madam, excuse, please,' he burst out. 'I must at once leave. Highly important business.'

'Well,' Dr Mrs Yadekar said, 'I'm glad to see someone in India's got some idea of prompt action.'

11

Ghote hurried down the hill from the Shrimati Usha Yadekar Clinic, head buzzing with an excitement he found hard to keep decently in check. He had got into his hands a line of investigation that looked better and better with every passing moment. And, he added to himself with an inward smile of pleasure, he had also succeeded in securing from efficient, America-returned Dr Mrs Yadekar more than the strict five minutes she had stated she could spare him.

He decided to make straight for the furthest point on the round of exercise that had been prescribed for Ramrao Pendke, the August Kranti Maidan. It was a place he knew well from when he had had to investigate a rather sordid blackmailing case involving a girl who had lived in one of the hutments in the nearby Papandas Wadi. In the park, he calculated, where all day long idlers sat or played he would stand his best chance of finding someone who had seen that tall, noticeably bald young man, Raghu Barde. Possibily someone who had noticed him following Ramrao Pendke.

He arrived, out of breath and feeling his sore side, at the wide stretch of scorched grass and looked about. Half a dozen games of cricket were simultaneously being played by a variety of youths, mostly dodging school he guessed. A ten-year-old equipped only with a massive, man-sized pair of ancient keeper's gloves, crouched with an air of immensely serious professionalism well back from a tottering pile of bricks that did service for a wicket. At the other end of the scale were young men dressed in proper, if dirtyish, whites, playing with as much intentness. Then there were schoolgirls, in the neat uniforms of the New Era School opposite, enlivening their strictly allocated play-period with a game that appeared to consist of nothing but the repeated English question 'May I?' and the scornful, invariable retort 'No, you may not.'

No likely witnesses here.

Perhaps, he thought, he would have done better to have stopped in his race down here and questioned the urchin he had seen out of the corner of his eye squatting on the pavement selling a basket of far-from-fresh prawns. Their sharp smell had just alerted him. There would have been a witness with time in plenty to take note of any passing oddity. Should he go back?

Then he remembered that on the far side of the maidan there was a hedged-off area where old men were always to be found sitting hour after hour whiling away the time. They would be yet better witnesses. Dr Mrs Yadekar had told Ramrao Pendke to walk round the whole maidan. If he had obeyed his instructions, as with someone as fiercely precise as the doctor he could scarcely have failed to do, he should have been seen by at least one idly watching observer there.

He hurried over.

And struck lucky at once. Only, he was not sure whether his luck was wholly good.

A voice had hailed him at almost the moment he set foot on the wide path round the enclosure.

'Ghote! It's young Ghote, by Jove.'

He turned to see, sitting sedately on one of the pink-coloured stone-chip chairs surrounding the enclosures, hands clasped over the knob of a stick, his former colleague, Inspector D'Sa, now long retired, one of the last of the band of Anglo-Indians and Indian Catholics who had once dominated the Bombay police officer corps.

His immediate reaction was leaden dismay. D'Sa had been a tremendous bore even in his last days in the service. Immediately after he had retired he had been worse, always drifting back and descending on anyone he could persuade to listen for long sessions of past-regarding gossip. What would he be like now?

But then a second thought had come to him. D'Sa was, after all, a trained police officer, and now, as well, someone with time in plenty on his hands. In short, an ideal witness to have taken notice of the suspicious circumstances of convalescing Ramrao Pendke being secretly followed by tall, young, bald Raghu Barde.

There was a vacant stone chair next to him. Ghote lowered his bruised frame carefully on to it, wincing as the stored heat penetrated his cotton trousers.

'Well, well, D'Sa sahib,' he said, making himself sound as friendly as he could. 'How goes the world with you these days?'

D'Sa shook his head sadly.

'Badly, young fellow. Damn badly. There are you, I suppose, looking forward to your retirement. To easy days, to no more duties, no more consorting with riff-raffs. Less ulcers, you think, less heart attacks. But, I tell you, retirement is not at all like that. Retirement is: What to do today? What to do tomorrow? Same as yesterday, same as the day before. You know what I am reduced to doing, young Ghote?'

'No, D'Sa sahib. What is that?'

'To checking up the times letter-boxes are cleared. Yes, just that. You know it states on each box at precisely what hour they are to be emptied, such as 17.38 etcetera? Well, I keep watch on a few boxes round about and see if it is done to time.'

'And – And is it?' Ghote asked, failing to find anything else to say.

'Never. No, it is not. Look, I keep notes.'

The old boy tugged out of his shirt pocket a tattered little spiral-bound notebook. He flipped it open, revealing that it was called a 'Sweety Pad'. Line after line of meticulously entered figures filled its pages.

Ghote seized his chance, such as it was.

'Highly remarkable, D'Sa sahib. Most. I see you have lost nothing of your old skills. I bet, for example, there is not one single person passing through this part of the maidan that you are not noting also.'

D'Sa made a deprecating face, but not much of one.

'It is true I have still got eyes in my head,' he said. 'We

were taught how to do things at Police Training School in my time, not at all like you youngsters of today.'

Ghote swallowed the insult with entire happiness.

'Well, tell me, D'Sa sahib,' he said, 'for example, were you observing any strange activities here in the maidan, shall I be saying, on last Tuesday?'

'Ah. So the Tick Tock murder has been given to Crime Branch,' old D'Sa answered smartly.

Ghote managed a grin.

'You are cent per cent right,' he said. 'As always. Yes, I am here on duty. So can you be helping me? I am thinking one AI Lobo, at the station up there, has been too quick to nab the suspect. So I am tracing out the walk the victim was taking on the morning of his death with altogether a different culprit in mind.'

D'Sa nodded sagely.

'I always said, Inspector. Slow but sure. Slow but sure is the way to handle a case.'

And, yes, Ghote thought with a pleasant revengeful swirl of inner malice, very slow and not too much of sure. That was why you ended your days as in-charge for the Vegetable and Flower Show, you old fool.

'And were you seeing the Tick Tock victim here on Tuesday?' he asked politely. 'Was someone perhaps following him only?'

'Yes. Yes, I saw him.'

'You did?' Ghote forgave in an instant all D'Sa's ponderousness. 'You are one hundred per cent certain?'

'Oh, yes, Inspector. I noticed the fellow. He was not walking fast, and he was stooping, although he was only a young man. I deduced he had been suffering from some illness. Then, after the murder, I saw his photo in the *Mid-Day*.'

'Very good,' Ghote said, meaning it to the last syllable. 'But, tell me, D'Sa sahib, did you not observe also that this victim was being followed?'

'Inspector, if I told you I had, I would be telling one damn big lie.'

Ghote experienced a jab of disappointment. And could

not refrain, though he knew he should not, from prompting his witness.

'Are you sure you were not seeing a young man, almost cent per cent bald, very tall also, who was following with evil intent?'

D'Sa laughed. With prolonged enjoyment.

'Oh, you young officers. Always wanting what you cannot have. Inspector, have you ever gone through the work of the great German criminologist, Dr Gross, as adapted by J. Collier Adam, sometime Public Prosecutor, Madras?'

'Yes, I – '

'If you had, Inspector, you would know what is meant by the term "expeditious investigator". It is an officer who jumps to conclusions, my friend. A jumper to conclusions.'

Despite the stinging rebuke, Ghote felt obliged to make certain beyond all possible doubt that tall, bald Raghu Barde had not been under D'Sa's eye that morning.

'You were not at all observing such person?' he asked. 'Not even at some distance from the victim?'

'Inspector, he was not here. Take the word of an old police officer who has had his successes in his day, more than some know.'

Ghote rose silently from his stone chair.

And, almost by way of farewell, asked one more question.

'D'Sa sahib, what time was it you were seeing Ramrao Pendke here? I would like to have that exactly.'

'It was at precisely 11.27 am, Inspector.'

For a moment Ghote did not take in what old D'Sa had actually said. His had been merely the politest of parting inquiries, and he had hardly been ready to take any particular note of the answer. But then that time, so exactly stated, impinged on his mind.

D'Sa had said 11.27. But there was the evidence of the smashed watch that the murder had taken place at 11.08. The old fool must be completely wrong about the whole business. He must never have seen Ramrao. He must have seen someone looking somewhat like him.

'It was at just exactly 11.27?' he asked mechanically.

'Inspector, I take good care to keep my old timepiece accurate to the minute. How else could I catch out those postwallas late in clearing their letter-boxes?'

Ghote turned away.

He ought, he knew, to go round the maidan looking for idlers similar to old D'Sa. But he would have to do that under D'Sa's eye, feeling him every minute thinking *There goes one expeditious investigator*. He could not face it. It had been bad enough realising under Dr Mrs Yadekar's cold gaze that he did not actually know that there were two separate kidneys in the human body nor whereabouts they were to be found. Ved had a book at home, *The Human Body in Pictures*, something like that. He must look for it. But it was worse, coming from old D'Sa, to be thought of as not even having read the book of Dr Hans Gross – he himself had probably lent it to D'Sa in the first place – and to be believed ignorant even of what constituted expeditiousness.

Then he asked himself, wildly picking at excuses, whether D'Sa could after all be right about the time. What if somehow that smashed gold Rolex on Ramrao Pendke's wrist, the gold Rolex Mike Lobo had claimed was no gold Rolex but a cunning fake, what if its hands had actually been altered? Altered like something in a film?

But if they had, what could possibly have been the object? If Ramrao Pendke had died earlier than had been thought, who could benefit from such a trick? No, for a made-up alibi the hands would have had to have been put back, not forward. If they had been put forward, a murderer would simply risk the body being found before the murder was supposed to have been done. There was almost certainly no fixed time for Mr Saxena to come to the Tick Tock Watchworks with his case of HMT samples.

Or was there? Perhaps the First Information Report he had yet to see would say something about that.

And, yes, surely that was what he ought to be making

122

his first priority. Going round the maidan looking for possible witnesses under D'Sa's knowing eye was not the most important thing just now. Certainly not.

And, by God, AI Lobo had better not put any difficulties in his way about seeing that FIR. By God, no.

He marched back to the police station as if he was God Hanuman leading his troop of fellow monkeys to rescue the beauteous Sita from the wicked demon Ravana.

He had half-expected to learn that Lobo had absented himself without leaving behind, as he was duty-bound to do, details of where he had gone. Which would, he thought vindictively most likely be down among the gay girls of Kamathipura, if it was not so early in the day. But, no, the fellow was there, sitting as he had been the day before on the corner of the big central table – why did he have to sit like that when there were chairs available? – idly swinging a leg and joking with a couple of fellow officers.

'AI,' he barked out at him, 'I am wishing to see the FIR in the Tick Tock Watchworks case.'

'Yeah, sure, Inspector. It's about somewhere, with all the other stuff, photo of the victim, Case Diary, you be naming it. I'll dig it out for you.'

But he made no move to get off the table and go.

'Now, AI,' Ghote snapped. 'At once.'

Mike Lobo looked at him with raised eyebrows.

'Okay, okay, Inspector,' he said.

And he simply shunted round on the table, pushed aside one or two piles of papers and extracted from under a third an FIR book. He flipped through its carbon-copy pages, put in a thumb to keep the place and handed it over.

'Thank you, AI,' Ghote said, grimly.

He pored over the faint blue-carbon writing as he stood there. But, if he had hoped to gain from the report any relevant details that AI Lobo had overlooked, he was disappointed.

All he learnt he had known, more or less, already. The body had been found, he read, by Sideshwar K. Saxena,

HMT Watches representative, at 11.41 (time checked by four watches worn by the said S.K. Saxena) calling at the shop by chance. So, he thought wryly, there would have been just long enough, if Ramrao Pendke had been at the August Kranti Maidan when that idiot D'Sa had thought he had seen him, for him to have reached the Tick Tock Watchworks in time to meet his fate. And, no, Mr Saxena had evidently no fixed time for visiting the shop. So no question of an alibi produced by putting back that watch's hands.

The said S.K. Saxena, he read on, had looked in the workshop below where the owner, Rustom Hootosh Fardoomji, sometimes worked, but seeing no one there had left and reported the finding of the body telephonically from the nearby Cane Emporium at Kemp's Corner at 11.44. AI Lobo had at once proceeded to the scene, arriving at 11.51. At the same time Constable B.R. Vaingankar (No. 2347), on point duty at the junction of SS Patkar Road and Balbunath Road, had arrived escorting the said R.H. Fardoomji, who had stated he had found the body at a time not recorded.

Ghote looked up.

'Fardoomji was stating it was himself who found the body?' he asked. 'Was he in fact reporting such to this – '

He glanced at the faded blue writing of the FIR.

'This Constable Vaingankar, No. 2347?'

'That's what it says in the FIR there,' Mike Lobo answered easily. 'But Fardoomji sang a different tune when I got that confession out of him.'

'Oh, yes? What was he claiming then?'

'Nothing, Inspector. Except to killing Ramrao Pendke. That was all I was wanting, man.'

'Well, I would have to see this Vaingankar,' Ghote murmured, returning to the FIR.

'Yeah, you should certainly see him,' Lobo said, 'so you'll know what sort of dumbo we have to work with. Look at what time he states Fardoomji came up to him.'

Ghote scanned the FIR once again. And jerked up in surprise.

124

'At 15.42? 15.42?'

'That's what the idiot said. Looked at his watch and noted the time. I don't suppose he really knows how to tell it.'

Ghote sighed.

'Yes, well, I have met constables nearly as bad myself,' he said, abandoning another hopeful line.

He read the remainder of the FIR. And learnt nothing more.

He handed the book back.

'Well, then, now I must see the prisoner,' he said.

He waited for Lobo's reply. Would the request be met with the same evasion as before? And, if it was, would that not indicate clearly enough that Lobo was in fact unsure about the confession he had obtained?

'Bless you, you can't see the fellow. Not now.'

Ghote straightened his back, feeling a ripple of sharp pain as he did so, and looked hard down at Lobo, still idly swinging his leg on the corner of the big table.

'And why cannot I be seeing, AI, if you please?'

Lobo gave him a grin.

'Because, Inspector,' he replied, glancing at the fancy Japanese compass watch on his wrist, 'I have an appointment – six minutes ago, to be exact – with your said S.K. Saxena at the Tick Tock Watchworks, and I dare say you'd like very much to come along.'

It took Ghote an instant to recover. Then he answered.

'Yes, AI, I would very much like. And I am hoping after to see Fardoomji himself.'

'Yeah, Inspector, sure you will. If it works out.'

Ghote decided not to pursue the point. Besides, Lobo had said the HMT Watches man should have arrived at the murder scene six minutes ago. If they were much later getting there, he might well have given up waiting and left.

'Let's go then, let's go,' he said to Lobo, still sitting on the table.

'Think our friend Saxena won't wait? Hell, man, he'd

125

be there if we didn't come till tonight. Never mind all those watches on his wrist, he still goes by IST.'

'By Indian Standard Time?'

Lobo jumped off the table with a broad grin.

'Indian Stretchable Time, Inspector,' he said. 'Indian Stretchable Time.'

Cursing himself for having fallen for a joke as old as any in the book, Ghote marched out ahead of his fellow investigator.

And outside the Tick Tock Watchworks there was Mr Saxena, not so much as consulting one of the four watches on his wrist. Mike Lobo unfastened the padlock on the shop's shutter and pushed it clangingly up.

The interior came as a surprise to Ghote. The chalked outline of Ramrao Pendke's body, still dusty on the floor, he had expected. But he had thought the place itself would be not unlike his familiar Big Ben Watch Stores, though he hoped not to encounter any moral exhortations. Instead, however, of having just a few clocks and watches waiting for repair on its shelves with a dozen or so new ones for sale, the Tick Tock Watchworks almost lived up to its name. True, after the enforced absence of its owner there were few clocks still ticking and tocking. But clocks and watches that must once have ticked almost to deafening point there were.

There was a large case of the new Tata Titans, with black faces, with gold faces, with white faces, with smart diagonally striped faces, with gold straps, with metallic straps, with leather straps, black, brown and white, smooth and embossed. Ranged in rows in the case were square-shaped watches, round ones, oblong ones, with hair-thin hands, with fatly thick hands, with roman numerals, with arabic numerals, with no numerals.

There was a case, somewhat smaller, of Mr Saxena's HMT watches. And there were clocks of every conceivable sort, electric and wind-up, cuckoo and carriage, marble and plain wood, grandfather clocks and wall clocks with long dangling pendulums – one of these on the customers' side of the glass-topped counter (under which were yet more watches, fobs and repeaters, watches with their works exposed and watches without any works at all) had one of its two long weights missing – tiny clocks and clocks almost lost in huge gold sunburst settings, clocks supported by statuettes, clocks embedded in chunks of raw rock. Clocks on the walls, clocks on the shelves, clocks on the counter, clocks on the floor.

And almost all of them silent. With no time to tell. Ghote thought suddenly of the mad bus-starter who had seized his arm just outside with his repeated demand of *Time kya? Time kya?* He would get a cold answer here now.

'Well, AI,' he said, 'your Mr Fardoomji was certainly very, very interested in his work.'

He recalled then that this had been the point one of the Dhunjeebhoy brothers had made to the DGP, that someone as devoted to the careful art of watchmaking was not likely to have brutally battered a victim to death.

'The fellow's damn interests don't bother me,' Mike Lobo replied. 'All I'm interested in just now is the weapon he used. Couldn't find it here at the time, so I reckoned Fardoomji had taken it away and thrown it down somewhere. But the bloody fellow wouldn't tell me where. So, I thought I might as well take another look-see here itself, with the help of Saxena sahib who knows the place.'

'Yes, AI. It would certainly be well to have the weapon as Exhibit Number Ek when you bring your case to court. What exactly was it? Did Fardoomji tell you at least that?'

'No. Never said.'

'He never said? But you must – '

Ghote broke off. His fellow officer was indicating, none too tactfully, the presence of Mr Saxena.

'Yes. Well, AI, we must discuss that at – No. Wait. I think I know what that weapon might have been.'

Turning, Ghote pointed, not without a touch of drama, to the pendulum clock on the wall opposite and the missing weight of its pair.

'Mr Saxena,' he inquired, 'was that second weight there

when you visited this shop before and could not sell Mr Fardoomji any of your own samples?'

'Yes, Inspector,' Mr Saxena answered with sharp assurance. 'I am well remembering it. And it would have made first-class weapon, long and heavy like that other there.'

Abruptly he strode over to the chalked outline on the floor, bent over it and brought his arm swinging down, time after time.

'I can just see him do it,' he shouted. 'One, two, three. Bang, bang, bang.'

'AI,' Ghote said, turning sharply away, unwilling to witness any more such antics, 'were the wounds on the body up to one hundred percent consistent with such a weapon as the second weight from that clock?'

'They were, Inspector,' Mike Lobo answered, with a tinge of astonishment in his voice. 'By God, they were. They won't be able to challenge that in court. So all we've got to do now is find that weight, check the prints on it and we've got Mr Fardoomji nicely wrapped up.'

'I was hearing you had done that already,' Ghote said.

'Well, bit of extra evidence can't do any harm,' Lobo replied cheerfully.

So the three of them began to search the little shop and the even more crammed workshop below it, littered with all the watches Fardoomji had been working on before he had been hauled away. It took them more than three hours before they were finished. But at last they were left only with the certainty that the missing clock-weight was nowhere on the premises.

'Still, can't be helped,' Mike Lobo said, when finally Ghote had conceded there was nowhere else to look. 'Won't make all that much of difference. I've got the bastard cold all right.'

Mr Saxena nodded in grave agreement.

'Ah, I would never have thought it of Rustomji,' he said. 'But he would be going in for those Tata Titans. He would go in for them. Something not sound there.'

Ghote felt this a sad summing-up for a man who, if Mike Lobo was right about him, would eventually meet the hangman's rope at Thana Gaol. His determination not to let that happen, unless some new hard evidence really proving the man's guilt came to light, fired up anew.

He turned to Mike Lobo.

'So now, AI,' he said, 'will you kindly take me to talk with your prisoner.'

And, more than a little to his surprise, Mike Lobo simply answered, 'Come on, then.'

12

Ghote would have liked to have gone with Mike Lobo directly to Rustom Fardoomji's cell to collect him. But arriving at the station Lobo had ushered him straight into the Detection Room, implying that Fardoomji was already there. And then he had quickly disappeared. So Ghote, when he found the room was empty, had to concede he had been neatly outmanoeuvred. Lobo would have a few good minutes to put the fear of future punishment firmly into his chosen culprit's mind should he be tempted to go back on his confession.

Provided, Ghote said to himself as he stood in the barely furnished room with its one high barred window, that Fardoomji has not truly confessed to killing Ramrao Pendke.

The door behind him was jerked open and the clocks-obsessed Parsi was thrust in ahead of Mike Lobo.

Ghote saw a slight figure in nondescript shirt and trousers with a worried-looking narrow face partly hidden by a large pair of spectacles – had they just been returned to him, Ghote wondered – placed rather crookedly on a thin hook of a nose. He was put in mind of nothing so much as an anxious parrot. There were no traces on that face or elsewhere of bruises or injuries. But then, as Shruti Shah had said, Mike Lobo was an expert.

'Sit there,' Lobo said to his prisoner, pointing to the chair secured to the floor on the far side of the small wooden table that with one other chair was the room's sole furniture.

Fardoomji scrabbled to obey, although Lobo had not spoken with any particular ferocity. Ghote noted the cowed look, and was reinforced in his belief that the interview ahead was going to be tricky.

It was a thought that was redoubled when Mike Lobo,

instead of leaving, simply perched on the table between himself and the Parsi and sat, as was his wont, swinging his legs.

'Thank you, AI,' he said sharply. 'I would not be needing you.'

Lobo favoured him with a knowing grin. But he did hop down from the table and move towards the door.

'Hope I can trust you not to leave marks on my boy, Inspector,' he said.

And then, with the door closing, he added a last remark addressed to his prisoner.

'Don't like getting hurt, do you, bhai?'

The Parsi, cringing on his chair, made no reply. Unless a loud gulping sound constituted an acknowledgement.

Ghote took the chair opposite, one of the bruises on his hip jabbing at him sharply. How differently different people react to pain, he thought. And there are some who shrink from even the threat of injury.

He gave a little cough.

'Well now, Mr Fardoomji,' he said, looking directly into the anxious parrot-face across the table, 'suppose you tell me, and myself alone remember, just what was happening in your shop on the morning of Tuesday last?'

'I killed him.'

The murmured response was so quiet it was difficult even in the small enclosed room to make it out.

'You killed him? Yes, I know that is what you have told to Assistant Inspector Lobo. But tell me why it was that you killed this visitor to your shop. What for, in fact, had he come into the shop?'

The anxious parrot opposite chose only to answer the second question.

'To buy a watch.'

'But I was asking why you killed this man who had come in, as you say, just only to buy a watch?'

'I killed him.'

'Yes, I know you have confessed to that. But why were you doing it? Why?'

Rustom Fardoomji simply looked down in silence at the scored surface of the wooden table in front of him.

'Do you smoke?' Ghote asked him. 'Should I send for cigarettes?'

Perhaps a smoke would relax the fellow. Get him to a state where he might let his fear of Lobo, if it existed, rise from hiding.

'No.'

'You do not smoke?'

'No.'

But even that monosyllable was spoken so reluctantly that it, too, was hard to hear.

Ghote sighed.

'Well then, tea? You would like some tea only?'

'No.'

'All right. No tea. But tell me now, why was it that you were deciding to attack this man? That you were battering him to death, as you told AI Lobo?'

'He is saying I wanted to rob the rich fool.'

Ghote pounced.

'The AI is saying that? Is it true? Is that why you attacked this customer coming in?'

'I wanted to rob him.'

'Yes, yes. You have said. But it was because he was a rich fool? You were thinking that?'

'It is what is in my statement.'

'But you said it? You yourself said it? Or was AI Lobo writing it, and you were signing?'

For a moment the anxious parrot looked up, and Ghote thought he was going to get at the truth of the matter at last. Learn what shrinking from physical punishment was perhaps keeping locked fast in concealment. But it was a momentary glance and no more, and then the beaky head sank again on the narrow chest.

'Did you say it, or did the AI just only write it?' Ghote asked again, though with little hope.

'I killed him. He was a rich fool.'

'I see,' Ghote said carefully. 'And what was it that made

132

you realise this customer coming in – He had not been into your shop before?'

He almost expected Rustom Fardoomji to answer once more with *I killed him*, but he did at least mutter a 'No.'

'Then what was it that made you think he was a rich fool, that he was perhaps asking to be robbed?'

Again there was a pause before any answer came, and again Ghote permitted himself a glimmer of hope that he was beginning to rip away the outer garment of a fear-imposed account.

But once more there came the same dulled reply.

'He was a rich fool.'

'But how did you know that? How?'

'He had a gold Rolex that was a fake.'

Better, Ghote thought. A proper answer. One small advance.

'A fake? One of those watches they are making out at Ulhasnagar?'

'Yes. Like that.'

'I see. And how was it that you were able to tell it was such a watch? He did not take it off his wrist, did he?'

'He was a rich fool.'

Damn, damn, damn. Back to that. Had Lobo done his work altogether too well?

He leant across the battered table.

'All right. He was a rich fool. And you thought he would be easy to rob, no?'

No answer now.

'Did you decide straightaway you would rob, as soon as he had come in?'

He thought then he saw a baffled look in the eyes behind the big askew spectacles. But when his question was answered he got no further.

'I have told. He was a rich fool.'

'So what exactly was happening? Did he refuse to give what you were demanding? Or did you attack at once?'

'Yes.'

'Which? Which? I was asking two things. Which did you do? Demand, or attack without demanding?'

'I attacked.'

Wearily Ghote tried another approach.

'Mr Fardoomji, I have heard the testimony of your distinguished cousins, Mr Homi and Mr Bomi Dhunjee-bhoy. They are saying that you are a person who was never thinking of anything but timepieces only. Is that so? You are that sort of person?'

'I killed him.'

In face of that assertion once again Ghote nearly gave up. But he was determined not to let the least chance go by.

'You killed him, Mr Fardoomji,' he repeated. 'So you are many times saying. So you were saying to Assistant Inspector Lobo.'

He had put all the emphasis he could on to those last words, and as he spoke them he had looked at the narrow-faced Parsi as intently as a wheeling kite piercingly surveying the ground below. But he saw not the slightest sign of any reaction. No twitch of fear. No tiny spark of hope.

He sighed and resumed his questioning.

'You killed him, Mr Fardoomji? What with did you kill him?'

'With the weapon.'

'I see. But what weapon?'

Once more an almost imperceptible pause.

'With the weapon he is saying.'

'Who is saying, Mr Fardoomji? Who?'

'Mr Lobo. Assistant Inspector . . .'

'But what weapon was that? Is it the same that you yourself are saying? The one you were truly using?'

'I killed him.'

'What with? What with did you kill him?'

'I killed him.'

And, though Ghote persisted for more than an hour after that, he got no more out of the anxious parrot than the repeated and repeated *I killed him*.

At last he had to admit defeat. If Rustom Fardoomji was not in fact the murderer of Ramrao Pendke, Mike

Lobo had worked on him too well. Unless a miracle occurred, the fellow was going to go before a Magistrate repeating his story, was going to repeat it in court, would perhaps deny it at last only on the day of his execution when no one would believe him. Certainly he was not going to go back from it now, when there was still the possibility that he would be put back in a cell and have Assistant Inspector Lobo enter it after him.

But failure with the frightened, brain-deadened man at the other side of the table only increased Ghote's determination to find an explanation for the murder by other means. An explanation that would show up as bare-faced lies everything Lobo had claimed.

And, he thought to himself with satisfaction, he had at least now acquired, from that FIR he had eventually succeeded in seeing and from elsewhere, a good many times and details. Now he could go, armed, to interrogate the man he saw as most likely to be the true killer of Ramrao Pendke, Raghu Barde.

The Tata Institute scientist, from what he had learnt out at Dharbani, believed his native-place village ought to be left in peace to make its baskets and weave its cloth and attain some small prosperity. Ramrao Pendke with his plan to mine manganese in the area threatened all the work Barde had devoted over the years towards achieving that aim. So had Barde put an end to Ramrao's life? It was surely possible. Had there not been that violent quarrel at the Shrimati Usha Yadekar Clinic the day before the murder itself?

He called a constable to take Rustom Fardoomji back to his cell and hurried out. At Kemp's Corner he spotted the yellow top of a taxi, hailed it and told the driver to take him to the TIFR.

Maybe there would be trouble claiming the ride on expenses. But, if he had to, he was prepared to pay out of his own pocket. Every last paisa.

The paisas and rupees, in fact, mounted up a good deal faster than he had bargained for because the journey turned out to be slow indeed. With Mike Lobo's borrowed, scarcely readable, copper-faced watch on his wrist, he had already lost the habit of frequently, unconsciously checking the time. So it had come as a surprise to find he was right in the middle of Bombay's evening traffic jamboree. The taxi kept crawling forward a few yards, then coming to a stop and waiting, engine economically switched off, horn going furiously, till for no apparent reason the ice-jam broke and they were able to make a little more progress. Only to come to a halt once more and have to sit fretting, with the stink of half-consumed petrol floating in through windows it was too hot to close.

The Hour of Cowdust, Ghote thought. My God, it should be the Hour of Car Fumes.

So it took over an hour for a journey which, even with ordinary day-time traffic, should not have lasted more than thirty minutes. From Kemp's Corner and its huge fly-over, wriggling down to Chowpatty Beach. Then the sweep of Marine Drive where at any other hour they would have zoomed along beside the sea fast enough to produce a wonderfully cooling breeze. Next, turning sharp left at the Air India building so as to work their way round Back Bay Reclamation, along Cuffe Parade. And finally, turning sharp right, rattling down the bare straight stretch of narrow road, like a country road with its dusty verges, that led at last to the Tata Institute at almost the very tip of downwards-plunging peninsular Bombay.

By the time they had reached the gate at the TIFR Ghote had convinced himself that Raghu Barde would not be there. But, when he inquired, the security guard on duty put through a call to Barde's room and, looking up, said grudgingly that, yes, he had answered. His was Room 342.

Leaving the taxi, Ghote made his way to the residential quarter of the big complex and found without difficulty Room 342. He knocked on its pale-wood blank door.

And, in response, from inside, causing him to jump back in alarm, there came a shriek of sudden wild fury. A moment later the door was flung wide.

Poised in the doorway Ghote saw, beyond doubt, the man he had come to question, young, very tall and prematurely bald with a high-domed skull at the sides of which tufts of unruly curled black hair protruded. And contorted rage had seized in knots of locked tension every feature of the face beneath that peaked bald skull.

13

Ghote took a step forward towards the enraged figure in the doorway in front of him.

'It is Mr Barde?' he asked, pitching his voice to a clear, quiet note. 'Mr Raghu Barde? They were ringing through to tell that I was coming.'

'I said. I told him. Not to be disturbed. Not. Not. I told the fool. No visitors. No visitors. Leave me alone.'

Ghote recalled that the securitywalla at the gate had been noticeably short in telling him that Raghu Barde had answered his phone. But the fellow had not passed on his name and rank. So Barde's rage, which he thought now despite its violence had in it something of mere hysteria, could not be accounted for by fear of a police inquiry.

'Mr Barde,' he said, doing all he could to infuse his voice with continuing calm authority, 'I regret but I am not able to leave you alone. I am a police officer, Inspector Ghote by name, and I am here to ask you questions concerning one very serious matter.'

His tone appeared to have the effect he had hoped. Raghu Barde did not answer him and his body still retained its fierce tension. But he did at least turn sideways so that it was possible to enter the bright, hygenically-furnished room behind him.

'Sit down, Mr Barde,' Ghote said as the tall scientist closed the door.

He had made the words all but an order. After an instant of hesitation Raghu Barde went over to the narrow bed under its bright cotton cover, sat down on it and tucked his bare feet up underneath himself.

'I – I am sorry, Inspector – Inspector – What were you saying that your name was?'

'Ghote. It is Ghote.'

'I am sorry, Inspector Ghote, I am afraid I was somewhat rude just now.'

More than rude, Ghote reflected. But he made no reply. With all the pent-up tension Barde had shown, this was, he calculated, one of the times when leaving a silence was likely to produce more from a witness than any number of direct questions.

And, sure enough, after the shortest of pauses, Raghu Barde spoke again.

'You see, Inspector, when you were knocking I was deeply engaged in a train of thought. I am a mathematician, you know. That is my employment here. I just happen to have a head for numbers. I do not at all know how I acquired such, but I have it. To an uncommon extent, though I say so. My father, you see, was altogether uneducated, a village weaver only. Perhaps, I am sometimes thinking, it was from weaving, which my family has done for many generations, my mother's also, that I was developing some sense of number. I do not know. But I have it, and just now I was working, thinking. I did not expect at this hour of the evening to have any interruption. I imagine you have no idea how a person of my sort works?'

The spate of autobiography seemed to need a jolt forward now.

'You – You write down figures? Add them up? Or, no, multiply and divide, other things also?'

Raghu Barde actually smiled at this, a smile of unexpected warmth in view of the tremendous rage that only a short time before had gripped his whole body from the crown of his high bald head to the curling toes of his bare feet.

'No, Inspector,' he said. 'It is not at all like that, I am assuring you. You see, for a person of my sort – and I admit that we are a rare breed – numbers are so much in our minds there is hardly any question of writing them down, let alone adding one to another.'

He leant forward eagerly on the bright-patterned bed.

'Let me give you one instance,' he said. 'Before I was

beginning work just now, I was taking a short stroll, and I happened to see a handcartwalla. Now, being the sort of chap I am, I of course noticed the number burnt on the side of the cart, 1729. Now, does that mean anything to you yourself?'

'It is the number on the cart,' Ghote answered guardedly. 'By law it must be there.'

Raghu Barde smiled his warm smile again.

'Ah, yes, the police view. But what do you think those figures meant to me? You would never guess. But the moment I was seeing them I said: Aha, the smallest number expressible as a sum of two cubes in two different ways. And, you know, if ever I am getting to marry, I suppose I will want a wife whose birth date comes to some number pleasing to me like that.'

'I see,' Ghote said.

And, although the mumbo-jumbo about cubes and expressibles meant nothing to him, and he could not help thinking that to choose a wife by number would be a much riskier proceeding than to let the astrologers choose one for you, he did dimly see what a different sort of life Raghu Barde lived from that of the common number-unencumbered man.

He thought he saw, too, now a way of getting to the business he had come here for without arousing immediate defensiveness.

'I am supposing you are always and always doing such tricks with numbers,' he said. 'Each and every time you are looking at your watch, for example, you must be seeing some expressibles.'

Raghu Barde smiled again.

'Well, I might,' he conceded. 'Though, as a matter of fact, I seldom wear a watch. When I go back to my native-place, as I often do – it is a small village in Vidharba, almost into Madya Pradesh State – I leave my watch behind. Time is altogether different back there.'

As he spoke a light shone in his eyes far removed from the glare of rage that had blazed in them when Ghote had first seen him.

Ghote, however, was intent on his cunning strategy.

'But when it is that you are wearing a watch,' he said, 'you are finding the times it says are meaning special things to you, isn't it? For instance, if I was saying 11.08 am . . .'

He waited, poised, for a reaction.

But Raghu Barde merely looked a little puzzled.

'Am or pm, Inspector,' he answered, 'it would make no difference to me. It is the numbers themselves only that I cannot help arranging in whatever mathematical patterns they happen to fall into.'

'Not even,' Ghote jabbed out, 'if it was 11.08 am on last Tuesday?'

A wary look did come into Raghu Barde's eyes then.

'Ah,' he said slowly. 'Yes, it was what was just passing through my mind when you were telling me you were a police inspector. It is the Ramrao Pendke murder, no? I was seeing Mr Pendke last Monday, the day before he was killed. You must have found out that at the clinic where he was.'

'And what was it you yourself were finding out at that clinic?' Ghote hammered in. 'Was it the time that Ramrao Pendke left each day for the exercise he was made to take? Was it the route he was given?'

For a little Raghu Barde sat cross-legged on the colourful bedspread in silence.

'I see what you have got into your head,' he said at last. 'You must have heard also that I was losing my temper when I talked with Mr Pendke, and you have decided that it must be myself who was killing him. At 11.08. Yes, 11.08. That is why you were asking that absurd question. I see it all now.'

Every trace of the warmth of his smiles had disappeared. In its place were ominous signs of another storm of rage.

'Never mind about absurd or not absurd, Mr Barde,' Ghote said with enforced quietness. 'What I am wanting to know is: where were you exactly at 11.08 last Tuesday morning?'

He could see the mathematician thinking, even as he

was putting his question. Was it only numbers that were running through his head? Or was he working out some lie?

'Yes, I can tell you that quite definitely, Inspector,' Barde answered after a moment. 'On Tuesday morning there was a staff meeting here at TIFR, and I was attending same. I was here and nowhere else.'

'I see. And when was this meeting taking place?'

'It began at 11.30 precisely, and since this is Bombay I was wearing my watch and took care to be there. So, you see, I could hardly have been at Kemp's Corner – Mr Pendke was killed near there, isn't it? – only twenty minutes before the meeting.'

Ghote was constrained to admit that this was so. His taxi here from Kemp's Corner had taken a full hour. But even in the middle of the night with no traffic the trip would take perhaps as long as twenty-five minutes, and in the mornings there was certainly plenty of traffic on the streets.

No, wait, he thought suddenly. The smashed hands on Ramrao Pendke's fake gold Rolex. At the back of his mind there had been the nagging thought all along that somehow that crime-film clue must be more than accidental. And surely altering a watch's hands was exactly what a mathematician might be expected to think of. Someone who thought always in figures. And was also somewhat impractical.

And then, with a thump, he realised that he himself was the one who was being impractical. And certainly nothing of a mathematician.

Because, if Barde had altered the hands of that watch before deliberately smashing it, all he could have done was to make the time of the murder appear earlier than it actually was. Advancing the hands of the watch before smashing it could only have been to risk the body being found before the hour the watch was showing. Putting them back would simply have spoiled the alibi he had just produced.

'Very well, Mr Barde,' he said, attempting a show of

grimness to cover his discomfiture, 'I will of course be checking to one hundred percent that you yourself were at this meeting which was starting at 11.30 am. But otherwise it appears you are no longer figuring in my inquiries.'

'Thank you,' Raghu Barde said, visibly relaxing again. 'And you have only to ask any other member of staff about the meeting. It was full house.'

'Very well.'

Ghote turned and left.

Only when he was closing the door behind him did the full force of what he had learnt come home to him. If Barde's alibi checked out, and it was surely likely to or he would not have put it forward so confidently, then his most promising candidate as the murderer of Ramrao Pendke was cleared. And Mike Lobo might be right after all.

As he walked despondently away towards the gate, his attention was caught by a young woman emerging from the building next to Barde's. What quite it was that made him at once sure she was on the TIFR staff he did not know. But, despite her sex, her age – which could not have been past the late twenties – and her prettiness, which was considerable, he had no doubt she was a scientist working at the Institute.

'Madam,' he called out. 'Madam, excuse me.'

The girl stopped and turned.

'Yes?'

'Please, I am wondering if you can assist me. You are a TIFR staff member, isn't it?'

'Yes. Yes, I am.'

'Achcha. Then can you tell me this? Were you present at a certain staff meeting that was taking place last Tuesday morning?'

A gleam of amusement appeared on the girl's face.

'I certainly was,' she said. 'Protest meeting at an Administration directive.'

'Oh, yes? And it was taking place at 11.30 hours?'

'It was.'

'And, please, was it beginning exactly to time? Often a meeting is failing to start at advertised hour.'

'Very often. But we are scientists here and accustomed to precision. We measure time in nano-seconds even. So when we call a meeting for any particular hour, you can be sure it will start at that time. Unless it's called by the Administration.'

'Thank you, madam. And one last question only. You are acquainted with one Mr Raghu Barde?'

'Raghuji? Of course.'

'And he was present at that same meeting?'

'Yes. I tell you, no one was going to miss it. There were going to be fireworks. And there were.'

'I see. Thank you. That is all I am wishing to know.'

He gave her a nod of a bow and turned to go.

'Wait a minute. You are not saying why you wanted to know all this. Who are you anyway?'

'Oh, very regret. I am a police officer, Inspector Ghote by name. Making some routine inquiries.'

'Police? We all know about routine inquiries. What have you got against Raghu? He's the sweetest guy. Is it his activities in his home village, helping the dalits there? I suppose you think anyone helping the downtrodden is bound to be some Naxalite terrorist?'

'Madam, madam, not at all. It is truly just only routine inquiry. I was wanting to know exactly where was Mr Raghu Barde at 11.30 hours last Tuesday, and now that I am knowing I no longer have any interest in the said gentleman.'

'Oh, yes? Well, to be strictly precise, you have got your facts wrong, Inspector. Raghuji was not at the meeting at 11.30 hours, if by that you mean that exact minute. He came late. I happened to notice. He came in, puffing and panting, five minutes after we had begun. A little more perhaps. I suppose he had been lost in thought. These mathematicians. I am an engineer myself.'

Ghote drew in a breath.

'You would swear to that?' he said. 'Please, what is your good name? This may be important evidence.'

He had been doing some rapid arithmetic. Given these seven or eight minutes extra, it was just possible perhaps that Raghu Barde could have left the Tick Tock Watch-works after smashing by accident Ramrao Pendke's watch and have reached TIFR when this girl had said she had seen him.

'I am Miss Amita Modi. But, listen, I am not wanting – '

Ghote swung round and left her at a run. He needed a word with Raghu Barde. Urgently.

Somehow he knew, though, even as he thundered back up to Room 342, that Raghu Barde would not be there. And, sure enough, when he thrust open the room's door he saw that it was empty. It even had an air of desertion.

He was at a loss to account for that impression, strong though it was. Then he registered that a large cotton shoulder-bag, typical of a student or intellectual, jutting at the sides with the corners of books, which he had seen without seeing earlier down on the floor beside the bed, was missing.

He knew then that Raghu Barde had made off. He had not gone down to the canteen for a cup of tea. He was not visiting some fellow staff member. He had fled.

The moment this had fully sunk in he guessed where his man would have gone. To his native-place. To Village Khindgaon. He had not mentioned the name of the village earlier. So, in all probability, he believed it would take the police some little time to trace him. He must think he had a safe refuge for some hours, even some days.

Then there was only one thing for it. To get out to Khindgaon himself as fast as he was able.

If he drove there, hard as he could go, he could arrive well before Barde taking the night train to Nagpur and having to wait in the morning for the bus out to Khindgaon. He could take him totally by surprise. And then he would get a confession out of him. He could hardly fail. A confession to put up against the one Mike Lobo had got in his own doubtful way. But his confession would be backed by facts, details, times. By God, it would.

14

More than once during the long, long drive through the night in a hastily ordered jeep Ghote thought he was going to have to abandon the attempt to get to Raghu Barde's native village before the tall, bald, rage-prone mathematician could reach its safety himself. The first part of the journey, out of the long, sea-bound peninsula of Bombay itself, had gone better than he had dared to hope. The great evening traffic snarl had almost come to an end and he had made faster progress than he had counted on. He had expected, once clear of the city, to drive at speed on the almost empty night roads. But he had reckoned without his grey-smeared tiredness after the turmoil that had begun with the motor-cycle attack out at Dharbani which had left him so badly hurt.

But eventually he realised he was passing that very point on the highway. He thought at once with a shudder then of how his body, had he not been found by Sitabai and had continued to lie there unconscious, might already have been ravaged by vultures there in the long, concealing grass.

But why had Ganpatrao chosen to attack him in that way, he wondered with weariness. It must have been purely on impulse. Not because he feared this Bombay police officer would prove he had killed his cousin-brother. After all, it seemed probable he had not done that. If Raghu Barde had fled, that was surely a strong indication that he rather than Ganpatrao was the Tick Tock murderer. No, it must have been because he believed that this Bombaywalla knew of the plan to mine manganese. He must have feared that through him the secret would get back to the Patil and lose him his inheritance.

Yes, that in all probability must be the answer.

At last, blank with fatigue and with his every bruise another point of fire, just after dawn he found the turning to Village Khindgaon, some fifteen miles beyond Dharbani. He drove then, lurching over the unevennesses of a path a good deal narrower and seemingly much less used than the one leading to Dharbani, as far as he thought it wise to take the jeep. When in the first thin white light of the new day he spotted a small grove of mango trees he at once swung the wheel and made for its shelter. Then at last, happy that Raghu Barde, when some hours later he would come walking from the bus stopping-place, would not spot the vehicle he clambered down.

For long moments he stood stretching and breathing in the night-cooled air, easing the sweat-clinging shirt off his back, scrubbing at his prickle of beard. His beardless boyhood days came flooding back to him then like a clean tide. Days when, waking early, he would creep out of the house to delight in the newness of everything before anyone else in the world was there to muddy it. Dawns when he had stood, like a sharp-prowed boat awaiting the moment of launching, welcoming the prospect of new experiences, new encounters, to be seized upon, taken in, fitted into the gradually emerging pattern.

Little had he guessed then that the pattern in the end would sprawl far from village simplicities and unvarying timelessness into the hustle-bustle of Bombay, its ever-ingenious criminal ploys, its minute-by-minute days, ruthlessly parcelled out.

But that had happened to him. He was caught up now inescapably in the clicking, tick-tocking world of duties and events. In the world of his duty to confront one Raghu Barde, and explode the times-cunning alibi he had concocted.

He set off along the dust-thick path towards the village.

But, barely had he gone a hundred yards, when he was brought to a sharp halt. There was some other person about at this empty hour. A man's voice, low and murmuring, was coming from behind a bank of earth at the corner of a field where a solitary palas tree grew.

He took a few steps forward, noiseless on the soft layer of dust, and cocked his head to catch the murmured words.

'Listen to my prayer, Churail. Hear me, great spirit. Forget my many sins. O Churail, I did not sacrifice a cockerel to you when it was the time. Churail, take away my misfortunes now, and, Churail, two cockerels, two, will be yours on the next night of no moon. Churail, I swear it. This I am promising. Promising.'

Ghote stood in startled wonder.

With the rational part of his mind he knew that in many places in vast India, far from the cities, their chronometers and computers, there must be people of primitive simplicity who still sacrificed animals to propitiate active malignant spirits. There had even been a case, famous in the annals of Crime Branch itself, when two Bombay detectives had eventually brought to light a group in the countryside practising human sacrifice. But to hear with his own city-attuned ears what he had just been listening to brought home to him abruptly just how far he was at this moment from the rational world he had been immersed in now for years.

At last he went, silent-footed, onwards, the murmuring of that frightened prayer gradually dying away behind him.

Khindgaon, when he came to it, proved to be hardly a village at all. There was a small crumbling badly-white-washed temple and just a cluster of huts, their sides plastered with drying dung fuel-cakes each marked still with the imprint of the hand of the woman who had slapped it there.

No one was about. Ghote went and sat behind the broken remains of a bullock-cart, which looked as if it had been there, slowly falling to pieces, weeds growing up through it, for years without number. And he waited till, with the first warm rays of the sun, one by one the villagers began to emerge and, each carrying a water-pot, make their way to the fields.

He sat on where he was, unobserved, and waited for

their. return. Then, taking care not to startle anyone, he stepped out and accosted the man he had thought looked most likely to be responsive.

'Ram, Ram. Tell me, which is the house of the weaver's son who goes all the way to Bombay?'

The man looked at him, took his time to decide whether this was a question he could reply to, decided that it was and pointed to one of the huts.

'Salubai Ma there only now,' he said. 'Raghubhai sometimes coming.'

Ghote thanked him and went over to the hut. On the mud platform in front of it stood a weaver's loom with a half-finished piece of cloth, intricate in pattern and rich with colour, still on it. In the dark interior, beyond the heavy time-gnarled plank of a door, pushed back to its full extent, he made out the dim shape of an old woman in a white widow's sari. Bent-backed and pottering, she was preparing to light a fire under the cooking stove.

After a moment he called out to her, asking if she was the mother of Raghu Barde.

She came hobbling out into the now warm daylight, tugging the pallu of her sari over her head.

'You are wanting my Raghu?' she asked. 'He is not here. He is in Bombay, far away. In Bombay he is very important sahib. He comes here only sometimes. He helps the weavers and basket-makers to sell what they are making.'

'Yes, yes. I know. But I believe he is coming back here today. I would like to wait for him.'

'Oh, no, no, sahib. Raghu has been gone only five-six days. He would not come again for some time.'

'But I think he will after all come today. May I wait in your hut?'

'Yes, yes, sahib. You are welcome, if you are wanting. I will have tea soon.'

The old woman tottered back in, and, before Ghote had even mounted the time-hollowed step up on to the platform of the hut, she emerged again dragging what was clearly her sleeping mat.

'Sahib, I will put it here for you. There is shade. Sit, sit. Take rest.'

'No, no,' Ghote answered, seeing his plan to catch Raghu Barde by surprise being innocently frustrated. 'I would like to come inside.'

The old woman made no objection to the curious wishes of the person from the distant city and dragged the mat back in again. Ghote followed her, ducking beneath the embroidered good-luck cloth strung across the hut's low doorway.

Inside, he had to come to a complete halt so dense was the darkness.

Raghu Barde's mother saw his difficulty.

'Wait, wait,' she said. 'I will light the lamp for you.'

Ghote would have liked to prevent her. The unstinting hospitality was doubly embarrassing. To begin with, Salubai was plainly poor. But then she was also the mother of the man he had come to Khindgaon to trick into confessing to murder. But there was nothing he could do.

In the darkness he heard the rattle of a match-box as the old woman reached it down. There followed the sound of her panting breathing. For a moment it puzzled him. Then he remembered how in his own boyhood it had frequently been necessary to blow on a match-head to get rid of the moisture that had accumulated on it during a night tucked away on a shelf scooped out of the wall of the house.

A few seconds later his recollection was proved accurate. There came the noise of the match being struck, and a little flare of yellow light sprang up. In a few moments more Raghu Barde's mother had succeeded in transferring the flame to the wick of an oil lamp.

'Thank you, thank you,' Ghote said.

Nor could he stop the old woman then setting to, getting the fire under her stove going and boiling tea.

He sat in the orangey light from the wick floating smokily in the oil lamp, sipping the milky brew. He hoped at least it would be finished before the old woman's son arrived and, in front of her, he had to extort from him an admission to committing murder.

But he need not have worried. The tea was long finished and there was still no sign of Raghu Barde.

Salubai left him in the hut and went to work at her loom. He remembered, as she began, that this was Sunday. Bustling Bombay would for a few hours of blessed quiet have come to a standstill. But here there were only days, each the same as the other.

Here there were hours, though. Hours that crept leadenly along while nothing at all happened. The hut grew hotter and hotter as the sun rose in the sky. Sleep nudged at him. He shook himself. He must stay alert. He must be ready for the least signs of Raghu Barde returning, ready then to descend on his prey with total unexpectedness.

To keep himself awake he began to make a mental inventory of all the objects in the hut. There were few enough of them. A small chest with an ancient brass padlock, containing no doubt the coloured saris Salubai had worn before her widowhood and perhaps a few other precious things. On the mud walls two pictures, varnished with the smoke of days and days of cooking fires, one of elephant-trunked Ganesha, one of Goddess Laxmi, serenely seated on Shesh, the snake of eternity. A few cooking implements, a tin grater, two flat metal thalis, a copper water-pot and another smaller one of brass, a heavy stone wheel for grinding spices. Then in a corner there was a large tin of vanaspati oil, *Only Pure Ghee Could Be Better* standing out in bright English lettering on the side facing him, no doubt mere signs to Salubai. A packet of tea, a small pot that had contained milk. Four cups and saucers precariously stored on one of the shelves scooped in the wall.

Then, as he went over this list for the twelfth or thirteenth time, suddenly the squeak-squeak-squeak, clack-clack-clack of the loom outside, which had gone on monotonously, continuously ever since Salubai had left him, came to a halt.

He shot to his feet, barged through the hut's low doorway and, straightening, saw Raghu Barde standing there, his cotton bag of books hanging from his shoulder.

'Mr Barde,' he said, bringing out his long-prepared words just as forcefully as he could have wished. 'You and I have got more to say to each other.'

Raghu Barde's mouth dropped open. His bag of books slipped from his shoulder and fell to the dusty, littered ground.

Into the eyes below that high domed forehead there leapt, plain to see, a look of animal fear.

'Yes,' Ghote said. 'You were hoping you had put me off the scent with a lie. You were thinking you could be tricking me by stating you had been at that meeting from its start only. Then, when I was saying I would check up your each and every claim, it was entering your head to escape. Here, to your native-place. Did you think, Mr Barde, the long arms of the police would not be reaching you even here?'

'But – But – It is not so. No.'

'No? It is not so that to stop Mr Ramrao Pendke bringing here manganese mines, with all their machinery, all their noise, all their wanting of coolies only, to this village you are wanting to keep as it has been always, that you were killing him in a rage? Come, tell the whole truth. It is too late for anything else.'

He had banged out his indictment, blow on blow. With each one he had seen that he was striking home. Until with those last words, *Tell the truth now. It is too late for anything else*, he thought he had seen at last, concentrating as he was on every least flicker of expression, a coming to a decision. There had been an internal straightening of the shoulders, the acceptance of black necessity.

'Inspector . . .' the man standing beaten and defeated on the dusty ground below the hut platform began. 'Inspector . . . Yes. Yes, I was lying.'

For a long moment Raghu Barde looked down at his feet, at the cotton shoulder-bag lying sprawled beside them, at a crude little pull-cart toy made from the tin lids of two old jars that some village child had abandoned there. Then he brought his eyes up to look straight at Ghote on the low platform of the hut above.

'Inspector,' he said, 'I do not know, I really do not know, why it was that I was lying. No. No. Yes, I do know. It was because I was afraid. Afraid of the police, as I had been in my earliest days. I had thought I no longer needed to be, that I had now made my place in the world. As a scientist, a mathematician. But I was wrong. The moment you told that you were a police inspector I felt the beginnings of fear in my heart.'

'You did well to fear,' Ghote said gratingly. 'You had committed a crime. The worst of crimes.'

But, even as he delivered the accusation, he saw from the face of the man he was accusing that, after all, he was not going to hear a plea of guilty. Barde had admitted to lying. But it was somehow plain that he was not going to admit to anything beyond lying.

'No, Inspector. No. I did not kill Ramrao Pendke. Oh, yes, you have been right in what you were saying. When I was leaving him on the day before he was done to death I was wishing to kill him. He was determined to kill this village that I love. Yes, kill it, kill the life that has been led here for years upon years. And so, yes, I am not sorry that he has been killed itself. But mine was not the hand that killed him.'

Despite what he had heard, and a tiny doubt that had crept in as he had listened, Ghote persisted.

'Come, that is so much hot air and nonsense. You were enraged against Ramrao Pendke. You were battering him to death.'

'No.'

It was not any shouted, hysterical denial. It was a simple, calm declaration.

Whether it was a declaration of truth or not, Ghote was unable to judge.

It is possible, he thought, that the fellow has just only at this moment succeeded to throw off his cowed-down fear of the police and has begun to defy me myself. It is possible also – he wished he could blot out the feeling – that this is not after all the man who has murdered Ramrao Pendke.

There was no telling either way.

'Very well,' Ghote went on, still the rock-hard accuser, 'if it is that you were lying before about where you were at the time of the murder, what is the truth of the matter? Or what new story are you going to give out?'

Raghu Barde licked his lips.

'Inspector,' he said, 'I am not at all giving out any story. This is the whole truth.'

A look that might have been calculation, or might merely have been an attempt to sort things out in his mind, passed across his face.

'I admit I did not reach back to TIFR until after that 11.30 meeting had begun,' he said. 'But the explanation is simple. I was in the city itself. All that I was doing was visiting – '

He came to a stop. Then resumed.

'All that I was doing was intending to visit a posh shop in Queen's Road where they are selling the cloth the weavers here in Khindgaon make. I was going to ask if they had new orders. But, when I was nearly at that place, I remembered the meeting, and saw that I was almost too late. So I went back as quickly as I could and reached just only some minutes after the starting time. You may ask anybody who was there whether in the end I came. They will tell you it was so.'

'Yes, very well,' Ghote answered. 'Someone has already vouched for it that you were there. But by coming as late as you did, I am well knowing, you had time first to have killed Mr Ramrao Pendke at the Tick Tock Watchworks.'

He stepped down from the platform and went up to Raghu Barde.

'I am taking you to Bombay,' he said. 'You have much more to answer.'

15

A look of horror, of fear almost as animal as that which had come over Raghu Barde when he had first been surprised, appeared on his face now.

'No,' he shouted. 'No. No, I will not go. No. Why should I be shut in your filthy lock-ups?'

'There is no question of filthy lock-ups,' Ghote answered. 'But you have once already lied concerning your whereabouts at the time of the murder. Why should I believe that you are no longer lying?'

'But – But – But I can prove I was not at that watch-shop. I can prove it.'

'With a proof like your tale only of being at the meeting at TIFR from its start?'

'No. No, with what is true. Listen, Inspector. When I was going back to the TIFR, hurrying because I was late, the dabbawallas were just arriving at Churchgate Station with their tiffin-boxes of lunch for people in offices there. You know the dabbawallas, Inspector?'

'Everybody is knowing them,' Ghote answered angrily. 'You cannot pretend that seeing those fellows coming with the lunches they had collected from housewives in the suburbs is proof that you were there at Churchgate Station then. They come there each day.'

'Yes, yes. But it is not just seeing those fellows. It is more. I was hurrying past where they are sorting the tiffin-boxes on the pavement there, and I was tripping over one of the long wooden trays they have. The men putting the dabbas into it abused me. They almost attacked me even, only in the hurry that they are always in to get the lunches to the offices in time they were returning to their work.'

'Well, what are you claiming now?' Ghote said, full of doubt.

'Inspector, it is obvious. Those fellows are sure to

remember me. And, as they are working always so much to time, not one minute to be lost each day, isn't it, they would be able to state I was there at, shall we say, ten past eleven itself. Because I was there, at just round that time. I was.'

Ghote pursed his lips in vexation.

It could be that Raghu Barde had at last produced a proper alibi. Certainly, if it turned out that there were dabbawallas at Churchgate Station who remembered the incident – and if it had taken place at all they ought to remember such an interruption to their day-by-day routine – then it looked as though Raghu Barde must have been at Churchgate Station at the time when, according to that smashed watch, Ramrao Pendke was being beaten to death. But Barde had lied before, hoping to get away with a tiny inaccuracy. It might well be that he was lying again now.

And there had been a moment of hesitation as he had begun to tell his story. He had seemed to be about to say that he had been in the posh shop in Queen's Road, and then he had claimed that he had remembered the TIFR meeting only as he was about to go into the shop. No, certainly he was not in the clear to one hundred percent.

'Dabbawallas and tripping over one tray,' he said, infusing his voice with a scorn that he hoped might push Barde into betraying the case he was beginning to make out for himself. 'What good is such evidence only? There are fifty-sixty dabbawallas at Churchgate Station each day exchanging tiffin-carriers from one tray to another as each train is coming in from the suburbs. How can the men that you say abused you be found there?'

'But they can, Inspector. They can. Those fellows do exactly the same thing each day, yes? Moving the selfsame marked cans from one tray to another each and every time, no?'

'Well, what of it?'

'Inspector, when I was tripping over that one particular tray I happened to notice the numbers painted on two of the tiffin-carriers. I was telling you yesterday how I am always spotting interesting numbers. And those on those two cans were quite interesting, 4049 and 4051, a pair of primes.'

'What primes?' Ghote shot back, a gust of fury springing up in him. 'What is this primes crimes?'

'Inspector, a prime number is one that cannot be divided into any other numbers. Even you should know that.'

Doubly angry, Ghote remembered dimly that in school he had indeed been taught this useless fact. And he had forgotten it, just as he had forgotten, if he had ever known, where the kidneys came in the human body – he must look for that book of Ved's – earning a similar rebuke from Dr Mrs Yadekar. But he did not have to take lack of respect from this fellow. No, by God.

'And what if you were seeing some magical numbers on a pair of tiffin-cans?' he said. 'What is that to me only?'

'But, Inspector, surely you must see. Those cans are put into the same tray each day. So if you are going to Churchgate Station on any day at about that time, you would find the dabbawallas who were abusing me. They would tell you I was there. They would remember.'

Ghote thought.

'Very well,' he said at last. 'I would check up. But until I have done so to the utmost I am going to hold you. It will be at Crawford Market Headquarters.'

The destination seemed to relieve Raghu Barde of his fears of lock-ups. He nodded agreement with resigned calm.

'Now you must come,' Ghote said sharply. 'I have a jeep waiting just only outside the village. Come.'

Allowing Barde a few minutes to talk with his old mother, who had sat watching uncomprehendingly their bristling exchanges in English, Ghote led him off out of the little, lost village. The village which, but for the death of the knowledgeable Ramrao Pendke, would almost certainly soon have become no more than a squalid settlement for casual labourers at the newly-opened manganese mines. Unless it were blotted out entirely by some wide road thundering day and night with huge trucks urgently carrying away the spoils of the earth beneath.

At the edge of the little collection of huts he saw Raghu Barde take a long, lingering look at a tall pile of baskets made by one of the villagers squatting patiently at work weaving the tough strips of grass into an age-old, intricate pattern. He was struck, looking in his turn, by the simple rightness that seemed to emanate from the basket in the man's hands. Baskets like this, he thought, must have been made in this place for generation on generation, exactly like the one being made now, unhurried by any pressures of fashion, of any here-today gone-tomorrow.

And he recalled abruptly a recent Sunday when back in Bombay he had taken Protima and young Ved to visit the Prince of Wales Museum and had seen outside it the market that had arisen to sell garments intended for Europe and America that had missed, by perhaps a day only, the deadlines imposed by sales organisations in the West. Protima had insisted on looking at the racks of bright shirts, frocks, skirts and long, full-flowing maxis, and had bought Ved a shirt. She had said it was at a very good price, and that latest-craze purchase had become the boy's special delight.

Or, he thought, a one-but-latest craze for the Europe it had originally been destined for.

He felt a growing cold bleakness entering him as, with Raghu Barde at his side, he made his way along the narrow path from the village towards the mango grove where he had hidden his jeep. It was a bleakness, he knew, not induced only by the prospect of the long, long drive back to Bombay.

A long and deeply wearying drive it turned out to be, however. Although he was in no such hurry returning as he had been to get out to Khindgaon before there was any chance of Raghu Barde arriving there, he had a sleepless night at the wheel behind him already. Now deadly fatigue swept up in him at intervals like a welling tide of oily black mud. He would have liked to have stopped at some convenient place and slept for an hour, for two hours, even three. But, though Raghu Barde was showing no signs of being anything but submissive to his fate, he did not dare take any risk with someone who had tried once before to escape.

So he contented himself with stopping as often as he could for tea or a cold Thums Up. He did not even feel it would be right to talk to his prisoner, other than on the most trivial matters connected with their journey. The fellow was after all still under suspicion. It was his duty not to allow him to try and influence the investigation.

Nor did Barde, sitting lost in thought, appear to want to talk. So mile after silent mile they drove onwards. Until at last they reached Bombay again.

Where, of course, they landed full in the middle of the Hour of Car Fumes.

Grimly Ghote battled his way through the traffic to Crawford Market Headquarters and at last disposed safely of his prisoner. Then he had himself driven home, already nodding off to sleep every two or three minutes, oblivious of jerky stops, frantic horn-blowing, everything.

At home he was barely able to find words to greet Protima and young Ved, only just managing to ask Protima to make sure he was up before ten o'clock next morning. He would need to be in good time to go down to Churchgate and check Barde's new alibi with the dabba-wallas there.

Then he lowered his battered, bruised-black body on to his bed and in an instant was lost in sleep.

Only a bare moment later, it seemed to him, to feel Protima shaking him by the shoulder.

'You were wanting to be wakened,' she said.

He shook his head muzzily, and the recollection of where he was and what he had to do came lumberingly back to him. The dabbawallas, he had to check up on them. And those numbers on two of their cans, 4049 and 4051. Thank God, he could remember them.

He looked blearily at his borrowed watch hanging from the nail on the wall beside his bed. He had no recollection at all of having put it the evening before in the familiar place.

But there was something wrong with it.

Then he realised. He had hung it face to the wall. All he was looking at was Mike Lobo's name and that damn, somehow taunting motto *First Past the Post*.

He unhooked the wretched thing, twirled it round and peered at its impossible faceted glass and copper face. Nine minutes past ten.

Nine minutes past ten.

He shot a furious glance at Protima.

'I said to be woken before 10 am,' he exploded. 'It is nine-ten minutes past already.'

Protima was undismayed. She gave a little shrug and looked down at him with mildly contemptuous pity.

'Just only ten minutes,' she said. 'What is to complain? Are you not knowing how long this world has been going on? Have we not passed through three yugas already and entered Kalu Yuga itself with all its evils? And each yuga is it not lasting three thousand celestial years, and each one of those is three thousand six hundred years of this world? What is your five-ten minutes to that?'

Ghote felt hot resentment bubble up inside him like water boiling over in a vessel. Protima and her beliefs. Kali Yuga mumbo-jumbo.

And, worse, he was again being scorned for his ignorance. Celestial years and world years, prime numbers and expressibles, and the damned kidneys somewhere in the body. Would it never end?

'All I am knowing,' he spat out, 'is that if I do not hurry like hell I am going to be late for a Number One important task. Late. Late. Late.'

Furiously he made his way stiff-limbed to the bathroom. Furiously he dragged on the fresh clothes Protima had set out for him. Furiously he banged out. Yet more furiously he kicked his scooter into spluttering life and shot off.

And I could have had time to eat something, he thought. And even I might have had a chance to look at that book of Ved's *The Human Body in Pictures* and have found out where are the kidneys.

But he was destined to be delayed even more before reaching Churchgate Station and the dabbawallas who might or might not be placing the dabbas numbered 4049 and 4051 in one of their long carrying-trays. As he waited impatiently, halted at a red signal at Flora Fountain almost within reach of his destination, a voice called out to him from the pavement.

'Ghote sahib. Inspector.'

He turned his head.

Mike Lobo was coming towards him, a cheerful grin all over his round face.

'Hey, God's grace seeing you here. Something I've got to tell you.'

'Yes? What is it, AI? I am in one hell of a hurry,' he shouted above the phut-phutting of his scooter.

'Oh, won't take a sec, man. Just this. I happened to pop up to the Shrimati Usha Yadekar Clinic yesterday. Thought I'd better find out just when Ramrao Pendke left there before he got himself and his made-in-Ulhasnagar gold Rolex hammered to bits.'

'Yes? Yes?' Ghote shouted.

The driver of a taxi, hemmed in because he himself had failed to move as the signal ahead turned green, had begun to hoot at him with wild gusto.

Mike Lobo flashed his wide grin again.

'Found out from that uppity, America-returned Doctor Mrs,' he said, 'you were interested in who visited Ramrao. Like his cousin and uncle from some backwood called Dharbani, isn't it? Then it came to me that, God bless you, you were thinking one of them could be fixed up with the Tick Tock murder.'

Red anger blew up in Ghote's head. And the taxiwalla behind was hooting even more venomously.

'Yeah,' Lobo went breezily on, 'so I made a few inquiries. And you can write them both off, Inspector. Got perfect alibis. They were together at the Rajabi Tower at just past 11 am. I spoke to the fellow from Lund and

162

Blockley, Watchmakers, who looks after the tower clock. He confirms it, all the way. Sorry for you, man.'

Ghote sat astride his scooter wishing he could at that instant do something that would annihilate Mike Lobo in one single act of vengeful fury. But nothing came to him.

Until, just as the taxi behind managed to ease its way past and its driver leant across to yell at him 'Shaitan!' he found a thing to do. He tore the unreadable, motto-garnished borrowed watch from his wrist and hurled it across at Mike Lobo – the bastard caught it – and then, wrenching his machine into motion, he yelled back 'Take it, take it, it's no bloody damn good whatsoever.'

16

The moment Ghote finally arrived at Churchgate Station he realised he very much needed Mike Lobo's watch. He had to have the exact time if he was going to be able to tell whether the dabbawallas Raghu Barde had claimed he had tripped over had been where he had said they were when he had said they were.

He cursed.

Cursed himself for again having given way to petty fury just because of Lobo's interference. Cursed Lobo for interfering, and worse, much worse, for having proved apparently that both Ganpatrao Pendke and the Sarpanch had been far away from the Tick Tock Watchworks when Ramrao had been battered to death.

But he thrust off the sullen, lightning-quivering cloud of depression which that knowledge threatened him with. Instead he locked his scooter under a patch of tree shade and hurried into the station itself. There he checked the time on the clock before going to look for the dabbawallas who, if Raghu Barde was telling the truth, dealt each day with dabbas numbered 4049 and 4051, the pair of primes.

Back outside round the corner, conscious that the time was just before ten past eleven, he walked rapidly along the yellow-tiled pavement. Squatting or hurrying dabba-wallas by the dozen were loading scores of their eight-foot long carrying-trays with hundreds of the round aluminium dabbas before they were whisked away to offices, shops, banks and markets, each one with its four inner containers, one on top of the other, filled with curry, rice, a vegetable, a chapatti or two – meat for Muslims, their own particular styles for Parsis and Christians – with sometimes nestling at the top inside a loving note from a distant new wife in the suburbs or a demanding or angry one from a distant old wife. He scanned the painted tops, coded in red, yellow, green or blue letters and figures.

Then suddenly he spotted the two curious numbers he had in his head. They were the more easily seen because their coding, he now realised, was for some reason different from the majority of the other cans.

But he still had to question the pair of white-capped dabbawallas crouched one on each side of the long wooden tray where dabbas 4049 and 4051 had just been placed. Had they been here at this time the previous Tuesday? At precisely this time? And had they then been tripped over by a very tall, quite bald young man? On this occasion he was not going to let a single, tiny detail go unasked about.

'Bhai sahib,' he addressed the nearer of the two dabbawallas, 'can you help me? I am wanting to know if you are here always at just this time.'

The man made no reply. Instead he rose from his squatting position, trotted over to a newly arrived supply of cans, picked out four of them, and, holding them by their swinging wooden handles, scuttered back, quickly as a monkey, to place them in the carrying-frame at Ghote's feet.

'Bhai sahib, I am asking.'

Still rapidly arranging the cans in the tray, the man continued not to offer any reply.

'Police,' Ghote rapped out. 'Tell me what I am wanting ek dum, or for once Bombay's great lunch delivery system will break down when one of its dabbawallas finds himself in the lock-up.'

The dabbawalla did now look up, his face dull with anger.

'Speak then,' he muttered.

'Is it that you are here at this time, with those two dabbas with those long numbers on them, each day?'

'Yes, yes.'

'Then you were here last Tuesday?'

'Monday, Tuesday, Wednesday, every day. Now, won't you leave me alone? Don't you know how little time we have? At the station where we load up, train is stopping just only two minutes. Calamities are happening, split-second work.'

'And last Tuesday,' Ghote persisted, ignoring the self-pitying plea, 'was there a man who was tripping over your tray here?'

'I do not know. Why should I know?'

But the man's companion, squatting equally busy on the other side of the long tray, looked up briefly at this.

'Bhai,' he said to his co-worker, 'you must remember. Young fellow with one bald head, bald-bald, walking like in a dream and tripping right over us. You gave him plenty of abuses.'

'Oh, yes. Him. I remember. Idiot.'

The surly fellow bent again to his work. But Ghote, with simple determination, got out of the pair of them names and addresses. Then he retired to where he had left his scooter on the other side of the road and began to think.

It seemed that this second alibi that Raghu Barde had produced was absolutely correct. If the fellow had tripped over the dabbawallas' carrying-tray at, to within a minute or two, 11.10 am, as checked by Churchgate Station clock, then he could not possibly have been battering Ramrao Pendke to death at the Tick Tock Watchworks at almost the same hour.

Yet, if he was guiltless of the crime, why was it that he had not produced this alibi when first questioned in his room at the TIFR? Why had he produced an account of his whereabouts that he must have known was inaccurate, relying on the hope that it would not be really closely checked?

Perhaps it was that he had said the first thing that had come into his head then. He had admitted that he had been put into a state of fear at the thought that he was in the hands of the police. Perhaps that was it.

But all the same he felt the faintest of uneasinesses at the back of his mind. It was as if, he thought, back in his village boyhood some sense of which he was hardly aware

166

had warned him that a snake was coiled asleep under a rock he was about to sit on. Even this new alibi, though for the life of him he could not see how it was not all that it seemed to be, was somehow unsatisfactory.

He sighed.

Yet, if the alibi was the simple truth, it meant conclusively that Barde was not the murderer of Ramrao Pendke. But then neither was Ganpatrao Pendke nor the Sarpanch: there was, so it appeared, the evidence of the clock mechanic at the Rajabi Tower for that.

Which seemed to leave only wretched Rustom Fardoomji. And Mike Lobo right after all.

A spasm of frustration and of determination flared up in him.

No, he would not go along to Headquarters and let Raghu Barde go, as he had begun to feel he ought to do. He would still keep a glimmer of belief that somehow the fellow's second alibi was as false as the first.

And neither, by God, would he give up Ganpatrao and the Sarpanch just on the strength of those few shouted words from Mike Lobo as he had sat there on his scooter at the red signal at Flora Fountain. He would go straightaway, yes, and see if he could get hold of the Rajabi Tower mechanic at Lund and Blockley Watchmakers. From his lips he would insist on hearing just what that no-good pair from Village Dharbani had done at the Tower. Just what time they had arrived and what time they had left.

At Lund and Blockley's – Ghote shook his head in wonder that this was the same firm whose Mr Lund, back in 1858, had constructed the extraordinary thirteen-dial timepiece, now permanently stuck at twenty-five minutes to one, which he had used up time contemplating when he had been too early for that first meeting with the DGP – he found he had run into a piece of luck. The mechanic in charge of the Rajabi Tower clock, he was told, had left to go there only a minute or two earlier. It was the regular day when the great clock had to be wound.

He hurried off in the man's wake to the University

building overlooking the Oval Maidan. In the porch of the big old British-days building with its statues in niches of the peoples of Western India as seen by their English sculptor, the mild Hindu, the shrewd Kutchi, the fierce Rajput, the prayerful Parsi, he caught up with the mechanic and his two attendant coolies. They were just about to begin their climb up to the top of the tower. He hailed the mechanic and explained his business.

'An assistant inspector, one AI Lobo, was coming to see you yesterday, no?' he concluded. 'I am just only checking up on one or two additional points.'

The mechanic, a sturdy, keen-eyed fellow in a neat check shirt and well-creased trousers, nodded in agreement.

'You are wanting to come up also and see the clock workings?' he asked. 'Your AI yesterday did not. Too much of hard work, he was saying. Well, I must go up myself every fifth day, hard work or not, week in week out, isn't it? Feast or festival, it is making no difference.'

'Achcha, I will come up also,' Ghote said, determined to accept a challenge Mike Lobo had declined.

Up and up they climbed, slowly and steadily. Ghote, to begin with, attempted to make some conversation.

'Tell me, bhai sahib, how old is this tower actually? It was here when I was coming to Bombay first, and even then it was looking ancient.'

'Oh, yes, it is dating from year 1869 and is in height 280 feet,' the mechanic intoned. 'It was taking nine years to build, gifted by one Mr Premchand Roychand who was known by the name of Uncrowned King of Bombay. It was his mother only who was one Rajabi, so it is Rajabi Tower.'

Ghote was feeling every step of those 280 feet now, on bruised back and aching legs.

'Used to have fail-safe electric mechanism,' his guide went remorselessly on, apparently not at all out of breath. 'Back in the 1930s. But the fail-safe itself was failing. Look.'

168

He gestured at a row of huge grimy switch-boxes on the wall beside him, greened over and fused with rust.

'All things pass,' he said with a touch of pomposity. 'All things excepting only Time itself. And my old clock that is recording its each and every minute.'

Ghote, grabbing a faint puff of cooler air coming in through one of the narrow vents in the tower's sides, was unable to get out any answer.

On they went. The mechanic stepping easily upwards, Ghote toiling just behind him, and two coolies padding on naked feet a few steps in the rear.

At last, when Ghote had almost come to believe he would have to cry off, they came to a narrow door and the mechanic halted. He drew a large key from his pocket and turned it in the door's lock.

'Machine Room,' he said.

To Ghote the place looked not unlike the navigator's cabin on some ship. It had, too, four small doors, one in each wall, leading out to balconies underneath the four gigantic opal-coloured glass clock-dials. Through the room from ceiling to floor there ran a massive steel rope, the centrepiece of the clock mechanism.

'Look downwards,' the mechanic said. 'You can see the metal discs we are putting on the bottom which as they descend turn these cogwheels.'

Ghote took a quick look down, stemming the first traces of vertigo.

'What is that loud noise I am hearing?' he asked, quickly straightening.

'Oh, it is what we are calling escape-mechanism. Look upwards and you can see it. It is regulating the clock, letting the weights drop only one little bit at a time. But my fellows are ready to begin winding the weights to the top again. I must just screw in the turning-wheel. One moment only.'

He jumped up on a plank and set to work. Then, at a signal, his coolies started marching round and round, winding the steel rope up on to its huge barrel above.

Ghote took advantage of the pause while they worked

to ask the questions he felt he had earned by his long climb.

'This clock of yours is keeping very good time?' he began cunningly.

'Perfect. Perfect time.'

'So, I suppose you yourself are always having a very good idea of what is the time?'

'Yes, yes. I am always checking my own watch. At office we have chronometers. Never one half-second out.'

'So you would know just exactly what time those gentlemen that AI Lobo was asking about came here and left also?'

'Oh, yes, yes. To the minute I am knowing.'

'So, kindly refresh my memory, what time was it you told the AI they were arriving and departing?'

'Oh, I was not at all telling him exact times. Did he inform you I was?'

'No, no,' Ghote said hastily. 'I was not explaining very clearly. AI Lobo told me only what you were telling him.'

'That those two gentlemen were here just only some time in the morning of that day? He was not asking precise times.'

'Yes, yes. That is it. So what were those precise times?'

Had Lobo once more been too expeditious, Ghote thought to himself. But what would the precise times reveal?

'They were coming at 11.32,' the mechanic said. 'It was arranged we would meet at 11.30. I was here, but they were two minutes late. And they were leaving at 11.57. I had said I could give one half-hour to them.'

Ghote felt joy running through him, sharp and biting as the fierce joy of a hunting leopard. So Mike Lobo had got it altogether wrong. Ganpatrao Pendke and the Sarpanch had neither of them an alibi for the time of the murder, that 11.08 marked out for ever on the smashed hands of Ramrao Pendke's fake gold Rolex.

Now he had under his hand two men, both more than ready to disregard any law that stood in their way, each with good reason for wanting Ramrao Pendke dead.

While, set against them, Mike Lobo's Rustom Fardoomji had as motive only that sudden seizure by greed which Lobo, in any case, seemed to have thrust into his mind. A man obsessed with his clocks and watches to the point of disregard for everything else, one it was hard to believe in as a brutal battering murderer.

And also, Ghote thought, I can release Raghu Barde now. Forget that niggling feeling of something being a little wrong with his second alibi.

But, damn it, he added, the hunting joy still coursing through him, Mr Barde can wait. What I must do now is to think just exactly what will be my next step so as to get myself a first-class case against those two, one of them or both. I want a case no one can blow away, not Mike Lobo, not the DGP himself.

Plan. Plan carefully. That is the thing. Get it right. From start to finish. Each and every time and detail.

And at the moment, without a watch, he knew from the clock in his stomach that it was time to eat. And where better to eat and to plan in peace and quietness than in his own home? And, besides, it would be a chance to look for Ved's book on *The Human Body in Pictures*.

At home, Protima seemed delighted to see him, despite the spate of rage with which he had left her at the start of the day. She made no difficulties about preparing him some lunch without warning, and appeared distinctly pleased to be going to do better herself than the couple of bananas she had intended as her own modest meal.

While she was busy in the kitchen, Ghote looked about for *The Human Body in Pictures*. He found it almost at once, and took that as a good omen. As soon as he had eaten he would get down to planning his operation in peace. He would see his way to success. Things had begun to go well from the moment that the Rajabi Tower mechanic had declared that he was such an accurate time-keeper. They were going to go on getting better and better.

He rifled eagerly through the big coloured pages of Ved's old book. And, yes, there they were, the kidneys.

171

There was a big diagram, on a left-hand page, of the body seen as a kind of factory. At the top someone sat in the head at a computer panel. Just below came two massive cogwheels, not unlike the black-greased cogs of the huge clock he had just been looking at, the teeth. Then there was a sort of downwards-plunging factory chimney, labelled *Oesophagus*, with at its foot two sewer-wallas busy shovelling away in the stomach. And, to the left and right of that, there came a pair of wooden presses, each worked by a merrily grinning boy, much like the old oil-mill of his village days, though much cleaner, the kidneys.

So now he knew where those were, at least.

And on the opposite page, to confirm his new knowledge, there was a more realistic representation of the inside of the body, an outline skeleton on a black background. And there again, printed in a cheerful blue, were the two kidney-shaped objects, with between them something lumpy in pink, the pancreas, whatever that did.

He felt yet more pleased with life, happy almost as the two grinning boys churning away at their oil-mill kidneys.

Protima brought in the meal she had cooked, delicious fried slices of spiced purple-skinned, pale yellow baigan with a quartered sweetlime beside them and curds with cucumber, cooling and nourishing. He tackled both with greedy pleasure. Filled with this, he would get down to his planning with double vigour.

'Sit, sit,' he said to Protima, through a mouth filled with aubergine. 'Eat also. This is delicious.'

'And for once you are at home,' she answered with the tiniest touch of sharpness, something he thought he would ignore.

'Take more,' he said, seeing how little she had helped herself to.

'Yes, today you come home. But where were you the night before last? And the night before that? Where were you again just only ten days before that? Away then for two nights and three days.'

'Oh, come,' he answered amusedly, 'that was when we

were questioning the culprits in the Bandra bank dacoity. That was three weeks ago, more.'

But, to his surprise and sinking dismay, temper flashed up at once in Protima's eyes.

'Three weeks? Three weeks? That is what you are thinking. That is how you look on your wife. Someone you cannot remember whether you were away from three weeks ago, or three months. I tell you, the time you were away those two whole nights and three whole days with your bank dacoity question-questions was just only ten days past. Not one more.'

Foolishly, hardly knowing why, he contradicted her.

'No, no. It is you who are wrong. That was at least three weeks ago. What day is it today? Monday. Well then, it was three weeks ago exactly. We began on a Monday. We broke them on the Wednesday.'

'No.'

He might have slapped her with a chappal, so outraged did she sound.

'Yes, I tell you, yes,' he answered, all good humour drained away as if from the oil-mill kidneys in Ved's book.

Protima sat and glared at him, reduced for a few instants to enraged silence.

'Wait, I will prove it,' she exploded then. 'Do not be relying on me. I am just only your wife. Your wife that you think cannot so much as count the days on a calendar. Your wife who has to stay in the house all day and every day until she is no more able to tell one from another. But I will prove it. I will go straightaway next door to Mrs Govekar. She is remembering everything, she can put one thing after another, she always is getting it right. You would see.'

At any other time Ghote might have taken up the challenge. They had consulted the Mrs Govekar oracle before, and he knew that the lady in her busy, clockwork mind did indeed keep a chronological list of every event in the neighbourhood. If sometimes after a little *No, that was the day your Radha Auntie came to see you* and some *No, no, the day before when in the market water-melons were so cheap,*

173

she could finally be relied on always to produce the correct facts.

But at this moment something Protima had ripped out in her rage had struck him dumb.

Your wife who has to stay in the house all day and every day until she is no more able to tell one from another.

That was by no means actually true of Protima who lived a life of not a little variety. But it was true of someone else. The dabbawalla he had spoken to at Churchgate Station. Dabbawallas lived lives that were truly ones of unvarying routine. Up each day at the same hour in order to be in time to collect the dabbas from the houses they served and get to the station when the train was due. Pushing the same racks of dabbas into the same compartment of the same train as on the day before and the day before that. Sorting the dabbas on the train, moving the same cans from one place to another without variation. Unloading at Churchgate Station on the same few square feet of platform each day. Taking the heavy laden trays to the same appointed spot on the pavement outside to sort them again. Handing the same dabbas to the same fresh dabbawallas to take them on bicycle or running with a head-load or trotting a loaded handcart through the unyielding mid-day traffic – different in individuality but the same always in its mass – to the same office buildings and shops. Taking the same lifts up to the same upper floors of the same high-rises. Collecting the same dabbas empty in just the same way again each day. A hundred thousand of them in all, so they said.

Their lives must be a blur, a whirl in a tiny endlessly self-repeating world, with only Sundays, day of blotted-out rest to interrupt it.

So how could such fellows mark out one day from another? How could they be certain that any particular incident had happened on a Tuesday rather than on the Monday before it or the Wednesday after?

And, in all likelihood, Raghu Barde, the mathematician, had worked this out in a moment when he himself had so unexpectedly demanded of him out at Khindgaon where

174

he had really been the previous Tuesday at 11.08. It was a risk to have taken, but it was one that had very nearly succeeded.

Thank goodness, he had not let the fellow go.

He was too dazed by the possibilities of this new revelation to do anything more than to say tamely to Protima that, after all, she was probably right about when it was that he had had to be away interrogating the Bandra bank dacoits. She did not seem altogether pleased at his sudden acquiescence. For a moment a tremor of his previous resentment quivered in him again and he thought of demanding if she was wanting him to go on claiming to be right so that she could have the pleasure of abusing him yet more. But he was too caught up by all that had just come into his mind to have the heart for that.

And, before he had had time to say something nice about how good the lunch had been, the telephone rang.

It was the DGP's secretary asking where he could be found. The DGP was wanting to see him urgently.

17

The urgency with which Ghote was wanted by the DGP turned out, when, sweaty and somewhat muzzed from dashing once more through Bombay's chaotic traffic on his scooter, he arrived at the DGP's office, to have been entirely in his secretary's mind. All that the DGP required was a progress report.

Ghote felt happy to provide it. Thanks, he felt, to his determination in checking every exact time of each suspect's alibi, he could say with confidence that Raghu Barde had twice provided false information. Coupled with the clear motive the man had, there was a very good case against him. And he was safely in custody, put there by himself. Even as a fall-back he had, too, ascertained that Ganpatrao Pendke's account of his movements at the time of the murder, and those of the Sarpanch, had almost certainly been deliberately vague. So, altogether he could present the DGP with three suspects, each of whom looked much more likely to be guilty than the Dhunjee-bhoy brothers' watches-obsessed cousin.

The DGP would surely be delighted to be given an explanation of the murder that answered the plea the Dhunjeebhoys had made. And now perhaps he would take a different view of the merits of a certain Assistant Inspector Lobo.

But, as he brought forward times and places one after another, Ghote saw the DGP's expression had not changed from the look of acutely critical attention he had assumed at the outset.

It was clear that each logical deduction was being asborbed. But none of them seemed, Ghote began increasingly to be aware, to be having the effect he had hoped for.

At last he brought his recital to an end.

'Hm,' said the DGP.

He propped his elbows on his wide desk – Ghote in front of it did not dare relax from his position of strict attention – and considered.

'Very well, Inspector,' he said eventually. 'I see you are determined to find the confession AI Lobo obtained was secured contrary to the regulations of the Criminal Procedure Code, as the brothers Dhunjeebhoy were unfortunate enough to allege here in your presence. That is your privilege, I suppose. But, let me tell you, I will not tolerate this investigation, which has attracted not a little public attention, being allowed to hang fire interminably.'

He flicked back the cuff of his shirt-sleeve and looked at the gleaming Titan Exacto on his wrist.

'I am going to give you just twenty-four hours, Inspector,' he said. 'Twenty-four hours exactly to come up with clear proof that any one of the three names you put before me did indeed kill this fellow at that Tick Tock place. It is now – '

Another scrutiny of the Titan.

'It is now precisely 14.19 hours. Unless by 14.19 hours tomorrow you have brought me that proof I shall order you back to normal duties. Understood?'

'Yes, sir. Understood, sir.'

It seemed to Ghote that it was only one half-second later that he was standing outside on the pavement, staring vacantly at the tall hedge surrounding the Oval Maidan across the wide road in front of him, with behind it vague figures in white moving to and fro, the inevitable cricket players.

Standing staring, and trying to get his thoughts together. Twenty-four hours. It was not long. Not long to come up with definite proof that one of those three had battered Ramrao Pendke to death. If only there was no choice. If only he could be certain, for instance, that Raghu Barde was his man. He could stand there then, for every one of the twenty-four hours if need be, and hammer a true confession out of the fellow. Or, if he was as certain that Ganpatrao Pendke was his man, he could break him

177

inside that time. Arrogance lasted only so long. Or the Sarpanch. Twenty-four hours would be altogether too long for him to go on wriggling and evading and lying. Before the time was up he himself would have pinned that greasy miscreant till he could squirm and invent no more.

But there was really so little to choose between any of them. And time was already passing. Some minutes already lost for ever.

He glanced at the watch on his wrist to see just how many. And found, of course, there was no watch on his wrist.

Achcha, he thought, that settles it. At least I know now what to do first. Get myself one watch. I cannot be all the time asking how long it is till the DGP's deadline when I am all along not knowing whether it is three o'clock or half-past ten.

Seizing his scooter, he rode as fast as he could, hooting his tweety little horn with the best of them, yet again through the jostling traffic up to the Big Ben Watch Stores.

Would prosing old Mr Big Ben have actually mended his own watch? Despite the time he had said it would have to take? It was possible. The fellow might have taken to heart what he had said to him about the importance of a police officer possessing a reliable means of telling the time, in spite of all that Shri Kipling stuff.

But, he thought, snaking his machine through a gap between a smart new red Maruti and a chugging, sides-scraped old bus, had he perhaps deserved to be Kipling admonished? With all that shouting and demanding in the shop that morning, had he not failed to behave as a Man, my son? Perhaps been a little childish?

Well, he would be calm and collected now.

But his resolution nearly went up in smoke before he had even entered Mr Big Ben's shop. In its window the card saying *Punctuality Is the Politeness of Princes (Raj-kumars)* had been replaced by another. It read *Forgiveness Is Better Than Revenge*. Was that aimed at him personally?

No. No, he must not get paranoid.

He entered the shop. Mr Big Ben had his back turned to the counter, bending over his workbench, watchglass screwed to his eye.

Ghote coughed.

No response, though there was a mirror in front of the bench in which customers entering could be observed.

He coughed again.

Still no response.

Well, concentration on the job in hand without worrying about the passing of time or any other consideration was deserving of praise. But, on the other hand . . .

'Bhai sahib,' he said loudly.

At that the old man did turn round.

'Ah, it is you, Inspector,' he said. 'But you have come too early. Too early altogether. And it is as bad, you know, to be too early as it is to be too late.'

Ghote very nearly banged out at the old man the retort he had had to suppress when the DGP had given him that same infuriating and not altogether logical advice. But his need to have a watch on his wrist once more was too acute.

'Bhai sahib,' he said, forcing himself to sound reasonable, 'I am very badly requiring to have a watch. Is it not at all possible for you to repair mine here and now only?'

Mr Big Ben looked at him with an expression of overwhelming piety.

'And all my other customers,' he said, 'why should they suffer?'

'But – But I am a police officer. My need is greater.'

'To know whether it is thirteen minutes past the hour or twelve only? My son, you should learn to tell needs from desires.'

Ghote swallowed that, with as much difficulty as a cat swallowing a hair-ball.

'Well, it is my bounden duty to note the exact times of certain occurrences,' he said. 'So, if you cannot mend my own watch, can you perhaps be lending me some other? One that is reliable.'

'If a watch is leaving this shop,' Mr Big Ben said with

179

a froth of indignation, 'it is guaranteed reliable. Kindly do not question that.'

'No, no. I am not at all questioning.'

For a daring moment then he actually contemplated laying out cash to buy a brand-new watch. There was a display of Tata Titans on the wall beside the old man, smaller by far than the one in the Tick Tock Watchworks but still impressive. And there was a case, too, of rather dusty HMT products, as carried by Mr Saxena, of the watches-covered, hairy forearm. But he thought of the economies such an impulse-buy would necessitate over the coming months, if not years, and was checked.

'Bhai sahib,' he said, 'I am asking. Can you find some watch to lend me while mine is repaired only?'

A gleam came into Mr Big Ben's squinty eyes.

'Yes,' he said, savouring the word. 'Yes, I have got one repaired watch here which a customer has not collected for three-four months. You can be having that. For a police officer the good citizen will always go to his level best.'

'Thank you,' Ghote said, striving for the right note of humility.

The gleam in the old man's eyes was plainly malicious now. It had been a terrible mistake to hint at the unreliablity of any of his work.

'Mind,' he said, 'what I am giving is an Ulhasnagar affair and no more. But those fellows cannot fool me with their name-stamps shame-stamps. I can put right all their workmanship, if I am wanting.'

Ghote knew he ought to reject the old man's challenge to accept a fake, however well repaired. But what the fellow had said had started in his mind a spark running fizzingly along a sprinkled gunpowder train.

Ulhasnagar watches, of course destined not to last in their imitation foreign cases given extra weight with slips of lead. Ramrao Pendke, the rich fool, as Rustom Fardoomji had been persuaded by AI Lobo to call him, with his fake Rolex. Fardoomji saying, as a mere aside during his interview with him, that the rich fool had come into his shop wanting a new watch. Why should he have needed a new watch, unless his present one had become broken? And if it was broken, it would have stopped. It would have stopped not at the moment Ramrao Pendke had entered the Tick Tock Watchworks, but some time earlier.

So the battered hands of the fake gold Rolex had not indicated the time of the murder at all. Any calculations based on it having taken place at 11.08 were meaningless. It must have happened at some altogether later time.

Mechanically he held out his hand as Mr Big Ben leant over his counter holding out the watch he had said he would lend him. Hardly noticing, he strapped it on his wrist and went wandering, still thinking, out of the shop.

Mr Big Ben found not a single moral sentiment to speed him on his way.

Then, standing on the pavement about to mount his scooter, the new watch ticking away unnoticed on his wrist, the full further implications of what he had just realised came to him. Like the swift darkening of a sun-bright day under an eclipse.

If old D'Sa had been right after all and it had really been Ramrao Pendke he had seen in the August Kranti Maidan at, as he had said, precisely 11.27, then the murder must have taken place at, more or less, 11.40, the time it would have taken to go on foot from the maidan to the watch-shop. And that meant, first, that Raghu Barde now had a complete alibi. He had been seen at the far-away TIFR meeting by that pretty engineer, Amita Modi, at seven or eight minutes past 11.30 at the latest. But, second, it meant that Ganpatrao Pendke, and the Sarpanch as well, had a perfect alibi. They had met the mechanic at the Rajabi Tower at exactly 11.32.

So, was it now certain, after all, that it had been Rustom Fardoomji who had killed his rich-fool customer? No. Not altogether. If, as now seemed certain, Ramrao Pendke had been attacked at the Tick Tock Watchworks at about 11.40, the gap in time between then and when the Parsi had spoken to Constable Vaingankar on traffic control duty at the junction of S. S. Patkar Road and Balbunath Road, a good distance away from his shop, was much less than it had seemed before. So Fardoomji's first story of having found the body when he came up from his workshop and having gone simply to look for a policeman to report the death was all the more likely.

It provided him with no real alibi, of course. Mike Lobo could still flourish that confession against him. But now it looked even more possible that the confession had sprung from acute physical fear and no more.

And there was worse.

He felt a sudden heaviness inside himself, as if some vital organ – would it be the pancreas? – had been abruptly stricken.

Now the business of providing clear proof for the DGP that someone other than Rustom Fardoomji was the murderer, and finding that proof within his twenty-four hours, had become a thousand times more difficult. More than a thousand times by far, because he must now look for his killer among all eight-nine million inhabitants of Bombay, plus also visitors.

He got on to his scooter and, kicking it into life, swung into the swirling, hooting stream of passing traffic. But he had no idea where to head for. Anywhere might lead him now to his murderer. Any one place was as good as another.

Then he thought there was one thing at least he ought to do. If Raghu Barde, behind bars at Headquarters, could not possibly have killed Ramrao Pendke, then at least he must be set free.

The doing of that did not take long, even when in a moment of curiosity Ghote asked the tall, bald young mathematician why it was he had produced his two false accounts of his movements on the morning of the murder.

Raghu Barde gave him the warm smile he had seen only once or twice before.

'Inspector,' he said, 'you are a better mathematician than you think if you were able to work out that those dabbawallas were unlikely to remember which day in a sequence it was when I tripped on their tray.'

Then he bit his lip in sudden embarrassment.

'But I see I must give you my explanation all the same,' he went on. 'Well, the fact is that I was down in Kamathipura that morning, and I am ashamed to say I was visiting a prostitute there. I don't know if you will understand. But, you see, I feel I cannot marry when I have responsibilities to the poor people I am born among. Yet I am a man and have the desires of a man.'

'You were going to a prostitute at eleven in the morning?' Ghote asked with visible astonishment, before wishing he had managed to keep his mouth shut.

'Oh, Inspector, why not? Needs of that sort are not regulated by the clock, you know. They do not take place only between the hours of, say, 6.25 pm and 11.55.'

It was Ghote's turn now to look shame-faced.

'Of course, yes, I know,' he said. 'And Barde sahib, may I be wishing you all good luck henceforth in selling those fine baskets and weaving-work. May Village Khindgaon never change. Best of luck.'

As if he was being rewarded for promptly freeing the Gandhian mathematician, Ghote found, as he left him, that he knew after all what his next step should be. It was no great advance. But it was the only thing that seemed to lie ahead. He would have to arm himself with a photograph of Ramrao Pendke and ask and ask anybody he came across in the vicinity of the Tick Tock Watchworks whether they had seen its subject on the morning of Tuesday last and if they had noticed anyone following him or entering the watch-shop at his heels.

It was the barest of possibilities. But such pieces of luck had come to him and his colleagues in the past. There were always, thank goodness, idlers in the streets of Bombay with nothing more to do than stare at passers-by. Perhaps one of them would have noticed something, might have remembered . . .

There was only one bright side: it was altogether certain

AI Lobo would not have undertaken any such time-consuming, wearisome task.

But first he had to get a copy of Ramrao Pendke's photograph out of Lobo. And, when he got to the station to ask for that, he found, as he had half-expected, he was not getting much co-operation from the man whose motto-inscribed watch he had so fiercely rejected. It was plain Lobo very much intended still to be *First Past the Post*.

'Photo, Inspector? What the hell do you want a photo of the guy for? I told you, your pet suspects are top-notch in the clear. There's nothing more to be done now, man, till I take our little Parsi friend before a Magistrate.'

Seething with vexation at the thought that his 'pet suspects' were indeed in the clear, if not for the reason Lobo thought, Ghote returned to the attack.

'Nevertheless, AI,' he said, 'I am wishing to check up to one hundred and one per cent on each and every circumstance. I need that photo to be taking to all the places near the Tick Tock Watchworks.'

'Well, sorry to God, man, but I haven't any more got a photo.'

'But, AI, you were saying you had the same. You were saying you had with all the other material on the case.'

'Was I, Inspector? Well, bless you, I think I must have been telling you wrong.'

Ghote fumed.

'Very well then,' he said, striving to keep his voice icy calm, 'I shall have to ask at *Mid-Day* newspaper. I am knowing they were using one picture.'

Lobo grinned.

'And who do you think gave it to them, man? One Mike Lobo. That's who. Got to make the most of a good murder inquiry landing on your plate, hey? And who do you think asked for the photo back? One Mike Lobo. And where it is now God alone knows.'

'I need a photograph of Ramrao Pendke,' Ghote snapped. 'Make a search, AI. Now. That is an order.'

'Okay, okay. If you're so set on it, though Jesus knows what you hope to prove.'

Watching Lobo go sauntering off, Ghote sighed and thought his chances of ever seeing a photo were almost nil. And he had now only – He looked at his borrowed Ulhasnagar watch. It turned out to be an imitation of an extraordinarily elaborate affair, a Seiko Sports 100, with no fewer than three inner dials, all ticking round, and a sweep second-hand that made it even more difficult to decide what the actual time was. But eventually he made it out.

He now had just over twenty-two hours of the DGP's twenty-four.

'Hey, Inspector, did I hear you asking about a photo of Ramrao Pendke?'

It was Sub-Inspector Shruti Shah. She had just come in, looking as always as if she ought to have been there ten minutes before, hair as usual falling down in front of her face, eyes as usual shining with active zeal.

'Yes,' Ghote said. 'Yes, I am very much wanting.'

Only some remaining sense of keeping discipline and good order prevented him adding that he never expected AI Lobo to let him have one.

'Well, I have got,' Shruti said. 'Mike was issuing a few straightaway after the murder, copies of one he was finding in the dead man's wallet. But then, when they were so pleased with the confession he had got, he asked for them back. But I was late coming that day, and he was missing me. So I still have mine. Do you want it?'

She began scrabbling in her handbag.

'Thank you very much, SI,' Ghote said.

18

Shruti Shah's photograph of the Tick Tock Watchworks victim brought Ghote no quick success. Ever aware of the minutes and hours slipping by on his complicated imitation Seiko Sports watch, he trudged here and there for all the rest of the afternoon and into the evening. He visited address after address in the area close to Rustom Fardoomji's shop to no avail. He stopped every passer-by he could, he accosted every idle onlooker, and still found no one who would admit to so much as having seen Ramrao Pendke the previous Tuesday morning. Let alone anyone who had noticed him being followed by someone else.

He was handicapped in his search, he knew, by not being able to conduct it at exactly the equivalent hour to that which, the week before, Ramrao had left the Shrimati Usha Yadekar Clinic, walked round the August Kranti Maidan where old D'Sa had seen him and, returning, had taken his stopped fake Rolex into the Tick Tock Watchworks. But to leave inquiries until next morning, precisely one week after the murder, would be altogether too much of a risk. There would then be barely four hours before he would have to leave to report to the DGP by his deadline time of 14.19.

No, there were some eighteen hours still remaining in total. He must, if he possibly could, use every minute of every one of them. Otherwise, Rustom Fardoomji would be taken before a Magistrate and – almost beyond doubt – in trembling fear would repeat the confession he had made to Lobo. And had repeated, again and again, to himself.

The evening drew on. The character of the people in the streets round Fardoomji's shuttered shop changed. Gone were the pavement vendors with their small collections of magazines and newspapers spread out in front of them or their tiny displays of items of cheap jewellery or little piles of wilting vegetables. In their place, down at Kemp's Corner itself, cars and taxis were stopping to disgorge the well-off on their way to the area's restaurants. No hope at all for a piece of luck there. Nearer the watch-shop the less affluent were busy with last-minute marketing, and disinclined, to say the least, to stop and answer questions.

The barber at the Decent Electric Hairdresser to one side of the Tick Tock Watchworks had long ago brought down his shutter. Even at the Sri Krishna Lunch Home on the other side the flow of customers had dried up leaving its proprietor moodily stirring at the remains of something on one of his big cooking vessels.

Ghote was tempted to abandon his search. It was almost certainly altogether unlikely now to be productive. But he could think of no other way to use up the remaining sixteen hours, those that came under the darkness of night.

Then, as he stood looking dispiritedly at the watch-shop's rust-streaked shutter trying to make up his mind where to try next, he saw the mad bus-starter who had accosted him at this spot on the first day of the case. The fellow was coming meanderingly right up to the shop again. Should he try asking even this wandering-witted, shirt-flapping, dirt-begrimed witness whether he had seen Ramrao Pendke? Show him his now curled and fingers-blotched photograph? The fellow, after all, had been on the scene much nearer to the time of the crime than anyone else he had so far managed to question.

But, no. Even though most harmless lunatics to be seen on the streets of Bombay kept to a single fairly small area, there was surely no point in attempting to get concrete evidence from such a fellow as this. What was it he kept demanding? *Time kya? Time kya?* No, all the poor wretch could think of would be what time it was. And, if he was given an answer, would be none the wiser, wandering lost as he was in a truly timeless existence.

'Time kya, sahib? Time kya?'

The madman had come up, suddenly advancing, and was peering at him in the face.

Well, perhaps no harm . . .

For what seemed the five or six hundredth time he pulled the photograph of Ramrao Pendke from his shirt pocket.

'Listen, bhai,' he said to the madman, trying to infuse calm and friendliness into his voice, 'you are often here, in this place? Near this Tick Tock shop?'

The eyes in the dirt-streaked, bushily grey-bearded face widened till their whites showed staringly in the light of the nearest street-lamp.

'Tick tock, tick tock. Time going, time going. Going, going, going. Bus starting, but long, long, long, long before Saturn passing from me. Seven-seven long, long years.'

With a grab the demented fellow seized Ghote's arm, his grip fierce with the unbridled strength of insanity.

Ghote thought for a moment of how Shruti Shah had dealt with him when he had first seen him. She had been a model of patience. He made up his mind to be no worse.

'Thik hai, thik hai,' he said soothingly. 'All right, bhai, all right. It will pass.'

The fellow seemed a little reassured.

'Pass, pass, pass. Seven years to pass.'

Ghote twisted round so that he could squarely present the blotched and smeared photo to this unlikely witness.

'Look at this please,' he said. 'Are you knowing this man?'

With a movement rapid as a mongoose diving for a snake's throat, the madman shot out his hand and grabbed. A moment later Ghote saw, to his fury, the photo clutched between both the fellow's dirt-encrusted hands as, a full yard away, he crouched peering over it.

Was he intending in his demented way to keep it? Did he think it was some sort of gift?

Could he himself get it back without an embarrassing

struggle? He had to have it. Without it his whole hunt for a witness would be useless.

He licked his lips.

'Bhai,' he coaxed, 'give it, yes? Give me the photo back.'

The madman, his mouth distorted into a tight grin, made no reply. Crouching still over his prize, he was murmuring incoherently, like a mother monkey obstinately nursing her dead baby.

'Give, bhai, give,' Ghote cajoled again.

'Saturn,' crooned the madman with wrenching despair. 'Saturn, Saturn. It is Saturn. You cannot stop Saturn. On, on, on he goes, through and through your house.'

Ghote made a plunge.

Quicker than any monkey, the tattered fellow swung away to hug his prize all the more possessively.

'Give it to me,' Ghote snapped. 'Give it to me now.'

'Saturn, Saturn, Saturn. It is Saturn.'

This is absurd, Ghote thought. I could all the time be showing that photo and asking. Just at this moment only someone might be here who saw Ramrao and whoever was with him last Tuesday.

He made another grab.

And this time succeeded in getting a hold on the thin, curly pasteboard slip. But the madman's grip was yet tighter.

If it gets ripped in half . . . Ghote thought, appalled. That would be worse. I will not have it tomorrow. Tomorrow when the same people who were here a week ago may be here again.

'Let go of this photo,' he demanded, thrusting his face into the madman's. 'Let go, I tell you.'

'Having trouble, Inspector?'

Ghote half-turned and looked up.

It was old D'Sa.

And, whether it was because another voice had intruded, or for some other reasonless reason, at that moment the madman simply let go of the photo and went wandering off along the edge of the pavement.

But Ghote's embarrassment at the situation D'Sa had caught him in did not go wandering off.

'A pagalwalla,' he said. 'I was . . . That is, he had to get hold of a photo I was using.'

'That I could see,' D'Sa answered drily.

Ghote decided there was only one way he could put himself on to a good footing again with the old detective. He must handsomely admit to the wrong he had done him in believing him hopelessly muddled about having seen Ramrao Pendke in the August Kranti Maidan. Little though D'Sa would know he had had such contemptuous thoughts about him.

'D'Sa sahib,' he said quickly, 'I am owing you one apology. You were cent per cent correct about seeing the Tick Tock victim last Tuesday. I am sorry to say I was believing you had mistaken his identity.'

'Yes, Inspector, I thought that had entered your head at the time. But not to mind. I am an old fool in many ways nowadays, so one person extra thinking the same does not much matter.'

'But – But no.'

'No, no. You are acquainted with the British saying *No fool like an old fool?* Well, I tell you, it is altogether true. Look at myself, spending my time checking up postal-wallas' letter-boxes. And, worse, do you know what time I get up in the morning?'

A little bewildered, Ghote could do no more than reply with such politeness as he could muster.

'No, D'Sa sahib. At what time is that?'

A gleam of something like triumph at the absurdity of what he had to tell entered the old man's eyes.

'At 5.59 precisely,' he said. 'Each and every day.'

'At 5.59?' Ghote could only echo.

'Yes. Not one minute before, and hardly ever one minute after. And do you know why that is? Let me tell you. I am old. I do not need much sleep. So I am awake perhaps as early as five o'clock itself. But I have decided it is not right to get up before six. That is a decent hour. So I lie in bed and look at my alarm-clock, waiting for

six. But then I say "What is one minute more or less?"
So as soon as the clock hand touches 5.59 I rise. What
could be more ridiculous than that?'

Ghote found it hard to answer. Though, dimly, he could
see how such a time-bound ritual could come about, might
one day come about for him.

But at least they had got away from discussing his
humiliating encounter with the bus-starter.

And, after a silence that threatened to become almost
equally embarrassing, he managed to see how to wrench
the talk back to his main preoccupation.

'D'Sa sahib,' he said, 'I suppose you were not having
some second thoughts about anyone who was following
Ramrao Pendke last Tuesday when you were seeing?'

'No, no. I have told you, young Ghote. That man was
not being followed when I saw him, and he was certainly
not walking with any person whatsoever. I would have
reported same if he had been, long before I happened to
see you there. I know my duty.'

'Yes, yes, well I am believing it.'

He gave a somewhat groaning sigh.

'Well,' he added, 'I must be getting on now. You know,
I am still not at all satisfied with the confession that has
been got out of the shop-owner here. What I am hoping
to do is find one witness who saw Ramrao Pendke enter
this shop in company with some person of malafide intent.'

'Yes,' old D'Sa answered sagely. 'Yes, that is the way
to go about it, young fellow. Slow but sure, that was what
I was always saying in my day.'

And the old boy looked so yearningly miserable at the
recollection of his former active life that a terrible possibility at once presented itself to Ghote. Should he ask
D'Sa to share his task? He could do with any help he
could get. The more passers-by who were questioned –
he had already knocked at every possible door – the better
the chances of finding a witness before he had to report
to the DGP at 14.19 hours next day. But, no getting past
it, D'Sa was the biggest bore in existence. And, once given
a toe-hold, he was likely to be insufferably patronising.

No, he would not do it. He could not do it.

'D'Sa sahib,' he found himself saying next moment. 'I am wondering, could you spare some little time to assist me tonight?'

Old D'Sa pondered for a little. Or, as Ghote clearly realised, put on a show of pondering.

'Well,' he said at last, 'I do not see why not. It is true I have nothing particular to do tonight. It would be a time-pass. Yes, a very good time-pass.'

So, after D'Sa had gone back to his home to collect the copy of *Mid-Day* with Ramrao Pendke's picture in it – 'I am always filing my newspaper. You never know when such may come in handy' – they began their joint operation. And, if working with the old detective did not prove quite as exasperating as Ghote had feared, it did not fall far short.

'We must go about this with some system,' D'Sa said as soon as he had returned with his paper. 'That is the key to successful police work, Ghote. System, system. I am always saying it.'

'Yes, yes, I agree to one hundred percent.'

He watched, leadenly, as D'Sa pulled out the little spiral-backed Sweety Pad which he kept for noting the times postalwallas emptied letter-boxes. With a green ballpoint the old boy then solemnly divided up a clean page into three columns.

'We will take one half-hour at a time,' he announced. 'Myself going in one direction, you, Ghote, in another. Then we will meet here outside the Tick Tock Watchworks itself and compare notes. After that I will go the other way, and you will go where I was, and so forth.'

'Very well, D'Sa sahib.'

'What time do you make it now?'

Ghote looked at the various dials of his imitation Seiko Sports 100. After a moment he made out the time.

'10.27,' he said.

'Yes. I have the same. Now, let us wait till 10.30 exactly and then begin.'

Solemnly they stood there in silence for three minutes. Then D'Sa took his folded *Mid-Day* from under his arm.

'Right,' he said. 'Go.'

Off Ghote went, trying not to feel too thankful to be out of the old idiot's way.

And precisely thirty minutes later he came back to the shuttered Tick Tock Watchworks to find the old idiot arriving there on the dot.

'No luck, Inspector.'

'No luck, Inspector.'

D'Sa put one tick in each of their columns in his Sweety Pad and entered the time of the next period in the third.

At 11.30 exactly they met again.

'No luck, Inspector.'

'No luck, Inspector.'

But then, just as Ghote turned disspiritedly to go off once more, he spotted, coming smartly up towards where they were standing, a familiar figure. Mr Saxena.

What could he be doing here at this hour of the night? Surely with those four watches strapped to his forearm he must know what o'clock it was.

He caught hold of old D'Sa's arm and pointed out the oncoming figure.

'Do you know who is that fellow, the one with that moustache like a brush only?' he said. 'It is one S.K. Saxena, the individual who was discovering the body. What can he be here for at this time of the night?'

A sudden pouncing gleam came into D'Sa's eyes.

'Young Ghote,' he said, keeping his voice low with evident difficulty. 'Young Ghote, have you never heard of the saying *The criminal is always returning to the scene of his crime?*'

'The crim— My God, D'Sa sahib, you are stating that Mr Saxena . . . That Mr Saxena is after all the Tick Tock murderer?'

'Well, you know, he is the person who was discovering the body,' the old detective answered. 'And that is another good old maxim, young Ghote. Very often the murderer is the one who has purported to be finding the body. He is, after all, a person who was definitely on the scene.'

Ghote felt a sharp flick of chagrin. Why had he not remembered that piece of special knowledge, less often a fact though it was than D'Sa had made out? And another thought came into his head then. S.K. Saxena had twice before come to look at the Tick Tock Watchworks. That was hardly because he was re-visiting the scene of the crime – that theory was surely nonsense only – but because he, as he had openly said, was wanting to take over the business when Rustom Fardoomji was no longer there. And, one other thing, had not the fellow shown altogether too much of indignation about Fardoomji not taking any HMT watches? Was that the indignation of someone going beyond the bounds of reason? Of someone at least half mad?

So S.K. Saxena had not one but two motives. Motives which D'Sa did not even know about. So was the old boy more right than he knew? And, when inside the shop behind them Saxena had gone into that play-acting business of being Fardoomji battering at his victim on the floor, had he been attempting to convince himself and AI Lobo beyond doubt that Fardoomji was the murderer?

But before he had time to consider more deeply Mr Saxena was upon them.

'Good evening, Inspector,' he greeted Ghote, with no trace at all of the discovered criminal in his cheerful tone.

'Good evening,' Ghote answered with caution.

Out of the corner of his eye he saw D'Sa sidling round so as to be in a position to pinion his suspect at the first sign of attempted flight.

'It is late to be seeing you here, Mr Saxena,' Ghote said. 'Do not be telling me you of all people are not knowing the time.'

He attempted a little laugh.

Mr Saxena laughed in his turn. More heartily.

'Oh, Inspector,' he said. 'You have caught me out.'

Fully behind him now, old D'Sa raised his hands ready to seize his man by both elbows.

'Yes,' Mr Saxena went on, 'you have caught me in the act. I was coming to have one last look at this shop.'

'One last look?'

Mr Saxena puffed out a brisk sigh.

'Yes, yes,' he said. 'I realised this very morning that, in truth, there is no chance of taking over here. Poor Rustom will find some relative to have it. These Parsis are always sticking together, you know. And why not? So I will never get to have such a place for myself. And, do you know, I realised too this morning that I am not wanting. No, a life on the road for me. That is what is suiting to my temperament. I was a fool to think anything else.'

So Ghote saw this momentary miracle of a discovery vanish in front of his eyes like a cinema screen image when the projector fails. And he realised that, in fact, the idea that anyone would commit murder solely on the doubtful chance of being able to take over a business like the Tick Tock Watchworks had been never very likely. While the notion that someone as brisk and cheerful as Mr Saxena was half mad had been purely ridiculous. Fit only for old D'Sa and his *The criminal is always returning to the scene of his crime*.

'Well, good-night, Saxena sahib,' he said. 'And good luck with your HMT watch sales.'

'Thank you. Thank you, Inspector. They are once more picking up, I am glad to tell.'

Briskly Mr Saxena walked off. Less briskly Ghote turned and left old D'Sa to tramp away on their renewed hunt.

At the stroke of midnight they met once more.

'Listen, Inspector,' Ghote said, as D'Sa made two more neat ticks on his Sweety Pad, 'there is hardly anybody about now. I am thinking we should give up until tomorrow.'

D'Sa shook his head gravely.

'Oh, yes,' he said, 'I am fully granting this line will not be yielding many results just now. But we must not give up. Never give up, Inspector. What I propose we should do now is return once more to those addresses you were visiting earlier. People may have reached home who were not there before. One of them may have seen something.'

'But, Inspector,' Ghote said, appalled, 'It is midnight. Each and every person there will be asleep. We would get one hot reception if we start to knock at doors now.'

'Hot reception or cold,' D'Sa answered, 'duty is duty. It is our duty to find any person or persons who saw one Ramrao Pendke in this vicinity last Tuesday at or about the hour of 11.40 am. We should carry out that duty to the utmost.'

'But, Inspector . . .'

'No, no, Ghote. That is the trouble with you young officers. You are shirking anything that is not going to be easy. Look at the way you were letting off that fellow earlier.'

'What fellow? I was not letting off any fellow.'

Then Ghote remembered the mad bus-starter. It was true he had let him go eventually without getting any answer out of him about the photograph of Ramrao Pendke. The whole mortifying episode was something he had pushed to the far back of his mind.

'The mad fellow you are meaning?' he asked. 'But what answer would I have got from him?'

'Yes, yes, the one I was releasing you from, with that long fresh-looking scar all round his side. You were letting him go walking off without completing inquiries. Well, that is not my idea of proper policework. Not my idea at all.'

'Yes,' Ghote said hollowly then. 'Yes, I was letting him go. D'Sa sahib, we must find him. Find him at once. He must be the man who was battering Ramrao Pendke to death.'

19

Old D'Sa looked at Ghote as if he was the one who was mad.

'Inspector,' he said, 'you are altogether fagged out. Let me go on with inquiries here. You go home and take rest.'

Ghote heaved a burdened sigh.

'No, Inspector,' he replied, 'I have got good reasons, many of them, for stating what I have just said. That fellow – Good God, I am not even knowing his name – is almost certainly the man who killed Ramrao Pendke. And you yourself put me on to him, D'Sa sahib. That big, fresh-looking scar you were mentioning, I had seen it also. Who could fail to be seeing it the way the fellow is always clad in such a torn, open shirt? And that scar, curving round under the ribs, it is just what would be made if you were taking from a person one kidney. Do you know where are the kidneys in the human body, Inspector?'

D'Sa looked affronted. Then wily.

'They – they are somewhere at the back,' he said. 'Or, more, towards the front.'

'Inspector, I am knowing. Definitely. They come one on each side of the stomach. They are like little oil – Well, never mind what like they are. The fact is that such a scar as that man has would be made when a kidney is removed to be sold to some rich person, a person like Ramrao Pendke, grandson and heir to the very, very rich Patil of Village Dharbani in District Ramkhed.'

D'Sa was beginning to look less openly sceptical.

'Yes, well,' he said, 'everybody is knowing that Ramrao Pendke was at the Shrimati Usha Yadekar Clinic receiving a kidney from a donor. It was in the *Mid-Day*. But, Inspector, is it that a donor is informed who is getting his kidney?'

'In ninety-nine cases out of a hundred he is not,' Ghote

answered. 'Even in nine thousand, nine hundred and ninety-nine cases out of one lakh. But when I was talking with Dr Mrs Yadekar at the clinic – she is running administrative side, and is also having American degrees in psychiatry – she was letting slip that in one case recently at the clinic a mistake had been made. She was giving a sack to one clerk because of same.' For a moment he thought of how once it had just entered his head that this clerk himself, seeking revenge for his dismissal, had for some reason committed the crime.

'And you think that this case was Mr Ramrao Pendke and this mad fellow?' D'Sa said. 'You are thinking that his madness was brought on in the end by having lost his one kidney and that he had one great grudge against Mr Ramrao Pendke?'

'Yes. That is it. To a nutshell. And I have some evidence also. Not good court evidence, but evidence. First, he was jabbering out once in his madness that he had received one large sum. It was stolen from him, he said, by his own son who was having gambling debts. Then, second, when I was showing him that photo of Ramrao just only three-four hours ago, it seemed as if I had put in front of him something altogether terrible. He was seizing that photo – you saw it yourself, D'Sa sahib – and looking and looking at it as if he could devour it only.'

'Well, yes, Inspector. You had one devil of a job to get it from him. If I had not come along . . .'

'But there is more, Inspector,' Ghote said. 'There is what the fellow was muttering. At the time I was thinking it was just only mad talk. But I am able to remember his very words. He was saying *Saturn, Saturn, it is Saturn* and *You cannot stop Saturn*. You see, it had come into his mind then that even beating to death the man he believed had brought that evil upon him, the man he was thinking was Saturn himself, even that had not lifted the curse he believed he was lying under.'

'Yes,' D'Sa said with slow thoughtfulness. 'Yes, I also heard him say those words, or words very much like. And at the time even I was wondering why the fellow was saying them with so much of despair. Inspector, I think you must be right.'

'Oh, I am right,' Ghote answered. 'It is plain enough. The fellow must have seen the man he remembered as having taken from him his kidney just entering this Tick Tock shop here. He must have gone in behind him, seized the heavy weight from a clock that is there on the wall and at once have beaten his victim to death, even in his frenzy smashing the watch on his wrist.'

But, as the very scene passed through his mind confirming him in the sudden insight he had had, he found himself spiralling down in an access of swift depression.

'But that is not the end of it, D'Sa sahib,' he went on, almost groaning aloud. 'You see, I have been given by the DGP himself just twenty-four hours to produce for him good proof that someone other than Rustom Fardoomji committed the crime. Otherwise DGP sahib will allow AI Lobo to take Fardoomji before a Magistrate to repeat his confession under Criminal Procedure Code. And, so frightened is that fellow I believe he would do it.'

'You are under the DGP's direct orders?' D'Sa said, visibly impressed.

'Oh, yes. But, you know, I have a feeling I was chosen for this duty just only because, if it was bringing trouble, mine would be an easy head to chop.'

'And it will bring trouble?'

Ghote thought for a moment or two then.

'Well,' he said, 'if we can find this pagalwalla and show that he was committing the crime, then, in fact, no one would be better pleased than the DGP. After all, some very, very influential people have told him they believe Rustom Fardoomji must be innocent, and we would be clearing the relatives of the Patil of Dharbani also, something DGP sahib is very much wanting.'

'Then, Ghote bhai, we had better begin to look.'

With evident relish D'Sa pulled out once more his Sweety Pad and drew new green ballpoint columns on a fresh little page.

'System is the thing,' he said. 'What we must be doing is to conduct a search in regular circles spreading out from this spot. Report back here at each half-hour as before. We will find him, bhai, never fear. A fellow like that will not have a home to go to.'

'Yes,' Ghote answered more pessimistically. 'I am hoping.'

They set off first, however, for the station to collect a couple of flashlights.

'If AI Lobo will not prevent us taking,' Ghote said.

'Let him just try,' said old D'Sa straightening his ancient back.

In fact, it turned out that Lobo had long ago departed, and Ghote was able to take a minute or two to telephone Protima. Once again he had to tell her he would not be home all night. He did not like to think, hastily replacing the receiver, what sort of reception this would earn him when he did at last get home. That was for tomorrow.

On the station steps D'Sa consulted his watch, not without some solemnity.

'Just past 12.20 am,' he said. 'But I think it would not be wrong to add ten minutes extra to the first half-hour. I will meet you outside the Tick Tock Watchworks at 1 am precisely.'

'Achcha,' Ghote said, plunging off into the velvety darkness.

Then began a long, long, miserable, fatiguing round of poking into every possible place where a wandering lunatic might have chosen to fall asleep. Ghote probed with his torch into doorways, under stairways, under handcarts left chained up outside by their owners or daily hirers. He looked at the broad window ledges of public buildings. He went along the stretches of pavement where the poor lay by the dozen in the comparative cool, sometimes with the comfort of a straw mat, sometimes without. He sent rats, squeaking and vicious, running from their hiding-places. He did not let sleeping dogs lie.

His pitch of determination soon became such that he unhesitatingly tugged aside a cotton sheet over a sleeping head, or even a sari if the form under it was not clearly feminine. And he was as ruthless in sending the beam of his flashlight circling round inside the frail plastic-sheeting or woven grassmat constructions of such pavement huts as led a precarious existence here and there in the area of his hunt.

And each half hour, to the minute by his mended Ulhasnagar Seiko Sports 100, he took care to be outside the Tick Tock Watchworks to meet old D'Sa. But neither of them once had anything at all to report.

Half-past one, two o'clock, half-past two, three o'clock. Tiredness dragged at Ghote like a huge, heavy-hemmed cloak. His bruised side, which till now had been hardly painful, began to tweak savagely at him with every movement. And the thought of the passing of time, of the steady running-out of those twenty-four hours he had been arbitrarily given, weighed on him like an unwanted crown.

He forced his way, pushing one aching leg in front of the other, along streets and lanes almost completely silent at this dead hour. Only the occasional fit of coughing from some troubled sleeper or the barking of a solitary dog disturbed the darkness.

He thought of the very different night he had spent under the huge old Patil's masterful orders out in Dharbani in the Sarpanch's courtyard, watching the calm moonlight advance and hearing the incessant creek-creek-creek of the crickets that in his infancy he had thought was the sound of the circling stars.

And Saturn is among those stars, he thought, a planet moving inexorably. A planet that must seem to the madman I am hunting to be moving with all the stately unswerving motion of an executioner coming to carry out the cruel commands of some long-ago all-powerful maharajah.

A car, bound on some mysterious errand at this late hour, swept by. Its pale headlights momentarily flickered across a slogan-scribbled wall beside him. Hastily he consulted his watch by their light. Almost time to be turning back for the next rendezvous.

Half-past three, and D'Sa was coming towards the watch-shop, walking more slowly now than even at the last meeting, his shoulders stooped.

'D'Sa sahib, you have done enough. More than enough. Kindly go home. Come again in the morning, if you are liking.'

'No, no, young Ghote. I have told you, an old man is not needing much of sleep.'

Ghote managed a sort of smile.

'At least today then,' he said, 'you will not be getting out of bed at 5.59 exactly.'

'No, no. Unless by then we have found our fellow.'

'Yes. We may have. Why not? He must be somewhere. See you at four then.'

'And not one second after.'

The old detective turned and trudged away, painfully slowly, into the darkness. Ghote tramped off to his next area of search, scarcely less slowly.

Four o'clock. Half-past. Five o'clock.

The first pale, pale signs of day had begun to show at the horizon where, down a street or up a lane, it could be seen.

Ghote thought now – his thoughts were moving with lumbering slowness as if they were not airy imaginings but lead-weighted lumps of hardly connected logic – of Khindgaon and the morning he had arrived there ahead of Raghu Barde and had come upon the man promising the spirit Churail to sacrifice two cockerels as penance for failing to sacrifice one. How different that tranquil dawn had been as he had stepped out of the jeep into the delicious fresh countryside air. How different from this dawn, grim indication of how the hours were passing in his hurried, mean, tearing, gritty, unpitying hunt for a man driven mad by the city and its harsh time-constricting demands.

Then, turning into the next yard-wide galli on his route, he saw, down at the far end in the pale light hardly different from the darkness it was dispelling, a figure moving away from him. It was hard to make out, even hard to know whether it was that of a man or a woman. But something in the way it was moving, a wanderingness, went like a dart into his grey-fuzzed brain.

New life spurted up in him.

He set off at a run, leaping from side to side in the narrow lane to avoid the rubbish littering it, a discarded red plastic bucket, a crumpled bicycle wheel, an old oil-drum, and as he got nearer and nearer to the wandering figure his hopes rose. That must be the same mass of bushy hair, even if from the back the fellow's beard was not to be seen.

He plunged on, slid wildly on a banana-skin or something, recovered, arms flailing, and turned the corner round which the madman, if it was the madman, had disappeared.

It was not the madman.

Little more than ten yards away, standing looking up towards the sun, which at that moment had risen above the horizon to send a glowing band of red all along the street in front of him, was a sadhu, loftily worshipping the new day. His hair, though bushy, was white rather than grey, and, though he did have a beard, it too was white, long and flowing instead of bushy and tangled. Nor was he wearing a shirt open at the front to reveal the scar of an operation to remove a kidney, but a flapping kurta in a dull shade of orange.

Sick with disappointment, Ghote stood for long seconds merely staring at the holy man as he worshipped in silence. He wondered, vaguely, about the time-freed life such a person must lead. Dimly he cursed him for not being the madman, freed in truth from time's harrassments yet obsessed with that reiterated, desperate question *Time kya? Time kya?*

Then, peering once more at the watch on his wrist, he decided he might as well begin making his way back to old D'Sa. To log up one more unsuccessful half-hour period.

There were others to record, too, as the light of day gradually strengthened over the sprawling, awakening city. And at each rendezvous poor D'Sa looked yet more drainedly fatigued, and yet more sullenly determined.

'Right then, off we go,' the old detective said, thick-voiced, at half-past eight. 'We do not want to waste time, young Ghote. There is not so much of it to spare now, you know.'

Blearily putting two more ticks in his Sweety Pad, he turned and plodded off.

Marching wearily away in the other direction, Ghote grimly acknowledged to himself that now their chances of finding the bus-starter were very many more times less. While the fellow had been asleep somewhere – but where? Where had he slept that they had found not one trace of him? – he would have been at least in one place. But now, almost certainly, he would be awake, and wandering. Either one of them could arrive somewhere the fellow had been half a minute after he had left. The madman, in his turn, could appear at some place which one of them had just searched half a minute before.

Why not just pack up? Let wretched, hopeless, stupid Rustom Fardoomji go to whatever fate awaited him. Let him take his passion for watches and clocks to the hang-man's rope at Thana Gaol if he was fool enough, and be damned to him.

But he knew he could not do that.

And on he went with his self-imposed, mountainous task. Wearily he pushed past bunches of schoolgirls in neat white blouses and neat grey or blue pleated skirts making their way to their various schools in time for the bells summoning them to their first classes. Wearily he avoided scrambling packs of schoolboys bound on the same errand, stringy striped ties at their necks, puppy-fighting as they went. He saw, without seeing, the pave-ment vendors setting out their wares for the day ahead with scrupulous care in ordered rows or carefully piled pyramids.

And, wherever he went, he forced his gummy eyes to stay wide, to dart looks to left, to right, forwards, backwards.

Never to any avail.

Where can the damn man be, he thought with dulled hammeringness. Where can he have hidden himself all night? Why is he not wandering up towards me now? Now? Now?

Surely he and D'Sa had been right in their assumption that the fellow would not stray beyond this immediate area. He had been present twice outside the Tick Tock Watchworks and he must have been there a third time when he had seen Ramrao Pendke enter the shop and had followed him in. So why was he not here somewhere now?

Nine o'clock rendezvous. Half-past nine rendezvous. Ten o'clock rendezvous.

Leaving once again, Ghote tried to force his stupefied mind into doing some arithmetic. Why, his mind absurdly insisted on asking, was Raghu Barde not here to do the sums for him? To produce some primes and expressibles. But, no, they were not what he wanted. He wanted just some times. At what time was he going to have to set out for the DGP's office? How much time would he have to allow for getting there from here? How many more rendezvous could he afford to make with old D'Sa, if D'Sa had not dropped dead before the last of them? At what time should he reach the Oval Maidan so as to be sure of knocking on the DGP's door at 14.19 hours precisely, neither early nor late?

At last he contrived to work out that he could safely leave setting off until after the 13.30 hours rendezvous. And if by that hour they had neither of them spotted the bus-starter, then that would be that.

He halted suddenly and began furiously winding his fake Seiko Sports 100. What if he had, in his utter tiredness, forgotten? Allowed it to stop? Had no idea that the time was nearer 14.19 hours than he believed?

He shuddered at the notion.

But, at the rendezvous at 13.00, as he watched in dulled hypnotism D'Sa make his one but last set of green ballpoint ticks in his Sweety Pad and looked up to ease the twanging ache across his shoulders, he saw, coming up towards the Tick Tock Watchworks, ambling and shambling, the flapping, bushy-bearded apparition of the madman.

20

Ghote could hardly credit what his bloodshot eyes were seeing.

He swallowed, dry-mouthed.

'D'Sa sahib,' he managed to get out. 'Look.'

D'Sa turned in the direction in which Ghote was staring.

'Ah,' he said. 'Yes. The criminal is always returning to the scene of the crime. It is an old truth. But never forget it.'

Nonsense before, Ghote thought, and double nonsense now. Only a madman would –

He licked his parched lips. The madman was still coming waveringly towards them, or towards the rust-streaked shutter of the Tick Tock Watchworks just behind them. Side by side he and D'Sa watched the quarry they had hunted so long. Neither of them able, it seemed, to move towards him or to step aside in case, seeing the men who had the day before shown him the photograph of his victim, he might suddenly take flight once more.

But the bus-starter, whether he had seen the pair of them or not, came meandering on.

At last he was near enough to be spoken to, coming to a halt and staring – was it with horror or with some sort of longing? – at the watch-shop's closed shutter. Then, before Ghote had been able to decide what to say to him, his wild eyes fastened on Ghote's own and there broke from his sores–disfigured lips the familiar words.

'Time kya? Time kya?'

The distended eyes were fever-bright with longing, as if it meant everything to the fellow – what is his name, Ghote thought in sudden panic – to be told what exact time it was.

And, as if an electric light had been clicked on in the

darkened room of his brain, Ghote knew at that instant what he had to say to the wretched bedraggled creature in front of him.

'Bhai, what time was it when you killed the man who had taken a piece of your body?'

'Yes,' said the madman.

Ghote leant towards him, almost on tip-toe. Did that *Yes* mean what it ought to mean? Yes, I killed him? Or was it just a word, a word issuing from a madman's brain? A word that might have been any other?

'Yes, yes, yes, yes, yes. He was Saturn. I had to put an end to him. What time it was? It was eleven o'clock and eight minutes after. Eight minutes, seven years. Seven years, eight minutes.'

Ghote risked a quick glance across to D'Sa.

And it was clear that he, too, believed he had just heard a confession to murder. It had even included precise detail, the exact time that the hands of the dead man's watch had shown as they were smashed. But that hour had not been, in all probability, the time Ramrao Pendke had been killed.

Carefully Ghote put another question to the demented creature in front of him.

'Bhai, how were you knowing it was eight minutes past eleven when that happened? How?'

'The watch, the watch,' the madman answered at once. 'I saw it there. That is what it was saying. I had to stop Saturn's march. I gave it one blow.'

'Yes. And what was it that you struck that blow with?'

'With – With – With that thing.'

'Yes? What thing? Tell me.'

'In the clock. In the clock on the wall. After I met him I was following him inside. And then I saw it. The long heavy thing hanging under the clock. I took it. I hit and hit and hit. Hit, hit, hit, hit.'

Again Ghote flicked a look at D'Sa.

'The very weapon, D'Sa sahib,' he said. 'A pendulum weight that is missing from a clock in the shop here. It is proof. It is truly proof.'

'Oh, yes, young Ghote. You have solved your case.'

Looking at it all now, Ghote could not see why it had not been evident to him long before that he had had the murderer under his eyes. The madman's presence had run like a jutting thread through his life ever since he had begun his search for the true murderer of Ramrao Pendke.

The fellow had been here outside the Tick Tock Watchworks, scene of the crime, when he himself had first come here. He had been there openly showing the long scar where his kidney had been removed, openly declaiming how he was cursed by Saturn. And kidneys. They, too, had kept coming into his mind. Time and again. At the clinic, where he had somehow been led to ask all those questions about transplants. And then, puzzling him all along until he had found that book of Ved's and seen just where the little oil-mills lay, there had been the question of where in the human body the kidneys were to be found. And again when Protima had lectured him about the yugas and he had exploded with fury at all he was expected to know about. Yugas, primes and expressibles and the whereabouts of the kidneys.

And the madman himself. Had not the thought of the fellow come into his head when he might least have expected it? Away in Village Dharbani when he had been trying to tease out sensible answers from that ancient, quarter-witted old soldier? Or when he had been striving to make conversation with the Patil's astrologer and had in desperation, as he had thought, asked him about the terrible influence of the planet Saturn in an astrological house? And, once more, when he had at last got inside the Tick Tock Watchworks and had been struck by the silence of its stopped clocks and watches. The thought of the madman and his *Time kya? Time kya?* had come vividly to him then.

It had all been there in front of him all the time.

D'Sa, he saw now, was once again quietly moving round till he was in a position to grip a suspect from behind if it should seem necessary. But now, Ghote felt totally certain, this was a suspect who truly had committed the crime.

The practicalities of what to do next brought him back to the present. What time was it?

He consulted the many dials of his borrowed watch.

Four minutes past one. Plenty of time to get to that 14.19 hours meeting with the DGP, armed now with proof of who had actually killed Ramrao Pendke.

But what about the proof? The word of a madman? Would the DGP after all refuse to believe in this fellow as the killer? Would he at last feel pleased at having responded to the Dhunjeebhoy brothers' plea? Or would he still insist on the validity of Rustom Fardoomji's confession as being that of a sane man?

'Right, Inspector,' D'Sa said, interrupting this swirl of pessimistic thought, 'what we have got to do now is to get this fellow certified as legally insane. We would need two qualified medical practitioners. I have dealt with three-four cases like this in my time. It is one hell of a business, I am warning you. You know what doctors can be like, wanting always to make altogether one big meal out of whatsoever they have to do.'

Ghote's new-sprung pessimism after that moment of exhilaration when the madman had come into his hands swirled yet deeper. The thought of all they had to do weighed on him. First to take their prisoner to a secure place, preferably not the nearby station but to Head-quarters, well away from any interference from Mike Lobo. Then to find D'Sa's two qualified medical practitioners. Next to get them to come without delay. Then, with time ticking out, wait during whatever lengthy examination they insisted on, as justifying some high fee.

It all might take hours. And – once more he peered at his Ulhasnagar Seiko – he had exactly seventy-two minutes before the DGP would decide, in his absence, that he had failed to produce any better suspect than Rustom Fardoomji.

He could not let that happen.

He felt himself as pressing with all the strength of will

he had up against some yielding but impenetrable wall. A wall he ought to be able somehow to burst through but could not.

Or could he . . . ? Yes, by God, he could.

'D'Sa, sahib,' he said in a flood of excitement, 'we do not have to go through all that. We do not. Remember, all that I have to bring to the DGP before 14.19 hours is just only better proof that someone else was murdering Ramrao Pendke than AI Lobo's confession from Rustom Fardoomji. And this is how I could do it. I can get a letter from a medical practitioner holding degrees in psychiatry stating this fellow is definitely mad, and that he had also admitted to battering to death Ramrao Pendke.'

'No, you are needing two doctors. I was saying.'

'No, no. Two medicos can certify the fellow later. Just now one letter, if it is first-class level, will do. And I know where to get such. Dr Mrs Yadekar at the Shrimati Usha Yadekar Clinic. She is having American degrees in psychiatric medicine. I have seen same framed upon the wall at the clinic. DGP sahib will hardly ignore that lady's evidence.'

D'Sa took a moment to consider.

'Yes,' he said then, 'you are right, bhai. Come on.'

He took the madman's arm in a firm hold. Ghote looked round, spotted a taxi at once and summoned it to the kerb. They bundled the madman in. He made no protest, and the taxiwalla did not make many. And in less than five minutes they were turning out of Altamount Road into the driveway of the Shrimati Usha Yadekar Clinic.

There they found, to Ghote's intense relief since, as they had chugged up the hill of Altamount Road, he had suddenly thought that Dr Mrs Yadekar might not even be at the clinic, that she was not only present but was willing to see him without delay. His hurried, businesslike departure on the previous occasion he had seen her had evidently left still a favourable impression. Mounting the stairs to her office, with D'Sa propelling the madman along in his wake, he attempted to get himself once more into a bustling, American, no-time-to-waste frame of mind.

But the moment he entered Dr Mrs Yadekar's clinically bare office, followed by an aged if still brisk companion pushing in front of him a wild-eyed, bushy-bearded human wreck, he saw that he had in an instant lost whatever good opinion of himself the doctor had.

'Inspector, what is this? Will you please tell me what you mean, bringing this – this creature in here like this?'

'Madam,' Ghote answered at once, 'are you not recognising same?'

'No. No, why should – '

Then she gave a sudden quick frown, and peered more closely at the shambling wreck in D'Sa's grip.

'Yes,' she said. 'Yes. Isn't it . . .'

She turned and tugged open one of the steel filing cabinets behind her, took from it a red-bound register and flipped furiously through its pages.

'Yes. Ram Bhavani, former kidney donor, paid 40,000 rupees plus diet allowance. Organ received by – Well, never mind.'

'Madam, no,' Ghote said. 'There is much to mind. This man – Ram Bhavani, you are saying is his name? – has now confessed to the murder of Mr Ramrao Pendke. That kidney he was selling was received by Mr Pendke, no?'

Dr Mrs Yadekar sat in silence behind her steel desk.

'Inspector,' she said at last, 'yes, you are correct in what you have stated. The implications are most serious.'

'Yes, madam.'

She sat in frowning thought for a little. And then looked up in puzzlement.

'But what I do not at all understand, Inspector,' she said, 'is why you have brought this – this individual here.'

She gave Ram Bhavani a suspicious scrutiny. Under it he shifted uneasily from foot to foot in D'Sa's grasp.

'Madam, it is quite simple,' Ghote answered. 'You must be knowing that the watchmaker in whose Tick Tock Watchworks the murder took place is under police custody. Madam, it is my duty to prove to – to – to the authorities concerned that it is this fellow and not the man who is being held who should be charge-sheeted under IPC Section 302, or, in the event of his insanity being duly confirmed, should be placed under proper confinement.'

'Well, yes, Inspector, I understand all that, but what is it to do with me?'

Ghote felt more than a little embarrassment in answering. But an answer had to be made.

'Madam,' he said, 'I have been given until – until, shall I say, about quarter-past two o'clock today to produce such proof. Time you see, is short. To get two qualified medical gentlemen to make their examination would perhaps be taking up too much of it. But you, madam, are having American degrees in psychiatry. So what I am asking is that you should provide me with a statement to the effect that you have examined this man and found him to be insane and know him also to be the murderer of Mr Ramrao Pendke. That would be all I am needing until 14.19 – That is, until this afternoon, madam.'

'Inspector, I cannot possibly do any such thing.'

The abrupt refusal hit Ghote as if a solid edifice had suddenly moved forward in its entirety and banged up against him.

It was just such a disastrous setback as he had feared coming up to the clinic in the taxi. But he had thought then that, if Dr Mrs Yadekar could see him, his troubles would be over.

Involuntarily he snatched back the cuff of his shirt-sleeve to see what the time was, how little remained of those seventy-two minutes he had had.

It was 13.19. He had just exactly one hour. Not a second more.

Not nearly enough time to find other qualified medical practitioners and let them examine Ram Bhavani.

'Madam,' he said to Dr Mrs Yadekar, almost weeping with the urgency he felt. 'Madam, you must do it. You must, you must.'

He received in return a look of pure coldness, chilling as ice.

213

'Inspector, I have my duties here. I don't have the time for any such course as you propose. I simply do not have the time.'

She had spoken with blank determination. American determination, Ghote felt.

But the force with which she had banged out that last *time* had an altogether unexpected effect. On the wretched madman standing there in D'Sa's quiet grasp, almost unheeded as they had discussed him.

'Time kya? Time kya? Time kya?' he screeched out.

'Inspector,' Dr Mrs Yadekar said, still icy. 'Will you kindly remove this person? Take him to some place of safety and have two regular psychiatric practitioners certify him.'

She rose abruptly from her chair by way of emphasising her request.

And the very abruptness of the movement must have sent some wild impulse through Ram Bhavani's head, because with a single frenzied jerk he broke free of old D'Sa's grasp and hurled himself on the white-clad figure who, weeks earlier, had questioned and examined him before agreeing to the sale of his kidney.

His hands, dirt-encrusted and sinewy, were round her throat in an instant. His wealed and wounded body was taut across the steel desk. His eyes blazed with fear and rage.

Ghote acted almost as swiftly. He ducked down, thrust his head and shoulders between the madman and the doctor, twisted, reached up, grasped the outstretched wrists and with all the sudden force at his command wrenched them apart.

Dr Mrs Yadekar fell back, tripped against her chair, clutched at her steel filing cabinets for support.

Ghote pushed himself up, heaved the now flaccid body of Ram Bhavani to a standing position and, with D'Sa, held him pinionned.

'All right, Inspector,' Dr Mrs Yadekar croaked from beside her filing cabinets. 'You no longer have to convince me this man is insane. What would you like me to say in any letter I give you?'

So, while D'Sa took complete charge of the now perfectly docile bus-starter, Ghote rapidly dictated a letter for the doctor to write on the clinic's impressive notepaper.

In less than three minutes he was urging D'Sa and his captive out of the office.

Under the portico of the big white-painted house they had a brief consultation.

'Listen, Inspector,' old D'Sa said, 'time must be getting on. So let us take a taxi to Headquarters where I would easily see to getting this fellow safely behind bars. After all, I am still remembered there, I should hope. You then take the taxi on and report to DGP sahib.'

He looked at his watch.

'You should have enough of time,' he said. 'Even some to spare.'

Ghote could only agree to the plan. He was not particularly keen on letting D'Sa take the madman into Headquarters. The old boy might find himself much less remembered there than he believed he was. But time was, indeed, pressing and he could see no other way of making absolutely sure he got to see the DGP before 14.19 hours.

It was possible, of course, that even if he was late in handing over his evidence the DGP would still rescind his order to Mike Lobo to take Rustom Fardoomji before a Magistrate to repeat his 'confession'. But it was not certain. It might not matter too much to someone as senior in the police hierarchy as the DGP whether one person or another was seen to be guilty in a case that had attracted public attention. And Rustom Fardoomji, after all, was apparently prepared to stand trial, even to plead guilty, for a crime he had not committed.

All seemed to go well as they set off. They found the same taxi that had brought them up to the clinic waiting only a few yards further down the hill. The driver, having had no trouble with their tatterdemalion fellow passenger before, was happy enough to take them.

He got through the traffic in fine style, too, and as Ghote looked at his Seiko Sports 100 after seeing D'Sa lead the mad bus-starter into the Headquarters compound, he found that it read only two o'clock. Somehow the time falling so exactly on the hour gave him added encouragement, too. All was going to go as well as it could go from now on.

'Oval Maidan, Mayo Road side,' he snapped out cheerfully to the taxiwalla.

And from that moment every sort of complication set in. The traffic, which till now had been lighter than usual, began catching itself up in snarl after snarl. Peering ahead, bobbing and weaving, Ghote was never able to make out why. But twice they were held fast for solid periods of five minutes. After the first Ghote simply sat with his sleeve pushed back, holding the Seiko Sports 100 in front of him and keeping a constant watch on its hands while, with the taxi engine cut off in the customary Bombay traffic-jam fashion, cars, buses, tempo trucks and vans all round hooted hard and edged inch by inch forward to lock the next hold-up yet tighter.

Then for some blessed minutes things began to go better again. They had reached the start of Marine Drive and were once more inextricably jammed up, it seemed, when they ought along that sweeping stretch to have been able to zoom away almost as fast as the taxi could go. But then, ahead, the stationary traffic, for no apparent reason, melted from its locked state. In a moment they were zipping merrily along. They sped round, unimpeded, into Churchgate.

Hardly any distance to go now.

Fourteen minutes past. They should do it. Just.

And then, at the very top of the Oval Maidan, but just too far away to make a sprint along the pavement worthwhile, they came to a blocked halt again.

Thrusting his head out of the window, debating whether by some Olympic sprinter's effort he might yet cover the distance in time, Ghote saw that the trouble was caused by a particularly large excavation, one among the hundreds always to be found in the roads of Bombay. This, he saw, was on behalf of the Telephone Nigam, the new organisation that had done not a little to improve Bombay's once appalling service. But improvement had meant laying new cables, and that had meant digging new holes. Nowadays the Nigam erected beside each new excavation a smart metal notice stating when the work had begun and when it was due to end. Ghote, his taxi stuck where it was, was able to read clearly the notice for this particular hole. It said that it was due to have been filled in eight days before.

Then, as miraculously as the hold-up had formed, it broke up. The driver eagerly re-started his engine, eagerly held his thumb on the horn. They shot forward.

But, keeping his Seiko steady with both hands in front of his face, Ghote saw it reach exactly the dreaded hour of nineteen minutes past two.

And it was one minute, perhaps a minute and a half, later that he shouted to the driver to halt, thrust the money he had long got ready into the man's hand, leapt out and ran inside.

The DGP's secretary was at his desk at the door of the great man's room.

'Ah, Inspector Ghote,' he said quite cheerfully. 'DGP sahib has been wondering if you would come. Please go straight in.'

Ghote, taking one last half-glimpsed look at his watch – 2.21, it read, unmistakably – entered the office.

The DGP looked up from his desk.

'Ghote,' he said. 'Inspector Ghote. Nothing to tell me, I suppose.'

At least no attention had been drawn to his unpunctuality. There might be hope yet, though that seemed altogether unlikely with a Titan Exacto ticking away on the DGP's wrist.

'Sir, yes,' Ghote said. 'Sir, I have much to tell.'

'Indeed? Well, you'd better get on with it then. I haven't got much time.'

And then the DGP did pull back the sleeve of his shirt

to consult his quartz-operated, never-wrong-by-a-second Exacto.

'Good God,' he said. 'Must have left the blasted thing on the wash-basin. Well, never mind, I don't suppose you were late for me, eh, Inspector?'

'No, sir, no,' Ghote instantly lied.

Well, he reflected as he began making his report, I am dead on time after all. In a way.

Bestselling Crime

☐ Moonspender	Jonathan Gash	£2.50
☐ Shake Hands For Ever	Ruth Rendell	£2.50
☐ A Guilty Thing Surprised	Ruth Rendell	£2.50
☐ The Tree of Hands	Ruth Rendell	£2.50
☐ Wexford: An Omnibus	Ruth Rendell	£5.95
☐ Evidence to Destroy	Margaret Yorke	£2.50
☐ No One Rides For Free	Larry Beinhart	£2.95
☐ In La La Land We Trust	Robert Campbell	£2.50
☐ Suspects	William J. Caunitz	£2.95
☐ Blood on the Moon	James Ellroy	£2.50
☐ Roses Are Dead	Loren D. Estleman	£2.50
☐ The Body in the Billiard Room	H.R.F. Keating	£2.50
☐ Rough Cider	Peter Lovesey	£2.50

Prices and other details are liable to change

ARROW BOOKS, BOOKSERVICE BY POST, PO BOX 29, DOUGLAS, ISLE OF MAN, BRITISH ISLES

NAME...

ADDRESS...

....

....

Please enclose a cheque or postal order made out to Arrow Books Ltd. for the amount due and allow the following for postage and packing.

U.K. CUSTOMERS: Please allow 22p per book to a maximum of £3.00.

B.F.P.O. & EIRE: Please allow 22p per book to a maximum of £3.00

OVERSEAS CUSTOMERS: Please allow 22p per book.

Whilst every effort is made to keep prices low it is sometimes necessary to increase cover prices at short notice. Arrow Books reserve the right to show new retail prices on covers which may differ from those previously advertised in the text or elsewhere.

Bestselling Thriller/Suspense

☐ Hell is Always Today	Jack Higgins	£2.50
☐ Brought in Dead	Harry Patterson	£1.99
☐ Russian Spring	Dennis Jones	£2.50
☐ Fletch	Gregory Mcdonald	£1.95
☐ Black Ice	Colin Dunne	£2.50
☐ Blind Run	Brian Freemantle	£2.50
☐ The Proteus Operation	James P. Hogan	£3.50
☐ Miami One Way	Mike Winters	£2.50
☐ Skydancer	Geoffrey Archer	£2.50
☐ Hour of the Lily	John Kruse	£3.50
☐ The Tunnel	Stanley Johnson	£2.50
☐ The Albatross Run	Douglas Scott	£2.50
☐ Dragonfire	Andrew Kaplan	£2.99

Prices and other details are liable to change

ARROW BOOKS, BOOKSERVICE BY POST, PO BOX 29, DOUGLAS, ISLE OF MAN, BRITISH ISLES

NAME. . . . .

ADDRESS. . . . .

. . . .

. . . .

Please enclose a cheque or postal order made out to Arrow Books Ltd. for the amount due and allow the following for postage and packing.

U.K. CUSTOMERS: Please allow 22p per book to a maximum of £3.00.

B.F.P.O. & EIRE: Please allow 22p per book to a maximum of £3.00

OVERSEAS CUSTOMERS: Please allow 22p per book.

Whilst every effort is made to keep prices low it is sometimes necessary to increase cover prices at short notice. Arrow Books reserve the right to show new retail prices on covers which may differ from those previously advertised in the text or elsewhere.